# Beach Holidays

## Rehoboth Beach Reads

### Short Stories by Local Writers

Edited by Nancy Sakaduski

Cat & Mouse Press
Lewes, DE 19958
www.catandmousepress

D0841387

## PERMISSION AND ACKNOWLEDGMENTS

Cover illustration/book design by Emory Au. © 2022 Emory Au.

REPRINTED WITH PERMISSION:

"As Gouda Story as Any," Jean Youkers. © 2022 Jean F. Youkers

"Big Wind and Big Water," Tony Houck. © 2022 Anthony E. Houck

"Blue House," Justin Stoeckel. © 2022 Lyle Justin Stoeckel

"DALD Day," David Strauss. © 2022 David Strauss

"Death by Chocolate," Renée Rockland. © 2022 Renée Rocheleau

"Ethereal," Steve Saulsbury. © 2022 Steven Saulsbury

"Fall Ball," Doretta Warnock. © 2022 Doretta Ann Warnock

"Fourth of July Fundango," Doug Harrell. © 2022 Douglas Gaines Harrell

"Holiday Hijinks," Lonn Braender. © 2022 Lonn Braender

"Home for the Hallow Days," Terri Clifton. © 2022 Terri Clifton

"Homebase," Anna Beck. © 2022 Anna Beck

"It Was a Good Friday to Fly a Kite," Michael Morley. © 2022 Michael Morley

"Labor (Day) of Love," Katherine Melvin. © 2022 Katherine Melvin

"Mummers in the Time of Y2K," Nina Phillips. © 2022 Nina L. Phillips

"The Power of Three," Mary Ann Glaser. © 2022 Mary Ann J. Hillier

"Slice of Pi Day," June Flavin. © 2022 June Flavin

"Sorry (Not Sorry), Wrong Number," Robin Hill-Page Glanden. © 2022 Robin Page Glanden

"Summer Valentine's Day," David Cooper. © 2022 David Warren Cooper, Jr.

"Take a Chance on Me," Madison Hallman. © 2022 Madison A. Hallman

"Taking the Plunge," Renée Rockland. © 2022 Renée Rocheleau

"The Bench," Krystina Schuler. © 2022 Krystina M. Schuler

"The Best Worst Holiday Ever," Jeanie P. Blair. © 2022 Jean Pitrizzi Blair

"The Cottage on Washington Street," Denise Stout. © 2022 Denise Marie Stout Holcomb

"The Eternal Ocean," Eric Compton. © 2022 Eric Bowman Compton

"The Hannukah Bush of Rehoboth," Mady Wechsler Segal. © 2022 Mady Wechsler Segal

"The Legend of the Waxing Crescent Moon," Linda Chambers. © 2022 Linda Chambers

"Tidings Of Comfort and…Lizards?!," Susan Walsh. © 2022 Susan Irene Walsh

## Table of Contents

## PREFACE

These are the winning stories from the 2022 Rehoboth Beach Reads Short Story Contest, sponsored by Browseabout Books. Writers were asked to create a story—fiction or nonfiction—that fit the theme "Beach Holidays" and had a connection to Rehoboth Beach. A panel of judges chose the stories they thought were best and those selections have been printed here for your enjoyment. Like *The Beach House, The Boardwalk, Beach Days, Beach Nights, Beach Life, Beach Fun, Beach Dreams, Beach Mysteries,* and *Beach Secrets* (other books in this series), this book contains more than just "they went down to the beach and had a picnic" stories. The quality and diversity of the stories is simply amazing.

## ACKNOWLEDGEMENTS

Thanks to Browseabout Books for their continued outstanding support. We are so lucky to have this great store in the heart of our community. They have supported the Rehoboth Beach Reads Short Story Contest from day one and continue to be the go-to place for books, gifts, and other fun stuff.

I thank both the Rehoboth Beach Writers' Guild and the Eastern Shore Writers Association for their support and service to the writing community. These two organizations provide an amazing array of educational programming, and many of the writers whose stories appear in this book benefitted from their classes, meetings, and events.

I thank this year's judges, Jackson Coppley, Lois Hoffman, Dennis Lawson, Mary Pauer, Dylan Roche, and Candace Vessella, who gave generously of their valuable time.

Special thanks to Emory Au, who captured the theme so well in the cover illustration and who designed and laid out the interior of this book as well.

I also thank Cindy Myers, queen of the mermaids, for her continued loyalty and support.

An extra-special thank-you to my husband, Joe, who helps on many levels and puts up with a great deal.

I would also like to thank the writers—those whose work is in this book and those whose work was not chosen. Putting a piece of writing up for judging takes courage. Thank you for being brave. Keep writing and submitting your work!

—*Nancy Sakaduski*

# Taking the Plunge

## By Renée Rockland

*Shoes,* Coco thought. How could she have forgotten shoes? The sand was so blisteringly cold she may as well have been standing on an ice block, and the waiting was only prolonging her agony. Coco shivered under an asphalt sky swollen with low-hanging clouds and chided herself as the steel-gray Atlantic foamed near her feet. The surf was unusually subdued, perhaps already acquiescing to the imminent onslaught of New Year's revelers poised to race into the frigid seawater.

"I'll bet this is what Han Solo felt like when he was frozen in carbonite," Coco said to her friend Michele, teeth chattering as she shifted her weight from one foot to the other, trying to stave off a cramp beginning to form in her left big toe. "I can't believe I let you talk me into this."

"What happened to your Wim Hof breathing?" Michele smirked. "I thought you said this wouldn't be a big deal."

The corners of Coco's mouth twitched upward. "Maybe I shouldn't have practiced in front of the fireplace."

"Ya think?"

"But I don't regret the spiked cider."

Michele giggled. "Nobody regrets spiked cider."

Coco blew into her hands and rubbed them together. "I'm officially a human popsicle."

"C'mon, new year, new you. Remember?"

"I should have opted for the green-juice fast from Twist. The new me is going to end up with hypothermia and have to spend my birthday tomorrow in the hospital."

"Well, you wanted your thirtieth to be memorable," Michele deadpanned.

Coco gave her a side-eye. "I think you're enjoying this a little too much. Either you're part Eskimo or you've got fur lining in that Wonder Woman costume."

Michele was one of several Wonder Women among the scrum gathered at the shoreline. There were also a few Yetis and polar bears, several Santas, some pirates, a group of boys wearing Viking hats (probably from Cape Henlopen High School), King Neptune (complete with a crown and trident), plenty of mermaids, an ice fisherman, and a small army of "I Dared to Dip into the New Year" T-shirts.

"Wonder Woman doesn't need fur lining," Michele said as she secured her crown against a bitter blast of arctic air that swept onto the Delaware coast. "But you're the one who's going to win the costume contest, Ms. Ice Queen. Have you noticed how many people are staring?"

In fact, Coco had. How could she not? She'd designed her costume as if Andrew Lloyd Webber himself had commissioned her to create a look for the finale of a lavish Broadway musical. Her color palette was shades of white with strategically placed metallic pops. For the frame of her headdress—which towered nearly two feet—she'd used lightweight aluminum wiring and then covered it in faux fur, feathers, and a staggering number of sparkling ornamental glass beads. Her collar, which was deceptively rolled, would double as a blanket when she emerged from Siberia and pulled the hidden rip cord, allowing it to cascade down her back so she could wrap the thermal material around her body for warmth—though at the moment, anything short of a fleece-lined sleeping bag would be as inadequate as stilettos on ice. The biting chill stung Coco's skin, penetrating directly to her bone. And she hadn't yet entered the water.

"I think it's pretty genius you used latex for your leotard," Michele said. "The people wearing T-shirts are seriously going to regret it once they get wet."

Coco's original design had included a full-body suit. "Like an ivory-clad Batwoman," she told Michele. But Michele said that would probably look too much like a wet suit and "wet suits are cheating," according to the rules of The Daring Dippers, the Rehoboth Beach winter ocean swimming club that was sponsoring the New Year's Day Dip.

So, Coco amended her costume, settling on a long-sleeved leotard with a plunging neckline. She'd debuted it triumphantly last night at the Rusty Rudder's New Year's Eve party, and everyone had laughed when she said, "I figured if I was going to take the plunge, my neckline should as well." Later, when they were dancing to Off 24, someone told her the costume looked like a Bob Mackie creation, and if compliments were tangible, Coco would have had it framed. To complete her look, she'd used metallic makeup on her eyes and lips and sprayed streaks of gold through her dark hair. The effect was both dramatic and jaw-dropping.

Once Coco had agreed to participate in Michele's wild and daring idea to kick off her "new year, new you" New Year, the Ice Queen costume had taken only four weeks from conception to completion. She'd tried to channel Susan Hilferty, the Tony-award-winning costume designer whose work on the Broadway musical *Wicked* had changed the trajectory of Coco's life when, during her sophomore year in high school, Coco's theater class had taken a trip to New York to see the show.

Coco had left the Gershwin theatre buzzing, an electric current pulsing through her limbs. While the rest of her classmates were reliving the spectacular choreography, Coco envisioned the costumes, recalling how the fabrics moved as they played with the light while the actors danced. And when everyone on the bus started singing "Defying Gravity" and "One Short Day" as they traveled south on I-95 on their way back to Rehoboth, Coco found herself wondering where the designer had concealed the actors' microphones.

Coco yearned to see the costumes and wigs up close, and when one of Elphaba's black dresses was gifted to the Smithsonian National Museum of American History, Coco's mother had surprised her with a day trip to Washington, DC. It had been a perfect day—like a day in the Emerald City—as Coco sat with her sketch pad in the American Stories exhibit, studying the costume from every angle.

No one was surprised then, when Coco earned a scholarship to the Yale School of Drama. She planned to study costume design and wig making, just like Susan Hilferty, and upon graduation, move to New York. Her first two years of college were like living in Oz, surrounded by color and light and imagination. Coco could see her future as clearly as if she'd donned a pair of polarized sunglasses. But in October of her junior year, while crossing the campus quad under the stippled shade of an elm tree, her cell phone had rung and five little words—"your father's had a stroke"—upended all her dreams and changed her trajectory once again.

She'd returned home immediately to help her mother. And when her father's prolonged rehabilitation eroded their savings, Coco had taken a job as a shampoo assistant at Bad Hair Day, Rehoboth's premiere salon. Eventually, she'd worked her way up to become one of their top stylists and was now known throughout Delmarva for her genius up-dos and makeup artistry, with a long list of clients who booked her for weddings over a year in advance. For her friend Piper's wedding this past Labor Day, she'd done hair and makeup for the entire bridal party, and during the reception at the Rehoboth Beach Yacht and Country Club, a guest had approached Coco and offered to put her up at The Plaza Hotel in New York if she'd come the following summer to do her daughter's wedding.

*New York.*

No matter how hard Coco tried to ignore the niggling, her dreams were always there, pressing at the perimeter, probing for an entrance. She thought they'd died the day her father had his stroke. And as the years passed, Coco had found a different outlet for her creativity. At least that's what she told herself.

Then this past summer, in a fit of restlessness, she'd reached out to the theater companies in Rehoboth and Milton. Most recently she'd helped Christopher Peterson build the costumes for *The Adventures of Priscilla, Queen of the Desert* at Clear Space, but instead of being satisfied by the praise, she was reminded of what she'd lost. And now, as she stood on the precipice of the big 3-0, nowhere near settled or sanguine, Coco's life didn't begin to resemble where she thought she'd be at this point.

Coco felt as if she were on skis that had gotten stuck in grooved tracks on a snowy mountain. It was too late to go back to school, but as her thirtieth birthday approached, she had dared to wonder if perhaps there might still be a place for her in the Big Apple. If perhaps she could adjust her skis, find fresh powder, and forge a different path. At Michele's insistence, Coco had even gone so far as to find a sublet starting next month, but she was still waffling, waiting for what?

"Are you ready?" Michele's voice pulled her back to the beach and the very real possibility that her dreams wouldn't matter, as she was becoming ossified on the sand.

Coco was cold to her core. "Every time I open my mouth I look like a chain smoker," she said, in a puff of crystalline vapor.

"All right, Joan Crawford." Michele snort laughed. "We go at the whistle. At least up to our waists. Right?"

Coco nodded, visualizing the piping hot cup of coffee she was going to savor in the Surf Bagel-sponsored warm-up tent after this was over.

She wondered if they'd consider an intravenous infusion.

The whistle sounded, and they were off, running and screaming with the rest of the questionably sane people on the beach. As soon her foot plunged into the surf, Coco's lungs contracted. She gasped but pressed forward, propelled by adrenaline and the promise of a hot beverage. The arctic water splashed up, piercing her skin like a thousand shards of ice. Coco was certain that if she cut herself at that moment, her blood would run as clear as the pristine waters off the coast of Iceland. By the time she was submerged up to her waist, she was panting, her breath coming in short uneven spurts as she imagined stalagmites forming inside her lungs. Coco couldn't feel her legs, but she felt Michele grab her hand and raise it into the air. They shouted in unison, "Happy New Year!" as Michele snapped a quick selfie before they turned and raced back to shore.

Coco exited the water feeling exhilarated, a rush of courage and confidence beginning to thaw her frozen organs. She looked beyond the wind-swept dunes to the boardwalk, slowly becoming aware of the crowd cheering in their down parkas, scarves, and stocking caps as she pulled her rip cord and the thermal cape waterfalled down her back. Coco wrapped it around her body, effectively blocking the wind. Volunteers (wearing shoes!) waited on the sand with stacks of "I survived my big dip" towels, and Michele snagged one on their way to the tent "since I don't have a fancy cape."

They entered the enclosure set up near the bandstand. Speakers blasted a New Year's playlist. U2's "New Year's Day" morphed into The Zombies' "This Will Be Our Year." Heat lamps were scattered throughout the space and volunteers stood at tables doling out congratulations and steaming cups of Swell Joe and hot chocolate. Coco gratefully accepted the caffeine and wrapped her hands around the paper cup, letting the warmth penetrate her fingers as she took up a position near one of the heaters. She sipped it carefully, moaning as the acrid fire flooded her system.

Michele found her a few minutes later. "Jalapeño with strawberry jam," she said, handing her half of a bagel.

Coco took a bite. Sweet heat. "Thanks." Feeling was slowly returning to her extremities, a burning, tingling sensation that reminded her with acute clarity she was alive.

"Excuse me." Coco and Michele turned in unison. The deep baritone belonged to a man dressed as if he were headed out for ski patrol, silver hair peeking out from beneath a stocking cap. His cheeks were ruddy, and his smile revealed dimples. "I couldn't help but notice your costume," he said to Coco.

"She designed it herself," Michele said.

His dimples deepened. "Quite something the way you concealed that cape."

"Thanks." Coco dipped her head modestly.

"Is this a hobby or something bigger?"

A hobby? Coco felt her spine prickle. And yet, it was a fair question. At this point, that's exactly what her dreams were and always would be…unless…"I've actually done some local theater productions," she said, straightening her shoulders.

The man smiled. "Ever thought about taking it to the next level?"

Coco took another sip of her coffee. "You mean like regional?"

"No, like a career," the man said as he reached into his pocket and pulled out his wallet. "Here's my contact info."

Coco took the proffered business card, the gold embossed lettering shining brighter than the lights on Broadway as she read his name. "Gregory Knowles." She looked up, stunned. "You produced *Kinky Boots* and *The Lion King.*"

He nodded. "Right."

Her next words came tumbling out in a breathless bolt of bravery. "I'm moving to New York at the end of the month."

Michele pumped her fist at her side. "Great! Next year we can celebrate New Year's *and* your birthday in Times Square."

Coco laughed. "We won't be any warmer."

"It's your birthday?" asked Gregory.

"Actually, it's tomorrow, but I'm not really celebrating this year."

Michele shook her head. "She's all 'ugh' because she's turning thirty."

"I just thought I'd be in a different place, you know?" Coco said. "And besides, January second is the single worst day of the year to be born."

Gregory cocked an eyebrow. "I've heard people complain about having birthdays close to Christmas, but that's a new one."

"Think about it," Coco said, taking another sip of coffee. "Tomorrow, everyone's going to be in a bad mood because they're going back to school or work, probably with a hangover. And they're feeling deprived because they've started their New Year's resolutions and are on a diet or off caffeine or sugar or alcohol. Do you know how many times someone has turned down a piece of my birthday cake? They indulge throughout December and then suddenly, January second rolls around, and they act like I've offered them rat poison. And don't get me started on gifts. It's the ultimate date for regifting. I've got enough candles and mugs and bath products to open my own shop."

Gregory threw back his head in unalloyed delight. "Well, how 'bout we make this a birthday to remember. You give me a call once you're in the city. I'll make some introductions, and I'll even spring for a belated birthday cake from Magnolia Bakery."

Coco stared, wide-eyed, as his offer circled her orbit. When it finally came in for a landing, she was rendered speechless. Michele put her arm around Coco's shoulders and squeezed. "She'll definitely give you a call, and red velvet's her favorite."

"Good to know. Hope to see you soon." Gregory disappeared into the crowd, and Coco exhaled, unaware that she'd been holding her breath.

"So?" Michele grinned. "You're welcome."

Coco drained the remainder of her coffee and playfully nudged Michele with her elbow. "I guess I owe you a spiked cider."

A group of revelers blowing party horns on the opposite side of the tent caught her attention. They were wearing silly New Year's hats and oversized numerical glasses, posing for pictures in their wet "I survived," T-shirts.

*Survived.*

The word lubricated her joints, easing the stiffness. An icy-hot serum that made her feel loose with possibility, like the Tin Man when he could finally move without creaking. Deep in her epicenter, Coco realized there'd been a seismic shift, as if the extreme of plunging into the Atlantic had finally caused her tectonic plates to align.

She crossed the room, feeling as weightless as the cape billowing in her wake. Coco lifted the plastic mouthpiece to her lips and blew with a resounding toot. The paper coil at the end of her horn unrolled and shot back in spectacular fashion. She laughed, a melodious burst that reverberated throughout the tent. Coco blew it again. Happy New Year indeed.

Renée Rockland grew up landlocked in Iowa and then spent almost two decades living in the Arizona desert until a job transfer moved her family to Maryland. Finally stepping foot in the Atlantic on a sunny August afternoon in Rehoboth Beach thirteen years ago, Renée is grateful for the lifeguard who didn't roll his eyes when she asked when the water would warm up. The Chicken Plungers are her people! "Taking the Plunge," however, is a mash-up of her twin daughters, who are navigating their 20's, wondering what the end of this decade will bring. One is a musical theater aficionado who has seen *Wicked* three times and the other participates in the Polar Bear Plunge in honor of her special education students.

Renée is thrilled to once again be working with Cat & Mouse Press and would like to thank Nancy Sakaduski for her eagle-eye editorial expertise as well as the judge who selected "Taking the Plunge" for an award.

## Judge's Comment

*This story immediately stood out to me, with its biting descriptions of the freezing cold, its fun and witty dialogue, and the charm of Coco's artistry as a costume designer. I couldn't help but root for Coco's success!*

# Sorry (Not Sorry), Wrong Number

## By Robin Hill-Page Glanden

Maria was adding garlic to her homemade Bolognese sauce when the phone rang. Usually, she let calls go to voicemail if she didn't recognize the number—so many spam calls these days. But she was expecting an important call from her publisher, so she quickly turned the heat down on the burner and grabbed her phone without first checking the caller ID.

"Hello."

"Hey there, baby! This is your lucky day. Clear your schedule for February 14th because I made plans for us to have the best Valentine's Day ever. It'll start with dinner at our favorite Rehoboth restaurant, Victoria's, at the Boardwalk Plaza. I mean, it's gonna be epic. Whatcha say?"

"Excuse me? Who is this?"

"Oh, come on, baby. Don't tell me you're still mad. I told you—it was only one dinner. You gotta believe me. And Monica just transferred to our Dover office. There's nothing for you to be upset about. C'mon, honey—celebrate Valentine's Day with me and let's reinstate our engagement."

"I'm sorry, but I have no idea what you're talking about."

"Don't shut me out, Shannon. You know I love you and only you. C'mon, let's give it another shot."

Maria moved the phone to her left hand, picked up a wooden

spoon, and stirred the sauce. "Oh, I think I see your problem here. And it isn't just that you cheated on your fiancée, it's that you can't dial a phone number."

"Huh?"

"What number did you dial?"

"The one I always call: 302-555-1951."

"You dialed 1591. You got two numbers reversed. And by the way—unsolicited advice here—your lines are really bad. Downright rude, in my opinion."

"Oh, crap. I am so embarrassed. Yeah, I misdialed. I'm calling on my landline, and I was so nervous that I dialed wrong. I'm really sorry."

"That's OK. I'm just stirring my Bolognese. At least you weren't calling about my car warranty expiring or offering me a lower rate on my credit card."

"You're stirring your what?"

My Bolognese sauce. You know, a red sauce that goes on pasta."

"Oh, yeah. You, uh, you really think my 'lines,' as you call them, are bad?"

"Yes. Very bad. I wouldn't give you a second chance with that 'Baby, this is your lucky day' baloney."

"Wow, you show no mercy. So, what would you suggest I start with?"

"Now, I don't know anything about your relationship, but I'd say that if you cheated on your fiancée, you might want to start out being a little more humble and sincere."

"Yeah. I guess you got a good point there. I'll rethink that opener."

"Good. Now see, it was lucky that you misdialed and talked to me. You get a second chance to use a better approach, and maybe *you* will get lucky, and the lady will give you a second chance."

"Thanks. I'll need it. Hey, my name's Tyler. What's yours?"

"Maria."

"Sorry I bothered you. Hope your sauce is OK."

"It's fine—it's simmering. I hope you and your lady work things out. I know it's cliché, but if it's meant to be, it'll be. It's great when you find true love."

"Sounds like you found true love. You're lucky—some people have it easy."

"I did, and it was really great."

"*Was* great? What happened? He leave you?"

"Yes, sort of. He died." She stirred the sauce to fill the silence.

"Oh, man, I'm sorry for your loss."

"You're original with the sympathy line, too, I see. But that's all right. Thanks. It happened a long time ago. My husband and I enjoyed thirty years of a wonderful marriage. Now look, I have to put the rigatoni on. Think you can take it from here, Romeo?"

"Oh, yeah. Again—sorry for the wrong number. I'll be more careful. So, here I go—second try. Have a good evening."

"You too. Talk to your lady, and don't be a jerk again."

"Ha, ha—'don't be a jerk,' she says. OK, I'll do my best. Good night."

\* \* \* \* \*

The following day, as Maria was having lunch and reading an article in the latest issue of *Delaware Beach Life*, the phone rang. She checked the Caller ID: *T Webster. T* for Tyler? The guy dialed the number wrong—twice?! "Hello. Tyler?"

"Yeah, it's me."

"You misdialed…again?"

"No, uh, I called you on purpose this time. You busy?"

"I'm just finishing my soup."

"I'd like to ask you for some advice."

"Advice? What kind of advice?"

"Well, I don't have any sisters, I work with a bunch of guys, and my mom passed away years ago, so I don't know who to ask. I need some, you know, female advice, and I thought of you. See, it didn't go real well on the phone with Shannon last night. I didn't say any of that 'Hey baby' or 'This is your lucky day' stuff. I took your advice. I was sincere and I apologized. I told her I love her and want to marry her, but she turned me down for Valentine's Day. She doesn't trust me."

"I'm sorry to hear that, but I don't know how I can help you."

"Well, Shannon really likes flowers. Yellow roses, especially. Do you think it would be a good idea for me to send her a dozen yellow roses to maybe get her to change her mind? Or do you think that's too much?"

"Tyler, I still don't know that much about you, your lady, and your relationship except that you messed up pretty bad."

"Look, it wasn't all that bad. This woman—Monica—came to work in our office, and she is model-gorgeous. We got to talking one day, and she asked me if I could recommend a good restaurant, since she's new to the area. I suggested a place and she asked if I'd join her there for dinner after work. I was flattered and kind of infatuated, I guess. I should have said no, but I didn't. One of Shannon's friends saw us together at The Cultured Pearl and told her. She was so upset. I apologized and promised I'd never go out with Monica or any other girl again. I even suggested we move our wedding date up to August instead of December because I can't wait to marry her. But Shannon wouldn't listen. Now she won't even take my calls."

"OK, so you made a mistake. Everyone makes mistakes sometimes, and it sounds like you want to make amends and fix the relationship. In my opinion, as a female who likes flowers a lot, I would always be happy to get my favorite flowers. And it does give your apology and your Valentine invitation a bit more substance."

"So, I should send the flowers, right?"

"Look. I can't tell you what to do, but maybe at this point it can't hurt."

"Yeah. Right. I'm gonna place that order right now. Thanks a lot."

"You're welcome. I'll send you a bill for my counseling services right after I finish my minestrone soup."

"Ha, ha, ha! Well, enjoy your Campbell's."

"No canned soup here. I make my own."

"Oh, that's cool. Sounds like you cook a lot."

"I'm Italian. I have my mother's recipes and my grandmother's recipes. Even though it's just me, I cook. It's what I do. It's what I've always done."

"OK. Bye."

"Good luck, Tyler."

\* \* \* \* \*

The next day, as Maria was finishing the edits on a magazine article, the phone rang. The Caller ID read: *T Webster*. She sighed, hesitated, then picked up the phone.

"It's you again?"

"Yeah, me again. I just wanted to tell you that there's some hope. Shannon got the flowers and she took my call last night, so we talked for a little while. This might be our second chance."

"Sounds promising. That's great."

"Hey, thanks for giving the flowers the green light. That might have helped convince her that I'm sincere."

"Well, as I said before—flowers couldn't hurt. But listen, I have to proofread this story. I have a deadline."

"What do you do?"

"I'm a writer."

"No, I mean what you do for work, to make money?"

"I told you—I'm a writer."

"You write stories? You make money doing that?"

"Well, yes, as a matter of fact I do. I write for a local magazine and a couple of national magazines. I also have two mystery novels that are doing pretty well, and I teach writing workshops. What do you do, Tyler?"

"I'm a supervisor at a landscaping company. I've worked there since I graduated from high school. It's hard work, but I like it. I like planting things and watching them grow. I like being outdoors. Hey, what's your author name? I don't know any authors. I want to check out your books online."

"Moretti. I write under the name Maria Arena-Moretti. Arena was my maiden name."

"Moretti? I had an English teacher my senior year of high school named Moretti."

"Really? Where did you go to high school?"

"Milford High. Class of 1980."

"You had my husband for English! Anthony Moretti. Anthony was in the Army, then he went to college. His brother moved to Delaware to work at DuPont, so Anthony applied for some teaching jobs in Delaware after he graduated. Right after our wedding, he got an offer to teach English at Milford High. We looked around the area to find a house, and when we visited Rehoboth, we knew that was where we wanted to live. So, we bought our house in Rehoboth, and Anthony drove to Milford every day."

"Yeah. All us kids were jealous of Mr. Moretti because he lived at the beach. Wow, he was your husband! Let me tell you—he's a big part of the reason I graduated. My buddy Mark and I were both failing English and History our senior year. Mr. M. stayed after school two days a week and tutored us. Gave his time for free. We both passed and graduated. All the kids liked him a lot. He started every class by telling a joke. Sometimes they were really corny jokes, but it got class off to a good start."

"Yes, that was my Anthony! He was quite a character, and he loved teaching. We didn't have any children of our own, but he always called his students 'my kids.'"

"I heard he passed away a while back."

"I'm sorry to say he did—almost ten years ago. I still live in our little Rehoboth house. I retired from my librarian job and started writing. I've been having a good bit of success with that. I miss Anthony terribly, but I'm doing OK."

"You know, I remember Mr. M. bringing in Christmas cookies you baked. They were the best cookies I ever tasted. He said his wife was the best cook in the world."

"He told me that all the time. Your mother didn't cook or bake?"

"No. We grew up on fast food, peanut butter and jelly, and Kraft macaroni and cheese. My parents did the best they could, I guess. Dad had a drinking problem, and I'm one of six kids. Born and raised in Milford. I can't believe you're Mr. Moretti's wife. What are the chances?"

"Oh well, you know—Delaware is like a big small town. But listen, I have to get back to work. Thanks for sharing that story about my husband. I got to know some of his students through the years, and I always enjoy hearing their stories about him.

"We never met, but I remember when you and Mr. M. chaperoned my senior prom. You were a good-looking couple."

"I remember that. Those were good times. I'm glad he helped you and your friend. Good luck with Shannon."

"Thanks a lot."

\* \* \* \* \*

Maria's phone rang two days later. *T Webster*.

"It's Tyler. Are you cooking?"

"No, Tyler. It's almost 10 p.m. and I'm watching TV."

"I didn't realize it was that late. I just wanted to tell you—Shannon is coming over tomorrow! The roses and a better *line* might have done the trick."

"Well, it sounds promising. That's wonderful."

"I'll keep you posted."

"Tyler, you don't have to do that. Just go mend your fences and get your relationship back on track."

"I'm sorry if I've bothered you, I—"

"No bother, Tyler. It's fine. I hope it all works out. Good night."

"I'm thinking positive. I'll send you an invitation to the wedding. Good night. And thanks again."

* * * * *

Maria turned off the TV and went into her office—the office that had been her husband's for so many years. She went to the bookshelf that held the Milford High School yearbooks. Anthony had worked with the students on the yearbook, and he kept a copy for every year he taught. Maria removed one of the yearbooks from the shelf and placed it on the desk. She turned to the section with the senior pictures and found Tyler Webster. The boy in the picture looked so young and was really quite handsome. His dark eyes were intense, but he had an uneasy, yet defiant, look about him—maybe he was camera-shy. He looked very serious in his dark suit and gray necktie. His dark wavy shoulder-length hair was cut in the layered shag style that was popular back then. Maria smiled at the image of the young man her husband had taken under his wing. She saw a boy who seemed insecure but was trying to hide it by staring down the camera and looking grown up in his Sunday-best suit and tie. From talking with him on the phone, Maria felt there were traces of that boy still living in the man today. Many of the seniors had written comments next to their pictures in her husband's yearbook. In neat, printed lettering, Tyler had written:

*Hey Mr. M.—You are the best teacher I ever had. You are cool and funny, and you really care. Thanks for everything. I'll never forget you. Ty.*

Maria smiled again and put the yearbook back in its place on the bookshelf.

* * * * *

It was a rainy Wednesday evening. As she chopped cucumbers for a salad, Maria thought about Tyler. She had been thinking about him a lot. It had been three weeks since he called to tell her about Shannon's impending visit. Just like a mother worrying about her child, she couldn't help but wonder what happened. She hoped he had worked things out. Valentine's Day was Saturday. She had said he didn't have to keep her posted on his relationship status, so she really shouldn't be surprised that he hadn't called. Finally, curiosity got the better of her. She dialed the number for *T Webster*.

The phone rang four times. Maria was about to hang up when he answered.

"Hello."

"Hi Tyler—it's Maria Moretti."

"Hey, Mrs. Moretti. What's up? I thought you didn't want to talk to me anymore."

Maria thought he sounded a little down. Maybe she had hurt his feelings. "No, that's not what I meant when I said you didn't have to call me. But anyway, I was wondering how it worked out with Shannon. She came over and you got everything straightened out, right?"

"Yeah, she did come over. She came over, thanked me for the roses, but told me that it was not necessary to send her flowers. She's dating another guy now. She's moved on. She returned my engagement ring. So, we're done."

"Well, Tyler, you gave it a good try. Live and learn. Don't get discouraged. I'm sorry it didn't work out, but like I always say: If it's meant to be, it'll be. I really do believe that everything happens for a reason."

"I was sorry too…at first. But then I got to thinking maybe Shannon and I weren't right for each other. I always felt kind of uncomfortable with her. I never could really talk with her. Not like I talk to you. And I hardly know you. But I feel like I can talk to you about anything. Shannon is always so serious. She doesn't joke around, and she gets upset real easy. I always felt like I was walking on eggshells around her. She's dating some guy who's a paralegal for an attorney in Wilmington. Sure didn't take her long to find a new guy."

"Well, that should tell you something, Tyler. If you two were in love and it was the real thing, you wouldn't have gone out with someone else, and she wouldn't have been so quick to find a new man. Better to find out now than after the wedding."

"You're right. That's exactly what I've been thinking."

"I just wanted to check on you. We've talked a good bit and I wanted to see what happened. Oh, by the way, my husband had a yearbook for every year he taught, and I kept them all. I looked you up."

"My stone-face senior picture. I always hated getting my picture taken."

"You looked great. But a little like a mortician in that dark suit with such a serious expression. I did like the shag haircut, though."

"That was the only suit I had. Haven't worn one since. No need to wear a suit in my line of work, but I did buy some fancy new duds when I thought I had a big date for Valentine's Day."

"Well, I work from home in front of a computer. My usual attire these days is home-office casual—sweatpants and a T-shirt with coffee stains on the front."

"Hey…do you like to go out for dinner?"

"Yes, of course I do."

"Well, how would you like to take a break from all that cooking you do and come to Victoria's with me for dinner? I've still got a reservation for two for Saturday night."

"Tyler Webster, are you hitting on me? I'm old enough to be your mother! Surely you know a lady your age you'd like to take out to dinner."

"Actually, there's no one I'd invite on a date right now."

"Well, what about the other one—Monica? You're free to date her now that Shannon officially ended your relationship."

"Oh yeah, about Monica. I found out she's dating the manager of the Dover office. I guess the transfer worked out pretty well for her. You know, Monica and I really didn't have much of anything in common. So, how about dinner with me on Saturday?"

"That's very nice of you, Tyler, but Valentine's Day is a holiday to celebrate love. You don't want to spend it with an old gal like me."

"Mrs. Moretti—far as I know, there's nothing saying that a day celebrating love has to be only about romantic love. I think it can be two friends having dinner together on a Saturday night that just happens to fall on February 14th, that just happens to be Valentine's Day. It's also kind of a thank-you gesture. Your husband helped me a lot—he got me to focus on the subjects I was struggling with so I could really learn and pass those courses. You helped me too. I feel like I'm a better man for having talked with you. I'm looking at myself and at relationships in a more positive way. I think I'll do a lot better going forward."

"Well, I'm glad I could help you, Tyler. I guess that dinner would be OK. Victoria's does happen to be one of my favorite restaurants, and it would be a shame to let that reservation go to waste. You'll dress up and wear those new duds you got?"

"Yup. I sure will. And maybe *you'll* ditch the sweatpants and coffee-stained T-shirt and wear something a little nicer?"

"I could do that—I have a couple of dresses I break out for special occasions. OK, then, we'll plan on dinner this Saturday.

"We'll drink a toast to friendship, to the love you and your husband had, and to the hopes that I find love like that one day."

"I think that's a truly wonderful idea. I'll go with you on one condition—you call me Maria instead of Mrs. Moretti."

"It's a deal. Text me your address, Maria. I'll pick you up at 7:00."

"I will. I'll be ready."

"Great. And Maria…I'm not sorry about the wrong number. Like you said: Everything happens for a reason. I think me dialing your number was no mistake. Turned out, the day I connected with you on the phone was *my* lucky day.

For twenty years, Robin worked in the entertainment industry and as a freelance writer/book editor in Philadelphia, New York, and Los Angeles. While in Los Angeles, she attended the UCLA Writers' Program, edited books for other authors, and wrote feature stories for two LA magazines. Family matters brought Robin back to her home state of Delaware, where she now works as a freelance writer and editor. Her short stories and poetry have won Delaware Press Association awards and have been published in numerous anthologies and magazines. She is also a regular contributor of nonfiction stories to two of the *Guideposts* magazines.

Robin is pleased to be included in another Rehoboth Beach Reads anthology. Her story, "Sorry (Not Sorry), Wrong Number," started as a result of the many wrong numbers and spam calls she receives. (Robin receives frequent calls for Seasons Pizza, as people often reverse two digits in the phone number and dial her home number by mistake.) The wrong number phone call idea evolved into a traditional, romantic love story. After she finished, Robin decided that the ending was too predictable. She wrote the story again, took it in a different direction, and added a new character—a high school teacher modeled after her father.

*Finding a family outside of the one you're born into is a gift, and this story celebrates how that can occur, by accident and then by choice. Delaware is a small state, and coincidences such as the one that opens this story are more common than an out-of-state reader might imagine. We think the guy is going to get the gal, isn't that how all love stories end? But the twist is just enough. Instead of finding his one true love, our hero finds a different, and as important, relationship. Teachers of subject matter can touch other aspects of a student's life and this story takes advantage of the impact of small gestures. Deftly written, sufficient detail to hold the reader's interest, and lively dialogue that carries the reader along. A pleasure to read and savor.*

# Death by Chocolate

## By Renée Rockland

As a general rule, Lu Stockley stayed out of her husband's home office. It wasn't so much that she actively avoided it, but when asked the secret to her forty-four-year marriage, her immediate response was, "a room of one's own." Lu felt strongly that the recent she-shed craze had less to do with contemporary decorating trends and more to do with women finally figuring out what men and their man caves have known for all of eternity: personal space promotes marital harmony.

Lu's husband had his office; she had her craft room with her beloved Cricut cutter, skeins of yarn, racks of punches and paper, and bins filled with all manner of buttons, baubles, and beads. And on the rare occasion her husband, Pete, deigned to enter, he usually started perspiring at the threshold. Several years ago, when Lu was recovering from knee surgery and had asked him to fetch some yarn for a sweater she was knitting, you would have thought she'd asked him to enter a radioactive room without a hazmat suit.

Likewise, with the exception of her occasional effort to keep the dust from growing thick enough to be considered a health hazard, Lu rarely poked her head into her husband's study. Even then, one could argue that dusting was futile, as every available surface was covered with reports and clippings and half-drunk cups of coffee. She had thought that when he'd retired last summer, much of the paper would have finally disappeared, but it hadn't. And now, in a desperate attempt to find her missing wedding ring, Lu was going to have to venture into his domain.

Her husband's office was not a logical place for the ring to be hiding, but she'd exhausted all of the logical places. At least twice. "I'm sure it'll turn up," Pete had said when she'd asked him about it a few weeks ago. "Have you checked the pockets of your gardening belt?" That's where she'd found her ring the last time she'd misplaced it. But it was February, and she hadn't been gardening since fall. Lu took off her ring frequently—to wash her hands, make sourdough bread, put on lotion or sunscreen, or go swimming in the ocean. The last place she remembered seeing it was near her bathroom sink when she'd removed it to put cream on her face before bed.

"You don't think it fell down the drain, do you?" she'd asked as she crawled between the covers one night.

"Doubtful," her husband had replied. And as if to emphasize his lack of concern, he'd closed his book, rolled over, and turned off the light.

Lu was at a loss, so she decided to take advantage of Pete's absence this morning. He'd walked from their beach cottage in the Rehoboth Heights neighborhood to the downtown public library and would be gone for a few hours. She wasn't really snooping—neither of them locked their respective spaces—but all the same, it felt like a bit of an invasion. Still, desperate times; desperate measures.

The room had south- and east-facing windows, and the sharp slant of winter light shone through, illuminating the piles of papers as well as the need for a good dusting. Lu wasn't sure where to start. Glancing around, an article from the *Cape Gazette* caught her eye. It was a recipe for chocolate cupcakes from Denise Clemons's "Cape Flavors" column. *That's weird*, she thought. Pete fussed if she asked him to stir a pot on the stove; she couldn't imagine him baking cupcakes. But then Pete had been acting strangely ever since he'd retired last summer.

Lu's friend Birdie had told her to Google "retirement blues," and sure enough, there were over one hundred thousand hits. Clicking on a few of the links, Lu discovered it was fairly common, especially among men. Birdie said her husband had gone through the same thing when he retired but that once he found golf, he never looked back. "Pete will find his way," Birdie assured her. "You just have to be patient." And so, Lu was practicing patience. Lots of patience, as Pete's moods jitterbugged between depressed and delighted. Lately though, his bouts of blues seemed to be less frequent. Birdie, it appeared, knew what she was talking about.

Lu set aside the chocolate cupcake recipe and started gathering coffee cups. Perhaps she'd removed her ring the last time she came to collect them. It didn't make sense, but then one morning, she'd found her cell phone on a shelf in the refrigerator, so it wasn't completely out of the realm of possibility either.

Lu carted four cups to the kitchen sink and returned to her husband's desk, patting the piles as if she were checking her pockets for keys. A small lump caught her attention. She lifted the papers, then sighed. It was only a pen. "This is a waste of time," Lu muttered to herself. As she turned to leave, she accidentally bumped the corner of his laptop. The screen came to life, and the word *poison* caught her attention.

Pushing her glasses up on the bridge of her nose, Lu squinted at the illuminated display. In the search bar, Pete had typed, "undetectable poisons." *How odd.* Then Lu noticed a paper on which he'd scribbled, "Arsenic—no taste, color, or smell. Consider western hemlock."

Lu was not prone to hysterics. Still, this gave her cause to pause. Why was Pete searching for information about poisons? Activ Pest Solutions took care of the mice that tried to use their home for a winter warm-up. Pete did have an ongoing dispute with their neighbors over their yappy little dog, but surely, he wasn't thinking about snuffing Fluffy!

Pete had been retired for almost nine months. Lu recalled the links in her Google search. Some of them included shocking headlines about men who hadn't been able to make the transition to retirement successfully and went on a rampage. She shook her head. This was absurd. There had to be a reasonable explanation. Rifling through a few more piles, Lu found a sticky note on which he'd scrawled, "Death by Chocolate." It was stuck to a piece of haphazardly torn paper, and when Lu turned it over, she gasped. In red pen, he'd written:

**Lu's Favorite Foods – Valentine's Day "Surprise"**
- Lobster mac and cheese
- Thrasher's with extra vinegar
- Bennett's peaches
- Rocky road ice cream
- Dark chocolate!!!

He'd even circled "dark chocolate" several times as if the exclamation points weren't enough. Lu tucked the paper back where she'd found it and left his study, pulling the door shut behind her.

* * * * *

The next morning, bundled up against a winter wind blowing in off the Atlantic, Lu met her friends Gemma and Birdie near the historic temperance drinking fountain on the boardwalk in downtown Rehoboth Beach. As members of the Silver Striders, they tried to walk at least one mile, five days a week—more when Gemma convinced them to register for a race. Supposedly, they were in training for the Shamrock Shuffle next month.

"Birdie's still got her cane," Gemma announced as they arrived.

Birdie shot her a death stare. The cane had appeared almost a year ago, shortly after Birdie's husband had passed, and Gemma and Lu couldn't figure out any reason for it other than Birdie felt she needed something to lean on. "But that's what friends are for," Lu had told her when they encouraged her to leave it behind. Birdie had grunted in response.

The conversation today, however, wasn't about Birdie's cane. Lu needed their advice. She'd been mulling over her discovery and had come to the only possible conclusion: "I think Pete's trying to poison me."

"That's ridiculous," Birdie said, tapping her cane on the boardwalk for emphasis.

"Why would he want to poison you?" Gemma asked, as she pumped her arms, a purple one-pound weight clutched in each gloved fist. "It makes no sense."

"It makes perfect sense," Lu said. "I've got two words for you: *life insurance.*"

Birdie wrinkled her silver brow. "But you've got plenty of money… Don't you?"

"I thought so." Lu tightened the cashmere scarf around her neck. "I don't think Pete would have retired if we needed money, but when he came to bed last night, he was reading a book on gambling."

"Did you ask him about it?" Gemma lifted her arms overhead. "Triceps," she said as they both looked at her.

"He said he was brushing up for our next trip to Atlantic City."

"Well, you have been going there a lot since he retired." Birdie tapped her cane again energetically. "Maybe he lost all your investments at the blackjack table."

Lu sucked in a deep, salty breath of sea air. This was all too much to consider, even as the pieces started clicking into place like tumblers on a padlock before it popped open.

"Let's say you're right," Gemma said, in a voice that clearly indicated she thought Lu was out of her mind. "When do you think he's going to do it?"

"Tonight. He knows how much I love chocolate, and it's Valentine's Day. He's even taking me to Salt Air for dinner."

"Hrmph." Gemma worked her biceps, thrusting her arms in front of her like a boxer. "At least you've got a date."

After their requisite mile, the threesome strolled up Rehoboth Avenue to Browseabout Books for a cup of coffee and a heart-shaped sugar cookie. They ordered at the window, and then Birdie went inside for her book club meeting. She had told them she was very excited because local author Ethan Joella was coming to talk about his debut novel, *A Little Hope*, which Birdie adored.

Lu waited with Gemma on the curb near The Coffee Mill's 1941 Chevy Chester. The truck was a fixture in its parking spot on Rehoboth Avenue and was always decorated for the current holiday. Today it was draped in red and white hearts. Next month it would be shamrocks and leprechauns. Gemma's granddaughter, Rynn, had just gotten her license and honked as she approached. "See you tonight," Gemma said to Lu as she opened the car door. "But for the record, I still think you're crackers."

Lu made a split-second decision as she watched the little Honda with its rainbow bumper sticker disappear down Rehoboth Avenue. Her husband, who'd rarely read a book until he retired, was suddenly spending a great deal of time at the library. He'd told her he was meeting friends, but in light of her recent discovery, everything he said and did seemed suspect.

Lu crossed at Second Street and entered through the library's automatic sliding doors. The stairs were just ahead. If she were quick, she could slip through, avoiding her friend Helen, who volunteered at the circulation desk. Lu didn't have time to chat. Once upstairs, she pulled her knit cap low and tucked her chin as she passed an open door where Lu spied Pete sitting at a table with a notebook in front of him. He was writing furiously, as was everyone else around the table. Lu observed from the shadows. When they put down their pens, a woman asked if anyone wanted to share, and she watched her husband raise his hand.

"Hi, I'm Pete," to which everyone responded, "Hi Pete." Lu wheezed audibly as the padlock in her mind sprung open. *A Gambler's Anonymous Meeting.*

The group broke up, and Lu hustled around the corner, trying to decide her next move, when she heard her husband's voice again. "Thanks for a great meeting, Nancy. See you next week."

Lu bit down on a gloved finger to keep from making a sound. Without thinking about it, she decided to follow him. She watched as he left the library, turned right, and crossed at First Street, waiting in the median as the light changed. Lu hung back, ducking behind trees and in shop alcoves as she'd seen people do on detective shows, but Pete never looked over his shoulder. He passed First and Anchor and went into Chocolate Wave, a boutique chocolate shop with hand-crafted confections. Under normal circumstances, Lu would have been thrilled. She considered chocolate a food group, and the Rehoboth Beach Chocolate Festival was her favorite annual event. But now she couldn't help wondering what nefarious plans he had for his purchase.

Lu turned and headed toward home. Twenty minutes later, as she was brewing a cup of peppermint tea to settle her nerves, Pete walked through the front door. "I've got a surprise for you."

Lu lifted her eyebrows.

Pete set a bag from Chocolate Wave on the counter. "Chocolate sea salt caramels and marshmallows. I couldn't remember which was your favorite, so I got both."

*Covering all your bases*, she thought, as he leaned over and kissed her cheek.

"Just the start of my Valentine surprises." He winked. "I'm looking forward to our date."

Pete was acting as if he'd taken a direct hit from Cupid's arrow, which, as far as Lu could tell, was even further proof that the end was near. He disappeared into his office, and as soon as she was alone with the confections, Lu inspected each one with a magnifying glass, looking to see where he might have poked a syringe to inject it with poison. They appeared to be unmarred, but Lu wasn't taking any chances. She dumped them into the garbage with a sigh. It was a shame. She really did love their chocolates.

* * * * *

Salt Air's décor was modern farmhouse with a relaxed beach vibe. Distressed wood, hand-hammered vintage signs and window seats with inviting cushions and pillows charmed both locals and tourists. Lu especially loved the tall black pepper grinders and milking-can-shaped saltshakers in little wooden crates on the tables.

They were seated near a large antique mirror with a white wooden frame, and in its reflection, Lu could see Birdie and Gemma at a cozy two-top near the front window. Even though her friends had made it clear they thought Lu was playing Chinese checkers without all of her marbles, they still agreed to show up for moral support.

"But if it turns out he hasn't gambled away your life savings, dinner's on you," Gemma had said.

"Of course," Lu had answered.

"Do you think we should go incognito?" Birdie had asked. "I've got a red wig."

"It's not the Sea Witch Festival; it's Valentine's Day," Gemma had replied. "We'll just hide behind our menus."

Once Lu and Pete were seated, Pete leaned across the table conspiratorially. "Did you see Gemma and Birdie are here?" He smiled at them and waved.

*So much for hiding behind their menus.* Lu scanned the dinner options. "I think I'll order—"

"The seafood stew. It's your favorite."

Lu bristled. "I didn't realize I was so predictable."

The waiter took their order, and Pete smiled at her. "Predictable's not so bad, but I'd like to think we've still got a few surprises left between us."

"That depends on the surprise." Lu narrowed her eyes as he reached into his jacket pocket, pulled out a red heart-shaped candy box, and slid it across the table.

"I think you'll like this surprise."

"You already gave me chocolate today."

"But this one's special."

Lu lifted the lid to reveal a single chocolate heart with her given name, Lucille, written on top. Warning bells clanged inside her head. Pete only called her Lucille when he was trying to be charming or seductive.

"I'm not eating that!" Her voice attracted the attention of nearby diners.

"I don't think you'll spoil your dinner," Pete said, nonplussed. "I was going to wait for dessert, but you know patience isn't one of my virtues."

"If you're so excited, why don't you eat it?"

Pete shrugged. "OK." And then he took his spoon and tapped the center of the heart, cracking it open.

Lu peered inside and saw a flash of white among the broken chocolate. Curiosity overruling reason, she reached in, pulled out a small slip of paper and carefully unfolded it. The words jumped off the page. *Will you marry me again?* Lu gasped and when she looked up, Pete was down on one knee, holding out a dazzling version of her missing wedding ring.

"Is that my ring?" she asked, wide-eyed.

"With some improvements. I had Harry K add a few more stones. I figured it's the least you're owed after putting up with me all these years."

"Does that mean we're not broke?"

Pete kitted his brows. "Broke? Where would you get an idea like that?" Lu shook her head as she reached for the ring, but Pete pulled it back. "I'm still waiting for my answer, and if I have to wait much longer, I may never be able to get up."

Lu laughed. "Of course, I'll marry you. Again."

Pete slipped the ring on her finger and then, as the other diners erupted in applause, he hoisted himself back into his chair. Snagging a piece of chocolate, he asked, "So why would you think we're broke?"

"Because you've been reading gambling books," Lu said. "And your library meetings. I thought maybe they were for Gambler's Anonymous."

Pete threw his head back in a full-throated laugh. "Wait until I tell my group about this," he said, shoulders still vibrating in amusement. "This is going to make for a great story."

Lu admired her ring. It twinkled in the candlelight, and she immediately forgave Pete for making her think she'd misplaced it. But then, as his words rearranged themselves inside her brain, she asked, "What story?"

"Lu," Pete's voice was suddenly very serious. "The meetings I've been attending…they're…FreeWrites."

"Free what?"

"FreeWrites. For people who want to write."

"But you've never said anything about wanting to write."

Pete dipped his head. "Well, I wasn't sure I'd be any good."

"Hogwash! You're good at everything."

Pete chuckled. "I'm sure there's some debate on that, but I did take a class from Maribeth Fisher at the Rehoboth Beach Writers' Guild, and she was very encouraging."

"Still, I expect your first story to be dedicated to me." Lu smiled. "After all, I'm the one who told you to find a hobby."

Pete reached across the table and took her hand. "You will always be my muse."

"So, what's your story about?"

"It's a mystery. A whodunnit."

"Somebody dies?"

"Yep," Pete said in a stage whisper, "by poisoning."

Lu nodded as she reached for a piece of chocolate, savoring the creamy complexity as it melted on her tongue. "I think you should put the poison in chocolate."

The waiter arrived with their dinners. After he left, Pete said, "I was thinking the same thing, but we probably shouldn't be talking about this in public. Someone could overhear and get the wrong idea."

Lu lifted a spoonful of fragrant seafood chowder to her lips. "Oh, I wouldn't worry about that. People jump to all kinds of conclusions that aren't true."

"Pardon me." Their waiter had returned. "The ladies over there," he inclined his head toward Gemma and Birdie, "told me to give you their check?"

Lu reached for the bill. "I thought we'd treat tonight, Pete."

"Of course. And let's invite them back to the house for champagne and chocolates." Lu did some mental gymnastics, trying to figure out how she could rescue the confections from the garbage. "Somehow they ended up in the trash," Pete said, "but I pulled them out before any damage was done."

Lu tilted her head. "Did Gemma call you?"

"Let's just say an overactive imagination is a good trait for a writer. Maybe you should take one of Maribeth's classes?"

"Thanks, but I think I'll stick to helping you brainstorm." She took another bite of her seafood stew. "You know, when we renew our vows, the reception would be an excellent place for a dead body to turn up."

"Never wonder why I asked you to marry me again." Pete leaned forward and kissed the back of her hand. "Happy Valentine's Day, Lu."

"It will be as soon as I get my caramels."

RENÉE ROCKLAND IS AN AWARD-WINNING SHORT STORY WRITER WHO LONGS FOR RETIREMENT SO SHE CAN MOVE PERMANENTLY TO HER BELOVED REHOBOTH BEACH AND BECOME AN EVEN MORE ACTIVE MEMBER OF THE INCREDIBLE REHOBOTH BEACH WRITERS' GUILD. UNTIL THEN, SHE LIVES IN MARYLAND, WORKING IN PUBLIC EDUCATION DURING THE SCHOOL YEAR AND PLAYING ON THE DELAWARE SEASHORE DURING THE SUMMER, DOING RESEARCH FOR HER NEXT STORY, WHICH LOOKS A LOT LIKE TRYING NEW RESTAURANTS, DRIVING AROUND WITH THE TOP DOWN ON HER JEEP, AND READING BOOKS ON THE BEACH. PREVIOUS PUBLISHING CREDITS/AWARDS INCLUDE *BEACH SECRETS*, *THE YEAR'S BEST DOG STORIES 2021*, *SNOW IN AUGUST*, AND *THE BREASTFEEDING CAFE*. IN ADDITION TO THE GUILD, SHE IS A MEMBER OF THE EASTERN SHORE WRITERS ASSOCIATION. YOU CAN CONNECT WITH HER ON FACEBOOK.

## JUDGE'S COMMENT

*A couple of a certain age has settled into routines after years of marriage, and the wife's sleuth work uncovers disturbing items in her husband's part of the house, only to conclude in a delightful ending. Well written and the roles are identifiable. "Death by Chocolate" is fun, fast-paced, and peppered with pointed and relevant details that made the story plausible and will make readers want to find out 'whodunnit.' The mention of various Rehoboth sights as well as local persons helped make the story feel real, and the twist, while predicable on some level, was handled with a delicate touch. Tight and light and just right. Excellent story.*

# Ethereal

## By Steve Saulsbury

*"Gentlemen, this is no humbug!"*
—Dr. John Warren, October 16, 1846

### Spring 2019

My wife, Dana, and I had taken the Jeep downtown and parked on Wilmington Street. She was training hard and needed a break. And she wanted to buy her cousin a T-shirt at Funland.

"Do you remember the green one I had? With the clown? I wore it to kickboxing."

"What happened to it?" Dana asked. "You don't throw anything away."

*Gone,* I mused. *Into thin air.*

It was late May, the briny breeze recalling countless summer memories. Vacationers and day trippers were starting to fill Rehoboth Beach. There were no clouds. The sun, like the house lights in a theater, made an abandoned beer can shine like gold.

We didn't stay long at the boardwalk. Later, I wondered if we should have.

That afternoon, at the Sussex Dance Academy, Dana came down on her foot exactly the wrong way.

Fifth metatarsal broken.

We didn't know if she would ever dance again.

\* \* \* \* \*

The surgery was scheduled at St. Joe's in Towson, Maryland. My sister Sue, an anesthesiologist, referred Dana. She drove us to the hospital.

"She'll recover," said Sue. "It's amazing what they can do with titanium."

We were sitting in an airport-sized corridor. Muted light came through the floor-to-ceiling windows. Outside was a garden sanctuary, like a miniature rain forest. I gazed at the ferns and bubbling fountain under a tinted dome. Peaceful.

"Is the anesthesia safe?"

"Of course. It's very safe. In the event of a problem, the team is fully prepared. There are always risks.

My mind was wandering. I swallowed the last of my lukewarm coffee. The echoing corridor reminded me of studios where Dana had danced. She had been training for an audition in New York. Now we just wanted to return to Rehoboth.

"She'll bounce back," Sue said. "Don't worry."

### Summer 2019

Dana called. Her mother had accompanied her to New York for some diversion. She was in Times Square, wearing a boot. The surgery had gone well.

Energy hummed within the city blocks. Dana needed that for her recovery, as much as the calming surf and vitamin D at home.

"We just saw the Naked Cowboy," she said.

"I bet your mother liked that."

The trip was also consolation for her audition, indefinitely postponed. They were going to see *To Kill a Mockingbird* on Broadway. I was busy in Rehoboth, helping a friend with his first major photography exhibit at Gallery 50.

"How's the foot?" I asked.

"Better. It's getting better."

That was all I needed to hear.

## October 16, 2019

Sue wanted to meet us in Rehoboth. She said it was so *appropriate* to celebrate Dana's recovery, *and* her own professional holiday at the beach. She didn't say why. That's my sister, being mysterious. Sue does things like show up with a pie from Dangerously Delicious and say, "Guess what? It's National Pie Day!"

Dana had fully recovered. Back in her red ballroom dance pumps, cautiously at first. She had worn her ortho boot religiously, only complaining when it got sand inside.

Thoughts of the painful break and surgery receded, like the smell of popcorn on the breeze. We went to Louie's for pizza before meeting Sue on the boardwalk. She greeted us with a bunch of balloons and a brown-paper package under her arm.

"Helium. No inhaling!" I attempted to pitch my voice higher and ended up sounding like Pee-wee Herman.

"Did you know that helium can be used to treat respiratory ailments?" Sue asked.

"Oh, you're here for a medical conference, right?" asked Dana.

Sue laughed. "Not exactly. It's World Anesthesia Day."

"What?" I said. "No way."

"Yep. We've taken over Rehoboth."

"Anesthesia," Dana said. "I'm certainly glad for that." She did a quick rumba step. Her fashionably chopped hair fell across her face, but I knew she was smiling.

"Oh, no." Sue said, nodding toward the bandstand. "There's some of the group,"

A quartet of guitarists shuffled into the performance area, all wearing scrubs. After conferring and tuning, they began playing "Classical Gas."

Sue laughed. "Those guys!"

"What else are you doing?" I asked.

"We've got some things scheduled at the convention center. Lectures, workshops. Usual stuff. They're showing an old movie—*Awake*. It was pretty controversial. Still a conversation starter."

"Who knew?" I said. "So, is this the first time for this?"

"No, it's every October 16. Anesthesia is a big deal. Surgery without pain," Sue replied. "In fact…" She handed Dana the package.

We sat on a bench and Dana unwrapped the brown paper, revealing a framed art print. It was a depiction of an operating theater. Bold lines and light cut through somber tones.

"That's it," explained Sue. "*The First Operation Under Ether*. By your hometown guy, Hinckley."

"Hinckley?"

"Yes, Robert Cutler Hinckley. His painting is famous. The original is in the Library of Medicine in Boston. He lived here."

"He lived in Rehoboth?" Dana asked.

"He did. Eighty years ago. Right on Wilmington Avenue. He died in 1941. We're having a little presentation about him and the painting at the conference."

"I never heard of him," I admitted.

I imagined an old artist on the boardwalk.

*The planks are a little rougher, the air a little cleaner. Clutching his easel and supplies, hoping the wind is mild. He spies a young dancer, her dress sparkling like whitecaps, the athletic lines of her figure as sharp as a blade. A blade whose edge bore no pain.*

"See the etherizer?" Sue was saying. "Like gold. And the surgeon, Dr. Warren."

Dana was looking at the ocean. Her foot traced a circle in the fine sand.

I touched her arm, my fingertips sensing the faintest impression of salt, as it escaped, cast into the ether.

A group of teenagers came near. I blocked Dana from their jostling.

We stayed a while, under the fragile sky. The soothing crash of waves lulled us.

A last repose before Dana danced again.

STEVE SAULSBURY WRITES FROM MARYLAND'S EASTERN SHORE. HIS WORK HAS APPEARED IN ONLINE JOURNALS SUCH AS *MUDROOM MAGAZINE, THIMBLE LIT, THE YARD,* AND *PRESS 53.* HE WON FIRST PRIZE IN THE 2021 REHOBOTH BEACH READS SHORT STORY CONTEST, AND HIS STORY WAS SUBSEQUENTLY PUBLISHED IN *BEACH SECRETS.* IN ADDITION TO WRITING, STEVE ENJOYS SEARCHING FOR TREASURES AT AUCTIONS AND YARD SALES, VISITING WITH HIS GRANDSON, AND CONSIDERING WHICH BAND'S DISCOGRAPHY TO EXPLORE NEXT.

WHILE RESEARCHING IDEAS FOR THIS YEAR'S CONTEST, STEVE DISCOVERED ROBERT CUTLER HINCKLEY, THE NINETEENTH-CENTURY ARTIST WHO PAINTED *THE FIRST OPERATION UNDER ETHER.* THIS LED TO OCTOBER 16, WORLD ANESTHESIA DAY. HINCKLEY LIVED OUT HIS FINAL DAYS IN REHOBOTH, ON WILMINGTON AVE, WHERE HE REPORTEDLY OWNED A COTTAGE.

IN AN UNFORTUNATE COINCIDENCE, STEVE WAS DIAGNOSED WITH A FRACTURED FEMUR AS HE WAS FINISHING HIS STORY. SURGERY SOON FOLLOWED…UNDER ANESTHESIA. AN UNPLEASANT TWIST OF FATE!

# Big Wind and Big Water

## By Tony Houck

*A week after the nor'easter of '62*

For two days the storm had parked off the Delaware coast, piling up waves that devoured the sea walls, scoured the dunes, and drowned the inland. The wind had roared. In Rehoboth, the boardwalk had been stripped of its planks, and along its skeleton the shops and eateries lay in shreds. But this morning the sky was clear and blue, and as the mid-March sun took the chill off the air, resilience and determination were again winning the day.

As the cleanup continued, an excavator tracked toward the bones of the boardwalk and rattled to a stop behind a pile of rubble near the Rehoboth Beach Sport Center. Owned by the Dentino family, the amusement park had opened in 1939, and it was—only Mother Nature knew how—still standing.

The excavator operator grabbed the cup lid of his thermos and took a sip of coffee. He stared at the facade of the sport center, continuing to sip. *The rest of that wall's gotta come down…and that part of the roof's shot*, he thought. *Bound to be more work around the back, but all in all it looks great.* He set down the coffee and reached for his Camels and lighter. *Got me how it survived.* He lit a cigarette and, after taking a drag, radioed his friend working down the beach. "I can't believe what I'm seeing here at the sport center," he said into the speaker microphone.

"Ay, it don't make any sense, does it?" his friend said, in a thick Irish accent.

"Them Dentinos must be livin' right."

"God bless 'em."

The two men discussed other matters related to the cleanup and then turned to their plans for after work.

"Where we gonna celebrate your holiday this year?" the operator said. "The pubs've been destroyed."

"But not my patio or my generator. My beer fridge's cold, and it's *chock lán* of bottles of Guinness."

"God bless that."

"God bless us all," the friend said warmly and then clicked off the radio, returning a few moments later. "The boss is here. He's on his way to you next. We better get back at it."

"Gotcha. What time tonight?"

"Come over around seven." He clicked off the radio again, but returned quickly: "Do you have any Candelas left? They didn't get wet in the storm, did they?"

The operator smiled, knowing how much his Irish friend loved those light-green cigars. "They're safe. I'll bring a few with me."

"And wear your green shirt."

With a "roger that" the operator hung up, rotated toward the pile of rubble next to him, and raised the boom. As the bucket reached forward, it spooked a black-headed gull off its perch.

The bird lit on the carousel just inside the sport center and began to straighten and clean its feathers using its bill. When it had finished preening, it sat contentedly, staring here and there almost as if it were pondering how the amusement park had fared so well. The bird cocked its head and squawked.

In the open-air rear of the park, Al Fasnacht and his family were also puzzled by what they were seeing, having just arrived from

Pennsylvania to assess the damage, along with members of the Dentino family, who had traveled up from Florida. Al adjusted his hat and sunglasses and smiled at his wife and then at their children.

The Fasnachts owned a small recreation park in Harrisburg and had been on a beach holiday in Rehoboth the prior year. During that visit, they had taken a liking to the sport center and had discussed buying it with the Dentinos. A deal had recently been reached between the two families, but the nor'easter had put the settlement in doubt.

"I'll let you talk among yourselves," Mr. Dentino said. "Take all the time you need. Look around, but I wouldn't go inside, though...until the building's been deemed safe."

Al nodded and thanked him.

Mr. Dentino nodded back and shuffled away.

A short while later, the two families struck a new deal that allowed for the damage and signed the documents. The Fasnachts renamed the park Funland. The games included six Skee-Ball machines: three that came through the storm intact, two that had been crushed and replaced with new ones, and one that needed a little help. Each play was a nickel.

No one, not even the black-headed gull with its keen eyes, had seen the tiny, triangular spaceship that lay underneath the carousel after the storm.

*****

The tiny, triangular spaceship hadn't stood a chance against the nor'easter, or the Big Wind, as Bip called it. He and his family were lucky to be alive. Looking back on it, Bip's grandfather, or Flumkie as Bip called him, shouldn't have entered the atmosphere over the Big Water, but he did manage to land. (*Land* might be too generous a word; *crash safely* was probably a better way to put it.) Regardless, a rain-soaked gravitational wave generator and a hole in the ship's body, which was made of an asteroid-mined metal, would have been next to impossible to repair without help from home.

No one on DP7—shorthand for Dwarf Planet Seven as it was called in their language—knew where they were. Typical of DP7 family units (adventuresome, industrious, self-sufficient), they had told no one where they were going to spend the holiday commemorating the unification of their multi-planetary system, not even the elderly couple living in the neighboring bog. Decent folks who kept to themselves, of course.

Worse still, during the cleanup from the storm, a Big One had almost seen them while they were inspecting and unpacking their ship. Trembling, they had feared that the Big One *had* seen them, but after rubbing its eyes and shaking its head, it had simply tossed out their ship, perhaps thinking that it was just another damaged prize no child would ever win.

Thank the stars that Flumkie's tools had already been unpacked. Without them, he couldn't have repaired the microswitches inside the machine that was now their home and that they had learned was called Skee-Ball. And even though he couldn't fix the ball return gizmo, as long as each family member did his or her job flawlessly, the Big Ones would never need to take the machine apart and, thus, would remain oblivious to Bip's family's presence.

Of course, the family missed their tiny blue-green planet, but at least for now Funland, which they called the Big Park, was their entire world. And, like the Fasnachts, they were all in the family business.

Bip had begun working when he was very little, even littler than he was now. He had shadowed Flumkie on unseasonably cool days, when the pains of Flumkie's old age overwhelmed his out-of-this-world work ethic. A little man himself, Flumkie had been stern yet patient with young Bip, and long before his back had rounded into a hump, the master had taught his apprentice to move swiftly and quietly while clearing the ball-jams and resetting the scores.

He had also instilled in him, and the other members of the family, a hearts-stopping fear (for they each had two hearts to worry about) of being discovered. *Always stay in your lane,* Flumkie reminded him and the others every morning.

For a youngster like Bip, steering large brown wooden balls from one place to another wasn't work: It was fun and excitement…and money, paid in handfuls of nickels, although he would have worked for free.

Although by day the building rang with cries of disappointment and shrieks of joy, Bip did as he was told and worked his Skee-Ball lane. Besides, the big world outside held nothing but danger for him. At night, however, when the creaky old building was lapped by the murmurs of the pounding surf, Bip explored, leaving his nine fingerprints high and low. His older brothers and sisters often joined him long after the coast was clear. Father and mother preferred to gather food and then retire to discuss other times and lives or to drift off to sleep and dream about the stars.

At least for now, Bip had no dream of being anywhere else or of doing anything else. He was happy inside his lane, inclined though it was. This was the only life he had ever known, even though he had been born so very far away. Maybe he hadn't been born at all, but rather had been grown or had hatched from some tiny egg. Flumkie had never telepathized with him about such things during his apprenticeship.

Because of the fear of being discovered that Flumkie had instilled in each of them, they were the ghosts of Funland. Not even the Big Ones who climbed up the other five machines to clear the balls or reset the scores had ever seen them. Flumkie shuddered to think what the Big Ones would have done to his little family of three-inch-tall out-of-this-worlders with nine fingers and two hearts. Bip didn't know if others of his kind were scattered throughout the big world outside. Flumkie had taken that knowledge to bed with him tonight, and Bip didn't dare wake him, when he might be dreaming of home. Bip could ask him tomorrow about that or about Dwarf Planet Seven or about other planets he had visited on other holidays. Or maybe Bip would just stay in his lane and leave well enough alone.

TONY HOUCK IS A FORMER SPANISH TRANSLATOR WHO NOW WRITES FULL TIME. HE IS A PRIOR RECIPIENT OF TWO REHOBOTH *BEACH READS* JUDGE'S AWARDS FOR SHORT STORIES THAT CAN BE FOUND IN *BEACH LIFE* AND *BEACH SECRETS*. HIS FIRST NOVEL, *THE PRECARIOUSNESS OF DONE*, WAS RELEASED IN 2019. HE IS CURRENTLY WORKING ON TWO OTHER NOVELS AND IS OWNER AND OPERATOR OF THE BLOG *UNSALTED GEMS* (HTTPS://TONYHOUCK.COM), WHICH FOCUSES ON TRAVEL, SPANISH LANGUAGE AND CULTURE, CRAZY FAMILIES, WRITING AND GETTING PUBLISHED, AND OBSESSIVE-COMPULSIVE DISORDER, FROM WHICH HE HAS SUFFERED FOR MOST OF HIS LIFE.

TONY EXTENDS HIS HEARTFELT THANKS TO AL FASNACHT, NINETY-THREE YEARS YOUNG, FOR TALKING TO HIM BY TELEPHONE AND FOR GIVING HIM BACKGROUND INFORMATION THAT HELPED HIM WRITE THIS STORY, WHICH IS *MOSTLY* FICTION. TONY RESIDES IN HARRISONBURG, VIRGINIA, WITH HIS WIFE, SON, AND THEIR POUND PUPPY.

# A Slice of Pi Day

By June Flavin

Dear Alice,

We all missed you at our annual Bash at the Beach. This would have been your first year with us and we were so excited. I hope your recovery doesn't take too long. We'd love to have you join us in the summer. Ben says it will be no problem to prop you up on the deck so you can watch the rest of us run around like idiots, as we tend to do. You'll most likely still be on crutches by then, giving you dibs on the bedroom behind the kitchen. That way you won't have to use the stairs.

Ben and I got down here on Wednesday night to open the house. We brought a few pies from Serpes in Elsmere for the next day (Pi Day!!!). Everyone else was expected on Thursday, grabbing pies from their favorite bakeries on the way. You can't really celebrate Pi Day without pies!

Everyone was here by dinner, so we grabbed some pizza from Nicola's (pizza counts as pie!) and settled in for game night, which is mostly solving math problems and puzzles, because we're nerds and proud of it.

I'm sure Mark told you about our silly little fun on the Ides of March. On Pi Day (March 14) we eat lots of pie, then while sitting around in a sugar coma, we choose who will play Julius Caesar and Brutus on the Ides of March (March 15). It's someone different every year, so everyone gets a turn. We pull names out of a hat and each person plays that character, though we always have more people than characters, so some of us happily become the audience. Nobody gets hurt unless they fall badly when they pretend to die. It's best to do it outside, if the weather holds up, and this year it did.

It was sixty-five degrees on Thursday, and we had pies melting all over the place. We had to eat them fast, before they all melted away—OK, a bit of an exaggeration, but that's my story and I'm sticking to it. Mostly so I could get into that Boston cream pie. Yes, I know it's cake, but it still counts as pie. I refer to it as pie-cake.

On Friday, the temps went all the way up to seventy-eight. It felt like summer was already here. We'd stocked up on eggs and bacon for breakfast, then we all took a walk down to the boardwalk to enjoy the beautiful weather (and walk off some of those calories). We stopped for our group photo in front of the Dolle's sign. There's been talk that it might be moving, so this may be our last chance to include it in our annual photo. I hope it's still here next year so you can be in the photos too. We spread out to pick up things for the party, then met up back at the house. Ben and I picked up a few pasta pails at Nicola's, Sean grabbed some pizza at Louie's (that's his favorite), and Kyle got Thrasher's fries for the party.

Once we got home and everyone had gotten into their toga costumes, we went out on the deck because the weather was so beautiful. It hit seventy-eight around four p.m. Then we acted out Shakespeare's *Julius Caesar*, but we didn't have any of those fake stage knives with the springs in them, so we just squirted ketchup all over Caesar. It was even more fun than usual because we have a new neighbor who saw what he thought was a fight and came running over to stop it. Once he saw we were all laughing (and realized we were all wearing togas) he laughed along with us. He asked Brutus why he stabbed Caesar, while Ryan was on the floor happily dunking his fries in the ketchup that was all over him. Sean looked at the neighbor and said, "He's dunking his fries in ketchup. Clearly, he has to die." The neighbor nodded in agreement and started walking away. We all burst out laughing and insisted he stay and eat with us.

Turns out he had just bought the house and was planning on living here full time. His name is Bruce (what are the odds?), so we've made him the honorary Brutus for next year. He did join us for dinner, which is a good thing because we had tons of it. And there was plenty of leftover pie for dessert.

The wind picked up just after we went inside and it didn't let up until after nine p.m., so Bruce stayed with us for a couple of hours. I think Mom is already set on marrying him off to one of my single sisters, so there were a lot of apologetic looks from us to Bruce. He took it all in stride. Turns out his mother has been doing the same to him for quite some time. Must be a mother thing. I'm sure I'll do the same one day when Ben and I have kids of our own.

So now you know how silly we are when we're together. I hope this doesn't put you off hanging out with us, and we really hope you can get down to the beach this summer. I've never had a broken leg, so I don't know how long it takes to recover.

I hope your recuperation is speedy and that you can join us soon.

Here's to better times,

Love, Andrea

June 13, 2019

JUNE FLAVIN IS AN ACCOUNTANT WORKING IN CAMDEN, NEW JERSEY, AND LIVING IN WILMINGTON, DELAWARE. SHE ENJOYS CREATING STORIES ON HER LONG DRIVE TO AND FROM WORK. SHE HAS ALWAYS BEEN ATTRACTED TO THE OCEAN AND SPENDS AS MUCH TIME THERE AS SHE CAN. BELIEVING THAT THERE IS NO POINT TO TRAVELING UNLESS YOU END UP WITH YOUR FEET IN THE WATER TOOK HER TO GALWAY BAY IN IRELAND AND THE BLACK SEA IN CONSTANŢA, ROMANIA. SHE HAS PREVIOUSLY BEEN PUBLISHED IN THE 2022 DELAWARE BARDS POETRY REVIEW.

# Holiday Hijinks

## By Lonn Braender

"See the TV news?" Wyatt texted Asher.

"OMG!" Asher's response was immediate.

Wyatt pushed the call button. "We're in trouble. My dad's going to kill me when he finds out."

"We should run away. I have a cousin in Montana," Asher whispered.

"Where's Montana?" Wyatt looked around as if someone were listening.

"On the other side of Pennsylvania. You can't drive there."

"I don't know how to fly." Wyatt's voice trembled.

"Did they mention us?"

"No. All the mayor said was Monday is officially National Parents Do Homework Day." Wyatt leaned over and absent mindedly scratched Hijinks, who rubbed and purred against his ankle.

"He didn't say it was a joke?"

"No." Wyatt looked around again. His parents were out back having coffee.

"Maybe, since it was your dad's computer, they think it's real."

Wyatt's father stepped into the house shaking his head. Wyatt gulped. "Gotta go." He popped up, the cat bolted, and he shoved his phone into his pocket.

"Wyatt," his dad said with a frown. "What homework do you have due on Monday?"

"An algebra worksheet and a report on *Lord of the Flies*." His voice was tight.

"Mom can help you with the report. Give me your algebra

worksheet." His dad walked past.

"Uh, OK."

On Monday morning, Wyatt carried two homework assignments into school. Both were perfect. In fact, every student in his class handed in homework, a first.

After school, Asher ran to catch up. "Wy! Wy! Wait up."

"Can you believe it? Everybody's parents did their homework!" Wyatt was wide-eyed.

"I know, what do we do next?" Asher grinned a wicked smile.

"Next? Nothing. If my dad ever finds out that I used his computer to make up National Parents Do Homework Day, I'll be grounded for life."

"But what if next Monday was Free Ice Cream for Eighth Graders Day?"

"No, they'd figure that out."

"OK," Asher said, "how about Free Ice Cream for All Kids Under Sixteen Day?"

"Why sixteen?"

"My brother's a jerk."

The two boys walked home, discussing ice cream and holidays. When Wyatt got home, there was a note on the fridge from his mother telling him she'd be late and to do his homework. Wyatt immediately texted Asher. "Alone. Bring your iPad."

"OMW." Moments later, Asher's bike skidded to a stop. He ran in and up to Wyatt's room, but the room was empty.

"Wy?"

"Down here."

Asher raced down the stairs and into Wyatt's dad's office. "What are we doing?"

"Mom's out until dinner. We have an hour to play Fortnight." Wyatt opened his father's laptop. The seal of the United States of America lit the screen but was suddenly hidden by the cat who jumped onto the keyboard.

"Hijinks, get down." Wyatt shooed the cat off the laptop and then placed his index finger on the touch-button.

"How did you get your fingerprint to work?"

"Cool—right? My dad was showing me how it worked and let me scan my finger, but then he got a call and forgot to delete it."

The computer came to life, displaying "Parents Do Homework Day" still highlighted in red.

"Dude, you didn't close the program." Asher pointed.

"I just shut the lid after Hijinks jumped on the keyboard and sent the notice. I have to delete that." Wyatt deleted the email to the Rehoboth mayor.

"I was thinking." Asher leaned in. "They can't have a free ice cream day, but…" He held up his index finger. "They could have a free second scoop day."

Wyatt stared at his best friend. Slowly, as he worked it out in his mind, his grin grew and grew. He turned, clicked on the following Monday on the government computer's calendar, and typed in "Free Second Scoop of Ice Cream Day." He clicked OK, and a window popped up. He slid down the row until he found Mayor Schorr's email and hesitated only a second, then hit send. He deleted the record of the email, launched Fortnight, and began battling his way through the catacombs of Mars.

Wyatt hit *command-Q* and slammed the computer closed as soon as the back door opened. The two boys raced out of Wyatt's father's office and into the kitchen, giggling.

* * * * *

That Sunday night, Wyatt's dad sat up quickly when WRDE, the local news station, broke into a *Sixty Minutes* interview of Tom Cruise with a special report.

"We will return to regular programming after this special announcement from Rehoboth Beach Mayor Cecil Schorr."

The TV feed switched, and Mayor Schorr appeared, standing behind a podium and staring into the camera. He announced that Monday would be National Second Scoop Day and decreed that anyone selling ice cream needed to give a second scoop to all who requested it. He went on to tell both residents and business owners how this kind of off-season event helps with community appreciation.

Wyatt's dad, brow tight with wrinkles, looked at his wife. "There's no such thing as National Second Scoop Day."

"He's making it up, just like that homework day," Wyatt's mother said.

"Yeah, but he's saying it's national, a Federal Government holiday. He knows as well as I there's no such thing. What's he got up his sleeve?"

Wyatt's mom shrugged.

After school on Monday, Wyatt's mother picked up Wyatt and Asher at school and drove downtown. The first empty parking spot was blocks from the boardwalk, rare in winter. When they reached the boardwalk, there were dozens waiting in line in front of Boardwalk Scoop.

At school the next day, Wyatt and Asher couldn't stop giggling. Everyone was talking about the free ice cream.

"Wy," Asher said, "we have to do something for next Monday."

"I know. But what?"

"What about a free pass from school?"

"We can't give everyone a day off. No, it has to be something small, that won't cost much."

"How about a no homework day?"

"We just did homework." Wyatt put his hand to his chin like his dad did when thinking. "I got it. Free Pepsi day!" He spun.

Asher shook his head. "I like Coke."

"OK, a free soda day." Wyatt hopped. "Restaurants have to give away soda."

"Come on." Asher grabbed Wyatt's arm and pulled him along.

An hour later, Wyatt closed his dad's laptop, grinning. "I'm going to Thrasher's; they have gigantic cups."

"I'm asking for no ice." Asher laughed.

As he did the previous week, Mayor Schorr announced National Free Soda Day. He read out the rules and explained how it would benefit the city's morale. But this Monday was different from the last few. Sure, there were lines in front of most restaurants, but there was also a crowd in front of city hall, demanding to see the mayor. Some carried cardboard signs protesting "Schorr's Shore Giveaway."

That evening, WRDE reported live from Rehoboth with two television trucks, one focused on the mob at city hall and the other on the throngs of thirsty people queuing in front of Thrasher's.

Wyatt's dad shook his head again. He turned to his wife, "What is Schorr thinking?"

No one protested Fist-Bump Day the following week, but the week after that, city buses and a Jolly Trolley blocked Rehoboth Avenue over Free Rides for Teens Day. The school board and teachers swarmed city hall on Teachers Take the Test Day.

News reports confounded the public; the mayor insisted the odd holidays were directives from the United States Government, though he couldn't explain why Rehoboth was being singled out. Schorr made certain to stress to the reporter that both Dewey and Bethany had jumped on board, not wanting to lose customers to Rehoboth.

On the first Sunday in April, as the mayor announced Free Sausage on Pizza Day, Wyatt's dad's head snapped, and he glared at his son. Rubbing his chin, he leaned in close. "Wyatt? What have you done?"

The color drained from Wyatt's face, and he started sweating.

"Wyatt, I heard you and Asher talking about sausage pizza yesterday. Did you do this?" Wyatt's father marched into his office, returning faster than he left, laptop in hand.

"What have you done? You've used the power of the federal government to force businesses to give away profits. You've embarrassed parents with homework. You've made teachers take your tests. But worst of all, you used a government computer to commit fraud. When the powers that be find out who did this, and they will, I could go to jail. Do you have any idea how serious this is?"

Wyatt's dad didn't wait for a response. He strode back to his office, slamming the door. Wyatt turned to his mom and they both stared at each other, eyes wide.

"You should go to your room," his mom said. "And lock the door."

Wyatt sat on his bed and pulled out his phone but didn't have time to text Asher.

"WYATT!" His dad's voice boomed.

Wyatt bolted out of his room. His dad's face was redder than he'd ever seen it.

"Put your shoes on. NOW!" His dad spun and marched away.

Wyatt slammed his feet into his sneakers, grabbed a hoodie, and nearly tumbled down the stairs trying to catch up to his dad, who was getting in the car.

Wyatt got in and kept his face perfectly forward, moving only his eyes to see his dad. His dad was so red, Wyatt worried he'd explode right there.

After parking on Rehoboth Avenue, Wyatt's dad grabbed him by his collar and marched him into city hall, Wyatt's feet barely touching the ground. His father said nothing as he dragged his son down the corridor. He knocked but didn't wait, pushing the door open and hauling his son in.

The mayor, a rotund man, rose from behind his desk. He slapped both palms on the desktop and leaned over so far that Wyatt thought the man would tumble down.

"Mr. Mayor, my son has something to say."

His father pushed Wyatt close to the ornate desk. Wyatt could feel the mayor's hot breath on his face. Instinctively, he stepped back, but his dad held him in place.

"Well?" The mayor demanded.

"Hijinks started it." Wyatt's voice was a warbly whisper.

"Hijinks?" The mayor boomed.

"Our cat. We were just goofing around when Hijinks jumped on the keyboard and sent the message. We weren't really going to send it."

"We? Who's *we*?"

"Me and Asher."

"Asher Collins, his classmate and future cellmate." Wyatt's dad growled.

"Son, do you realize what you've done? You have this entire city in a riot. Business owners are mad as hornets, teachers and parents are arguing about tests and homework, the Jolly Trolley had to hire drivers, and…" he leaned over even closer, "everyone is mad at me. What do you have to say for yourself?"

"Sorry?" Wyatt squeezed out. "I only wanted a scoop of coconut."

"Wait outside young man!"

Wyatt slunk out, quietly pulling the door shut. He slumped against the wall. The words were hard to make out, but the sounds were certainly angry. Then suddenly the room went quiet. Wyatt was imagining being on death row when the office door flew open. His heart thumped hard as his dad ordered him in.

Mayor Schorr sat behind his desk, scowling. "Young man, we can't tell anyone about this. It could ruin your father's career, not to mention yours. But that doesn't get you off the hook."

Just then, there was a knock on the door. Asher's father stepped in, dragging Asher by the collar. Asher, eyes as wide as Wyatt's, looked at his friend, then back to the mayor who was once again hulking over his desk. The mayor berated Asher much as he'd done Wyatt.

"Neither of you will ever mention this to anyone. Do you understand?" Mayor Schorr's voice was menacing.

The boys nodded feverishly.

"Because I want to keep this quiet, I won't throw you in jail. But since you spoofed me, I decide the punishment. Starting this Saturday, until Halloween, you're on beach duty. Every Saturday morning, rain or shine, before the lifeguards arrive, you start at Poodle Beach and work your way to Deauville Beach."

"You want us to walk all the way up the beach?" Wyatt looked confused.

"Not just walk, son," Schorr barked. "You'll pick up every bottle, stick, and cigarette butt in the sand. You will pick up anything left or washed up. I want that beach spotless."

"What time do we have to start?" Asher asked.

"Sunrise. Have you seen how much garbage washes up?"

Asher looked to his dad, whose face was pinched and red. "Don't even think of asking for a ride."

"But Dad, that's like miles."

Asher's dad stood, towering over his boy. "Take your pick, walk a few miles to the beach or walk a few feet in a jail cell."

Asher's hand slammed over his mouth; his eyes bulged.

Wyatt spun to look at his dad but was yanked back as the mayor cleared his throat. He leaned so far across the desk, that both boys leaned back. "If you boys ever breathe a word of this, you'll wish all you had to do was clean the beach."

Wyatt's dad stood. "Apologize." He smacked the back of Wyatt's head.

"Sorry, Mr. Mayor."

Asher did the same.

The mayor pointed at the door and barked. "Remember, not a word!" The two dads marched their boys out of city hall and into their cars.

Little was said that night. In addition to the beach punishment, Wyatt was grounded; his phone and iPad were locked away tight, and his fingerprint had been deleted from the government laptop. After doing the dinner dishes, now a permanent chore, Wyatt stopped on his way to his room as the special announcement from the mayor flashed on the TV. He hid outside the den and listened.

"Ladies and gentlemen, it has come to our attention that these recent Monday holidays are in fact not government mandates but a scheme by hackers from Moragovia looking to provoke chaos and anarchy." The mayor glared into the camera as if looking for Wyatt. "We have reason to believe these nefarious *hoodlums* were testing their scheme in Rehoboth before launching it nationwide. Fortunately, city experts shut down these criminals. There will be no more silly Monday holidays."

The mayor looked annoyed when a reporter called out a question. Others followed suit, asking how, who, and why. Schorr deftly responded without answering a single question and quickly thanked the business owners and teachers for their patience. He ended with, "Sausage Day will still happen because many have already made plans."

Wyatt's shoulders slumped. He desperately wanted sausage pizza.

Saturday, Asher was on the beach, trash bag in hand, when Wyatt arrived. They looked at each other but said nothing. As they began walking up the beach, they searched for the secret cameras Mayor Schorr said lined the boardwalk and moved apart when they thought they saw one. Two hours and two full trash bags later, Wyatt and Asher collapsed on a bench at the end of the boardwalk. They were cold, hungry, and their backs hurt from bending down.

Asher looked around; it was a little after eight on a chilly Saturday in April, and there was no one around. "I was kinda hoping my mom would pick me up."

"My dad put his foot down when my mom offered. He said I did the deed and had to pay the price." Wyatt slumped.

"I'm just glad he didn't put us in jail. I heard stories."

"They have to have special jails for good kids, right? We really aren't hoodlums, are we?"

"They have to, right?"

"Well, I'd better get home, I'm still grounded."

"Yeah, me too."

The boys trudged through town until they reached Asher's street. Not wanting to get caught talking, they nodded and parted ways.

The following Monday, on what would have been Free Dessert Day, the city was quiet. The evening news ran a short segment showing a deserted boardwalk, reminding viewers of the crowd that had been there a week earlier. The following Monday, WRDE's Monday holiday mention was missing.

Two and a half weeks after the beach-walk sentence was levied, business owners attending a chamber of commerce meeting commiserated about how slow business was. One woman, the manager of Grotto Pizza, remarked that even though they'd given away a lot of sausage, it had been the best sales day that winter. The ice cream shop owner agreed and said Second Scoop Day had been his best day since summer. Ami from Thrashers said Soda Day was better than some summer Mondays. Across the room, business owner after business owner agreed that Monday holidays had been a boon, and they wanted them back.

A committee was formed that surprised Mayor Schorr the next day. They demanded the city reinstate Monday holidays. They didn't care about the hackers from Moragovia, they needed the business.

Mayor Schorr shook his bulky head, reminding them that the hackers didn't just attack restaurants, but buses, schools, and parents alike.

"Mayor Schorr." A tall woman in a bulky sweater stood. "That

Parents Do Homework Day got me more involved in my kid's schoolwork. I can't tell you how proud my daughter was when she helped me with algebra."

An older man stood. "My grandson got a part-time job driving the trolley—in March. When was the last time the trolley ran in March?"

"It never has," someone in the back yelled.

"We can't have teachers taking tests," Schorr retorted.

"Why not?" A well-dressed woman stood. She raised her hand and began speaking. "Mr. Mayor, my daughter teaches at Cape Henlopen, and she challenged her students to come up with their own test on the course materials. She offered extra credit for any answer she got wrong. Do you know she gave that same test to her students the next day, and every student got a B or better?"

"Yeah, but did she pass the test?" someone heckled.

Some laughed as the woman turned and grinned. "She aced it and challenged her students to do the same."

The crowd applauded.

The murmuring in the room was growing and so was the mayor's perspiration. He raised his hands. "Folks, folks, you don't honestly want me to contact these thugs and get them to take over our businesses and schools, do you?"

"Monday holidays were kind of fun. We had locals in our shop, and we don't even sell food," the owner of Sunshine Sandals responded.

"Get them to make next Monday Tootsie Roll Day," the man from Candy City called out. "We're overstocked."

"How about Whip Cream Day?" someone shouted.

"Doughnut Hole Day!"

"Take the Trolley to Work Day!"

"Cheese On Your Burger Day!"

The room was loud with ideas; Mayor Schorr tried but couldn't quiet them.

"FOLKS! Folks!" The mayor looked around and saw that the crowd had grown to well over fifty. A WRDE van was pulling up outside. "Folks, let me talk to the council and see what we can do." The mayor stepped away from the podium and quickly exited the noisy room.

* * * * *

"Wyatt?" his father called. "Come downstairs."

Wyatt put Hijinks on the floor and forced himself up off the bed. His father probably had yet another chore for him to do. But as Wyatt trudged down the stairs, he saw Mayor Schorr standing next to his father.

Wyatt stopped short and began speaking fast. "We only talked about our punishment, nothing else. I swear, we won't do it again."

"Calm down, son, it's not about talking." Mayor Schorr wrung his hands "Turns out the townspeople got a kick out of those made-up holidays. So, we're thinking, maybe we should keep it up, you know, just until summer."

"But what about Moragovian criminals taking over the country?" Wyatt asked, fighting back a grin.

"Don't you worry about them. You and Asher need to start thinking up holidays again and make sure one of them is Cheese On Your Burger Day—I do like Swiss on my burger."

Wyatt laughed. "Next was supposed to be Dads Clean the Toilet Day." Wyatt's dad glared at him.

"Let's start with Cheese on Your Burger Day. I'll expect an official email on Saturday," Schorr said, "after you finish walking the beach."

The mayor shook hands with Wyatt's parents and left. They traded looks, then turned to Wyatt.

"This doesn't mean you get off scot-free, young man," Wyatt's dad said. "You're still grounded. You'll give me the holiday names and I'll pass them on to the mayor. Now, back to your homework."

Grinning, Wyatt raced up to his room, but stopped halfway up and turned. "Um, Dad, can I have my phone back? Asher always helps me with Monday holidays."

His dad glanced at his wife who nodded and went to retrieve Wyatt's phone. When they were alone, Wyatt's dad fought to keep a straight face. He wagged a finger at his son. "Do not, and I'm not kidding, do not propose any dads do *anything* days."

LONN BRAENDER'S FIRST PUBLICATION WAS A SHORT STORY IN THE 2016 REHOBOTH BEACH READS ANTHOLOGY *BEACH NIGHTS*. SINCE THEN, SIX OF HIS SHORT STORIES HAVE APPEARED IN CAT & MOUSE PRESS BOOKS. HE HAS WRITTEN TWO YET-TO-BE-PUBLISHED NOVELS (ONE THE CONTINUATION OF HIS *BEACH NIGHTS* STORY) AND IS CURRENTLY WORKING ON TWO COLLECTIONS OF STORIES CENTERED ON THE EASTERN SHORE. THE IDEA FOR THE STORY "HOLIDAY HIJINKS" WAS TRIGGERED BY SEARCHING FOR OBSCURE HOLIDAYS FOR THIS CONTEST. THAT SEARCH UNVEILED SCORES OF SILLY AND COMMERCIALLY INVENTED HOLIDAYS THAT BEGGED THE QUESTION, *WHY NOT USE THEM ALL?*

BY DAY, LONN WORKS FOR THE COUNTRY'S LARGEST BOOK PRINTING COMPANY; ALL OTHER TIMES HE LIVES AND WRITES IN BUCKS COUNTY, PA, WITH HIS HUSBAND AND MUSE, BRUCE. TO READ EXCERPTS OF HIS NOVELS AND STORIES OR TO DISCOVER MORE ABOUT THE WRITER, VISIT WWW.LONNB.COM.

*This story will touch the heart of anyone who remembers being caught playing a prank and lived to tell the tale. But in this example, the creators of the hoax hijinks become heroes. And who can say no to a second scoop of ice cream?*

# It Was a Good Friday to Fly a Kite

### By Michael Morley

We were running two hours behind schedule.

This year we had done everything right. Our bags were packed almost a week in advance, and the car was loaded up the day before departure. The alarm clock buzzed at four a.m., and we were on the road before dawn. Yet despite doing everything right this year, nothing could prevent the dreadful beach traffic.

Stop. Go. Stop. Go. Stop. Go.

Apparently, every road in my home state of Virginia was under construction. Never-ending lines of signs taunted us between each mile marker. Between Road Work Ahead and Different Traffic Patterns Ahead you could feel the collective sigh of the neighboring drivers and passengers, feeling each other's pain, as we sat bumper to bumper. This convinced me even more than before that we would never arrive at our destination, Rehoboth Beach, for our Easter weekend, and I was even more sure that we would be too late to catch any of the kite festival in Lewes.

"I've never seen it this bad before," my wife, Rachael, said, trying to sneak a peek past the never-ending sea of stopped vehicles.

I shook my head. "This is just ridiculous. Don't they know we have places to be?"

My wife looked my way and smiled, letting out a slight laugh. "Shawn, construction stops for no one."

Attending the Great Delaware Kite Festival was one of my best memories as a kid, and now that I had my own two boys, I wanted to share this event with them. It had been a long time since we'd vacationed in Rehoboth as a family, but when I found out they were doing something special for the fiftieth anniversary of the kite festival, I immediately began planning our Easter holiday.

It took some convincing.

"Come on," I said. "It's going to be great. It's in a huge field, and there are all kinds of kites. I remember this one year there was a giant parrot that flapped its wings in the wind."

"Don't parrots already do that?" my youngest son, Nate, asked, with a raised eyebrow.

"Not a twenty-five-foot parrot," I said.

His eyes got wide, beaming in a way that only an eight-year-old's can. It's part of the wonderment that seemingly gets lost once they jump into the double-digit years.

I nodded. "Yeah. Only one person controls the kite, and that's going to be you."

My oldest son, Daniel, chimed in without taking his gaze away from his iPhone. "I don't know; it still seems boring."

I turned toward my wife and gave her a pleading look. "Rachel, please help me convince our kids that it will be fun and not boring."

"Daniel, we are going to the beach for Easter. We just have to stop and see some kites first. And there's an egg hunt afterwards." She winked at me in a way that said she did her part.

"It sounds fun," Nate said to his older brother.

Daniel paused to think it over. At twelve, he understood it would make his parents and brother happy. He put his device away. "Fine. Let's do it, Dad. Kites at the beach. But only if you promise you'll take us to get those boardwalk fries with vinegar after the egg hunt."

"Thrasher's Fries?" I asked him. "We have a deal."

Snapping back to reality, I glanced at my watch and shook my head. "Is that really the time?"

"It's a few minutes shy of quarter to nine," Rachel said.

We'd been on the road nearly four hours, stopping only once for a quick call-of-nature and a fuel fill-up—gas for the car and coffee for me. I didn't think we'd make it to Delaware by ten a.m. for the kick-off festivities, but if we didn't make any more stops, we might arrive in the nick of time.

Driving down Highway 29, I glanced at the rear-view mirror and noticed that my boys had fallen asleep. Traffic was looking as though it might now be working in our favor and the worst was over. The weather, however, didn't seem to be working in anyone's favor, as dark clouds had begun creeping into the mid-morning sky.

As if she were reading my mind, Rachel said, "The weather isn't looking too good."

"No, it's not," I said, shaking my head.

As raindrops began to appear on the windshield, I let out a quiet sigh. Soon, the drops turned into buckets.

My wife and I had to yell over the sound of the rain.

"I can't see anything, Rach."

"What?"

"I said I can't see anything. It's too hard to see ahead," I yelled and glanced once again in the rearview mirror, noticing the car behind us had its hazard lights on.

I adjusted my hands. The steering wheel vibrated from the rain pounding the car.

"Should we pull over?" Rachel asked.

"What?"

"Pull over," she yelled.

"No. I want to keep going."

Just a few miles down the road the rain started to let up and we began to see the sun pushing its way through the storm clouds. We were only about twenty minutes from Cape Henlopen State Park, where the festival was being held, and it looked as though we would make it in time after all.

"Are we there yet?" Nate called from the back seat.

"Almost," I replied.

"Will we be in time for the egg hunt?"

"Yes, Nate. It'll be right after the kites," I replied.

"We made it," Rachel said.

"Yes, we did," I said, more to myself than to Rachel.

I smiled as I began to remember being here with my father. The field, the people, the colorful kites dancing along the blue skies, all washed over me like a wave at high tide and I returned to my childhood.

"All right, Shawn," my father said. "Hold it, hold it."

With the wind picking up, it was difficult to keep the massive eagle kite I had attached to string from going everywhere but up. It suddenly dove, nearly missing two kids running with their kites, and then climbed, making me back up and nearly run into some bystanders watching their families trying to have fun.

"Be careful there, son," my father said, watching me struggling to control this impossible bird.

"I'm trying. I'm trying, but the wind is so strong."

"I know, but I know you can do it."

I started to run.

"Hold it, hold it," he called.

The wind died down, and then a gust hit me. The kite, with one quick swoop, flew up, and it stayed in the air.

"Is this it?" I asked, grinning.

"It is, buddy," my father said. "It is."

I returned to reality as we pulled into a parking spot. "It's as though nothing has changed," I said to myself.

As soon as we got out of the car, the warm spring air pillowed our faces. I could feel a bit of lingering dampness in the breeze, but the sun was shining bright.

"Nate, go grab your kite," I said, as I motioned him to the back of the car and popped the trunk.

Nate made a face.

"Dad, I got this." Daniel turned to his younger brother. "Nate, come on, we don't want to miss it. "There's still time before the egg hunt."

Across the field, dozens of people with different kites, each with friends and family grouped around, gazed at their kites flying across the sky. Glancing over at my sons, I saw them staring in awe.

Daniel and I both noticed a kid who looked about his age, trying to get his dragon kite up into the sky.

"Dad, how do we do this? The wind is so strong," Daniel said, holding his shark kite in one hand and the spool of thread in the other.

"Let me show you how it's done," I said, as he handed me his shark. Holding the kite to my side, I started into a light jog and within a few strides, I lifted it above my head and let go. The shark flew up into the sky.

Daniel's eyes grew wide, and his jaw dropped. "Why didn't you tell me this was so cool?" As he took the spool from my hands, his smile grew even wider.

"Are you a magician?" Nate asked me.

"I might be," I said, "and I want to let you in on my secrets. Let me show you how to do it."

Nate walked over to me and looked up at the sky. He shielded his eyes with his hand and then glanced back down at his dolphin-shaped kite and reluctantly handed it over.

I showed him how to start into a light jog and then launch the kite into the sky.

"Here," I said, as I passed him the handles.

"I don't think I can do it."

"Yes, you can."

He slowly took the first handle as he looked up into the sky.

"It's OK," I said. "We're going to do it together." I led him into a slight jog and together we released the kite into the sky.

Nate looked up at me. "What if it falls? What if I can't hold onto it? The wind is so strong."

"I know, but I know you can do it. Just look at the dolphin and feel the handles; you can't watch the dolphin if you are looking down at the handles."

"I'm trying," he said.

He looked up and saw the dolphin dancing in the wind alongside his older brother's shark.

"Shark attack," Daniel said, as he laughed, watching his kite alongside his brother's.

Nate looked up at the sky. His dolphin flew higher and higher.

Suddenly, the weeks of planning, miles of traffic, and buckets of rain fell from my mind.

"Dad, is this it?"

"It is, buddy," I said. "It is."

WITH AN AMBITION FOR READING ANYTHING WITH WORDS, FROM ALPHABET SOUP TO HIGHWAY BILLBOARDS, MICHAEL MORLEY NEVER DREAMED OF BECOMING AN AUTHOR. HAILING FROM GERMANY, HE GREW UP IN WEST PALM BEACH AND EVENTUALLY SETTLED INTO A SMALL TOWN NORTH OF PITTSBURGH. IT WASN'T UNTIL HE TOOK A CHILDREN'S LITERATURE COURSE WHILE STUDYING ELEMENTARY EDUCATION AT YOUNGSTOWN STATE UNIVERSITY THAT HE WAS INSPIRED TO BEGIN WRITING HIS OWN STORIES. MICHAEL MADE HIS FICTION DEBUT EARLIER THIS YEAR WITH "SAY HELLO TO HENRY," FEATURED IN *SHELL HOUSE*. FOLLOW HIS WRITING ADVENTURES ON INSTAGRAM: @AN_ACCIDENTAL_AUTHOR_COUPLE.

# As Gouda Story as Any

### By Jean Youkers

If I'd known I was going to end up in jail with a fat lip and fractured ankle, eating a bologna sandwich without cheese, I would never have agreed to go into business with my brother. My lawyer asked me to write down everything I remember about the whole mess for my defense, so that's what I'm doing while I sit here rotting away and hoping to make bail.

Pete's idea of opening a gourmet cheese shop and lunchroom held great appeal but proved to be much better as a fantasy than the reality once we began planning and fighting.

Our first disagreement was about the name.

"Let's call it Jack and Pete's Cheese Shoppe," I said hopefully.

"Jack, have you no imagination, no class?" Of course, my little brother's vision demanded a more pretentious French name. Hence our new business became Fromagerie Chez Pierre et Jacques. After we argued over whose name appeared first, he shot down my expertly drawn logo and most of my ideas for the menu. He always wanted to be the big cheese.

He even believed Rehoboth Beach would allow us to construct a small shop on the boardwalk, about the size of the Santa Claus house that appears there every December. I managed to talk him out of that; the idea would never fly, even if we could get a permit. Our operation required a larger space. Plus, the idea was stupid. People walking or running on the boardwalk won't stop long enough to buy cheese in the middle of racking up their steps.

The kid never listened to me in his entire life, so why would I expect him to start now? (Like the time we explored the woods when we were in middle school, and I told him not to touch the poison ivy. I knew he'd do the opposite so—ha, ha—the joke was on him.)

I never thought we'd find a location we could afford, but Pete miraculously found a spacious storefront on Wilmington Avenue, minutes from the ocean. So, we signed the lease and spent the next month painting and decorating the place to make it worthy of its elegant French name. We ordered exotic cheeses from Wisconsin, Holland, and Switzerland. Another expensive proposition. I suggested taking out a loan or selling shares in the enterprise, starting with Mom and our two most gullible uncles. But that would've been too easy.

Robbing a bank to get the necessary funds was never on my list of options, but Pete convinced me we'd return the entire stash anonymously once we made our first profits, maybe even with interest. He had nerve, I'll give him that, strutting into the place, unarmed, with an N95 mask as his only disguise. Against my better judgment, I acted as the lookout while he strode up to the teller and demanded "all the cheddar."

When alarms blared, I hissed, "Cheese it," as Pete was stuffing bills into his duffle bag.

"Say cheese," the teller, a hefty blonde with a huge bow in her hair, called out, smirking as we stumbled out the door while the security cameras flashed. Police sirens came closer and closer, but we managed to get away. I knew our pictures would soon appear on wanted posters, so we began to grow beards and wear thick dark glasses to hide the parts of our faces visible outside our masks.

We kept a low profile while we waited for the shipments of cheese and experimented with different recipes to develop the world's greatest grilled cheese sandwiches in time for our grand opening. It was set for April 12, National Grilled Cheese Sandwich Day, the perfect tie-in.

My favorite combo was cheddar with jalapenos, arugula, and caramelized onions. Cream cheese with mayo was also a sumptuous delight. Pete's garlicky cheddar and gouda with strawberry jam was not in good taste; in fact, it sucked. Crispy bread, slathered with butter, made every sandwich special, and I tried them all. Of course, we would offer the traditional Kraft American cheese grilled cheese sandwich that has been a favorite of Americans for the past one hundred years.

We sent out promotional flyers and ran ads in the *Cape Gazette*, and *Delaware Beach Life*, promising a two-for-one deal on any gourmet grilled cheese sandwich for National Grilled Cheese Sandwich Day. We put announcements on lampposts, where perching sea gulls called attention to them, in libraries, stores and such, letting the public know that Fromagerie Chez Pierre et Jacques would melt their hearts. I thought that, for once, one of Pete's harebrained ideas was going to pan out, not like the time he had me selling ice sculptures on the boardwalk in July.

As the big day loomed and our largest delivery still had not, we rushed out to buy all the cheese we could find in every Safeway, Giant, Acme, Walmart, and local gourmet shop. We needed a hell of a lot more cheese to accommodate the customers who would stampede into our establishment on April 12 and thereafter.

Soon, word got around that there was a severe cheese shortage in Delaware. The populace began hoarding, creating an unprecedented demand for cheese due to the shortage we had accidentally created. There were reports of people going to Maryland and Pennsylvania and all the way to Virginia and New Jersey in search of cheese.

Otherwise sane people were seen buying *Who Moved My Cheese?* at Browseabout Books in search of answers, only to learn the book was merely a business tome featuring metaphorical cheese. Thoughts of local mice making off with the cheese did not seem possible due to the careful packaging of the stuff that often made opening it impossible. No tactless mention was made of either Minnie or Mickey Mouse.

Yesterday, with only two days left before National Grilled Cheese Sandwich Day, I braved the crowds lined up at an Acme's deli counter in search of just a bit more cheese for our grand opening. Some jerk was making cheesy remarks about my efforts to push my way to the head of the line. He was ordering the last two pounds of Primo cheddar from the showcase, plus the only available portion of Swiss! I wanted to cut his face with the sharp cheese, but there was none. I simply shoved him out of the way, I admit it, and protested to the clerk that one customer should not be given the store's entire remaining inventory of cheese.

"After all, there's a shortage," I yelled.

The rest is kind of a blur. I went crazy, threw the first punch, wrestling Cheese Breath to the floor and taking possession of a single jar of Cheez Whiz. He smacked me hard with the cheddar, and the Swiss went flying overhead. Customers scrambled to catch it with all the determination of a bridesmaid sliding in to catch the bridal bouquet. Others were opening packages of crackers to enjoy with the cheddar.

My mouth felt numb, and when I swiped a hand across my lips it came back bloody. Disoriented, I tripped over a shopping cart, causing an intense young woman who'd been watching to start screaming that I was one of the bank robbers. Her head was bobbing so hard that her tacky bow flew off and landed in a vat of pickles. *Oh, shit!* It was the teller, and she was about to tell all. If only I could've buttered her up with one of our special grilled Swiss and cheddar combos with the crushed potato chips and anchovies.

The cops were already storming into the store and heading toward me. They could not be bribed with a double-decker grilled cheese sandwich or a cheese doughnut. I knew my luck had run out—if I'd had any to begin with. I struggled to get up off the floor, only to trip over my feet. That's when I must've broken my ankle because they had to cart me off on a gurney.

Now I'm in this hellhole jail cell, sandwiched in with criminals who don't own a classy fromagerie or have a brother full of great ideas. Grilled cheese is supposed to be comfort food, but here I am, locked up and about to be grilled. I've truly learned my lesson, counselor.

I have to stop writing—I just got an urgent text that says the delivery truck is waiting outside our shop with the biggest order of cheese. I'll text "Pierre" and tell him to get his butt over there and get help to unload it—we must not let the cheese stand alone.

Opening day is going to make us grate.

JEAN YOUKERS WRITES FICTION, HUMOROUS NONFICTION, AND POETRY. HER STORIES HAVE APPEARED IN THE REHOBOTH BEACH READS CONTEST ANTHOLOGIES, *DELAWARE BEACH LIFE* MAGAZINE, *DASH* LITERARY JOURNAL, *BROADKILL REVIEW*, AND LOCAL PUBLICATIONS. HER NOVEL *LUNCH BUCKET LISTS*, PUBLISHED IN 2021, FEATURES CHARACTERS WHO ENJOY LIVING IN REHOBOTH BEACH.

PROMOTING HUMOR AND OPTIMISM IS A GOAL IN MOST OF JEAN'S WORK; THIS OFTEN DERAILS HER EFFORTS TO STICK WITH SERIOUS SUBJECTS! FOR THIS YEAR'S CONTEST, SHE WAS FRUSTRATED TRYING TO WRITE A BEAUTIFUL CHRISTMAS STORY OR TOUCHING MOTHER'S DAY TALE, SO SHE PLANNED TO SKIP THE CONTEST. HOWEVER, ON APRIL 12, WHEN WORKING OUT IN HER WATER AEROBICS CLASS, JEAN WAS ZAPPED WITH HER STORY IDEA WHEN SHE HEARD THE INSTRUCTOR ANNOUNCE THAT IT WAS NATIONAL GRILLED CHEESE SANDWICH DAY. THANK YOU, SHELLY.

JUDGE'S COMMENT

*Excellent comedic timing delivered a story that kept me laughing.*

# Take a Chance on Me This Summer

## By Madison Hallman

> **6:59 AM**
> hey can u come in 2day

> **7:03 AM**
> Am I on the schedule?

> **7:04 AM**
> we need all hands on deck

> **7:06 AM**
> Am I on the schedule?

> **7:06 AM**
> ive got an author coming in 2day

> **7:07 AM**
> Am?

> **7:07 AM**
> Kasey, I am your boss and I am telling you to come into work to do your job.

> **7:08AM**
> I?

> **7:10 AM**
> This isn't cute. You are replaceable, you know. I could go out today and find a hundred other recent graduates with useless degrees and much better attitudes than yours.

**7:10 AM**
On?

**7:11 AM**
Please?!?!?!?

**7:11 AM**
The?

**7:11 AM**
Aimee is working today.

**7:20 AM**
Kasey?

**7:24 AM**
See you soon.

**7:24 AM**
:-)

**7:25 AM**
;-) *

I get to work at around 7:45. It's after May 15th, so parking isn't free anymore. Which means I had to ride my bike. Which means I'm sweaty and tired before I even clock in.

After locking up my bike and taking my helmet off, pausing briefly to look in the window to make sure my hair doesn't look stupid, I take a deep breath and open the door to my place of employment. The second most successful bookstore on Rehoboth Avenue: Starbooks.

"Happy Stacy McGowen Day!"

I blink a couple times and take in the scene before me. There's Brian Grossman, my boss, wearing a T-shirt with a woman's face printed on it. The face of a white, blond, middle-aged woman with a smile that doesn't reach her eyes. I assume that's Stacy McGowen.

"That's not a holiday."

"It is now." Brian reaches over the counter, grabs a similar T-shirt, and tosses it to me. Despite my best efforts, I catch it.

"I'm not wearing this."

"Yes, you are. Everyone is."

I look down at my outfit. Dark-blue short-sleeve button-down with khaki shorts and a leather belt: The Soft Butch Special. The SBS. The only formal wear I look decent in. You don't mess with the SBS. I even wore Sperrys for God's sake.

But the stern look on Brian's face isn't changing, so I guess I am. I throw the shirt over top of my outfit and succumb to wearing Stacy McGowen's face on my body.

"Alright, what needs to be done?"

He grins. "Actually, would you mind unboxing in the back? We got a whole pallet of Stacy's newest book."

"A *pallet*? Brian, that's like sixty boxes. You bought sixty boxes of one single book?"

"These are going to fly off the shelves. We're probably going to sell every single one of them today. She's coming in herself to do a signing and a meet and greet. Just like we talked about."

I must look confused because he sighs at me before continuing.

"Don't you remember the meeting we had when I was asking everyone about what we could do to drum up business? We have tons of people coming into the store, but not a lot of sales."

"Brian, tons of people only come into the store because they think it's a Starbucks. You even designed the sign so that the two Os look like a U and a C. People think they're getting coffee when they come in here, Brian. The first time I walked in I thought I was going to walk out with a Pumpkin Cream Cold Brew."

"And instead, you walked out with a job. A job you may very well lose if you don't get to unboxing those books right now."

With that, he produces a sandwich board with "Stacy McGowen Day: Embrace the Stace" written on it in chalk, and brushes past me out the door, ending the conversation.

I march into the back room and throw my backpack and helmet into the corner, grabbing the boxcutter and starting on the pallet. When I break the seal and peel back the cardboard flaps, I see it again. That face. Mocking me. *Stacy McGowen.* This time she's wearing a sundress and holding a bichon frise. All around her hover quotes from varying authors and literary critics, applauding her "rich, vibrant prose," her "unbelievably real characters," and her "unspeakably hot romances."

"Bite me."

"What?"

I whip my head around and there she stands. Worn out Chuck Taylors and mismatched socks. A long skirt with outlines of honeybees sewn into the fabric. A loose T-shirt with text asserting that Pluto was indeed a planet, and homemade earrings made from old piano keys (*G* and *F*, respectively). Her curly hair partially tucked into a beanie that is decorated with an assortment of enamel pins, advertising to the world her pronouns, her pansexuality, and her love for The Grateful Dead.

Aimee pushes up her thick-framed glasses, not seeming to care whether her fingertips smudge the lenses.

*God she's fearless.* "Oh, I said…uh…umm…'Bite me.'"

She looks around for a second before raising her eyebrow and pointing to herself.

"No! No. I just was…looking at the…her face. It…it's…th-the quote here." I gesture around wildly, hoping that I'll be able to come up with a point that won't make me sound insane, but I come up empty. I just sort of sputter ten or fifteen more words before closing my mouth and letting my hand fall to my side.

She walks to the corner and gently places her backpack next to mine before coming over to me. She takes a book out of the box and looks it over.

"Yeah. My grandmother loves her. I can see how she's not for everyone."

Aimee turns the book over to the front cover. On it is an illustration of a couple holding each other closely while standing on a pier. The title is written in cursive above the scene: *Take A Chance on Me This Summer*. We both stare at the title. Aimee traces her finger over the illustration absentmindedly.

*Is she waiting for me to say something?* "So...your grandmother likes Stacy McGowen?"

Aimee doesn't look up from the book. "Yeah, she loves her whole Jodi Crabapple series."

"I'm guessing that's the protagonist?"

"You're guessing right."

She flips the book open and I'm able to see the list of books in the series:

    *Lay All Your Love on the Beach*
    *Just a Notion in the Ocean*
    *I Can Be That Sailor Woman*
    *Does Your Mother Know You're at the Shore*
    *Angelfish Eyes*

I sense a theme, but I can't put my finger on it. My mind takes me back to a musical that Clear Space Theatre put on a few summers ago. Aimee looks over at me. Again, I must look confused because she takes a breath and points to the first book title.

"See, this one is a—"

"What are you two doing? We're opening in like one minute. Kasey, boxes. Aimee, I need you out front." Brian has reappeared, now sporting a Wilmington Blue Rocks baseball cap with Stacy McGowen's face crudely stapled over top of Rocky Bluewinkle.

Aimee quickly hands me the book and walks to her assigned station, on the complete opposite side of the store.

I finish with the boxes at around 10:30, sleepier and sweatier than before. By that time, Kendall and Maya have shown up to work the registers.

A bunch of people are in the store now. More than I've ever seen, actually. It makes the already small space feel downright claustrophobic. I spot Aimee sitting and reading in the middle of the aisle, a gigantic tome in her lap that she's already halfway through. I'm probably biased in my thinking, but I can't blame her. She does have a good work ethic, more of a work ethic than I've ever had, but she just can't help herself when it comes to a good book. Asking her to organize books on a shelf is like asking an astronomer to peer into the night sky to check the weather. I feel a tug on my sleeve.

"Excuse me, do you work here?"

"Yeah."

"When is Stacy coming in?"

"No idea."

"Well…that seems like something you should know."

"OK."

The random woman looks at me a little longer, and I look back at her. This is why I'm usually in the back of the store, shelving or cleaning.

"But I'd be glad to find that out for you, ma'am." It's a lie.

She gives me a small nod. I walk away to find Brian, who is standing in the corner, nervously checking his phone.

"Hey, when is Stacy McGowen coming in?"

He immediately hides his phone behind his back. "What?"

"Stacy McGowen. The woman for whom you've invented a holiday. What time is she coming to the store?"

"Noon."

I turn around to walk back to the lady.

"We need gifts," Brian says.

"What?"

"We need something to give to the customers. A memento. Like…a party favor."

"We truly do not need to do that."

"Stacy McGowen does it at all her events. Everyone is supposed to leave with something."

"Other than the 720 books I just unpacked all by myself?"

Brian gives me a look and my smarmy sense of self-righteousness falters. He's nervous. He's a metaphorical shrimp boat captain who somehow talked himself into running a luxury cruise. He's got a million things on his mind. A mind that is only programed to run like four things, max. Looks like that remind me that if he weren't my boss and was ten years younger, I would still think he's an annoying little trust-fund baby. But I'd let him crash on my couch.

"OK, look. She writes beach reads, right? And we literally live in the most beachiest beach town in America. We could go and get a bunch of little things from Mod Cottage or Bella Luna and hand them out."

Brian's head perks up and he nods.

It's encouraging, seeing someone's mood affected positively by my words. Maybe I should do it more often. I put my hand on his shoulder. "Rehoboth is unique and charming. Let's just give them a little piece of it." My voice is softer than I would like it to be, but whatever.

Brian speeds down the aisle and out of the store, leaving me in charge. I look over to where Aimee is sitting, now excitedly rocking herself as she reads, a huge smile on her face. I smile sadly and wish I cared about anything half as much as she cares about the written word.

My view of her is blocked by a pair of legs. Legs belonging to the same woman who wanted to know when Stacy McGowen was arriving. She clears her throat, but Aimee doesn't look up.

"Excuse me. Do you need help?" the lady asks, in a tone all too familiar. Imperious and disdainful, haphazardly disguised as genuine concern.

I get a bad feeling in the pit of my stomach. Aimee pauses her reading, holding her place with her index finger and looks up, smiling. "Can I help you find anything?" she asks in her perfect customer service voice.

"I just…you're aware that you're…you're…" The woman puts her hands to her chest and starts mimicking Aimee's movements, complete with an exaggerated toothy smile plastered on her face.

Aimee's face goes red. "Sorry, I didn't notice."

"OK, well everyone else did." The lady gives a passive-aggressive chuckle and gestures to the other customers, all of whom, coincidently, were minding their own business. "I just wanted you to be aware of that. Seeing as there are kids around and—"

I walk up and tug on the lady's sleeve. She immediately jerks her hand away as if offended.

"Hey, so you wanted to know about Stacy McGowen, right?"

"I'm sorry, are you aware that your employee—"

"It looks like she won't be able to make it today."

The lady's eyes go wide. "What?"

"Yeah, apparently, they found her this morning passed out drunk at Funland? I guess she broke in last night after they closed and tried to learn the patterns of the Whac-a-Mole machines so she could maximize her ticket output. Then…yeah…then I'm pretty sure she tried to take a bumper car out of the track and drive it around the boardwalk, and then when she realized she couldn't do that, she tried to make the Sea Dragon do a 360, in which she was also unsuccessful. I'm told they found her in the Haunted Mansion, cuddling up with one of the animatronics. Nude."

For a moment, I feel like I may have gone a little overboard.

Then, the woman leans in close and whispers to me. "Was she at least cuddling one of the skeletons?"

I shake my head. "No. It was the gigantic spider they have at the end."

She puts her hand over her heart and looks to the ceiling, fighting back tears.

I look down to see that Aimee isn't there anymore. I glance over at Kendall and Maya, who point in the direction of the bathroom—the secret one that we have to pretend we don't have when customers ask if we have one, so she might be in there for a while.

At around 11:45, I see Aimee come out of the bathroom. She starts straightening decorations, clearly wanting to be given some space. All I've been doing in the meantime is putting out copies of *Take a Chance on Me This Summer*, trying to read some of it but finding myself physically unable to make it past the third page.

While my hands are busy, I try and think about what to say to Aimee. How much did she hear before she walked away? Did *I* make her uncomfortable? Was it *my* fault she felt the need to retreat into the bathroom? Was I too loud? Did I walk over too quickly? Should I apologize? Was she embarrassed that I saw that woman being a jerk? Did she think it was creepy that I was watching her? She didn't need my help. She didn't need me white-knighting her, coming in to save the day to stroke my own ego and treat her like a child. This is why I don't get involved. It never works out the way I intend. Forget helping Brian out, that was a fluke.

"Hey, Kasey, I need you to unload our party favors from the truck."

Speak of the devil.

I turn around, and there he stands. His face is full of joy, his underarms full of sweat, and his fists full of...

"Brian, how many hermit crabs did you buy?"

"None. They come free when you buy the cages."

"Brian, how many hermit crab *cages* did you buy?"

"Every single one in Rehoboth, Dewey, and Bethany. You were right, we needed to be unique in our gifts." He has a huge smile on his face. He's clearly proud of himself. "Now come on, we gotta get them all ready before Stacy McGowen arrives." He scans his eyes over the store until he spots a beanie in the crowd. "Hey, Aimee! Kasey needs help unloading the gifts!" Brian gives me two winks and two nudges.

Aimee and I silently take the cages and place them next to the books as the customers stare at us. I try to give them a small smile, acknowledging the oddness of the situation, but no one reciprocates.

An older gentleman with three books in his arms clears his throat and steps forward. "Um...excuse me, are you selling hermit crabs?"

"No. They come free with every book."

"That seems a bit unusual."

I shrug. "It's Stacy McGowen Day."

Stacy McGowen shows up at noon, and I don't know why I'm surprised. She sits on her throne, which is a folding chair with seashells and sand glued onto it, and signs books for about four hours. Brian stands next to her, taking pictures and directing traffic. It's a successful event, no doubt, but we ain't selling 720 books.

Other than keeping the copies of *Take a Chance on Me This Summer* and the crabs stocked, there isn't much for Aimee and me to do. We just stand next to each other. I wait for her to break the silence when she's ready. She doesn't. I can't stop wishing she would.

The event's over at 5:30 and the store is dead, as usual. I'm sweeping up, as usual. Some of the hermit crabs escaped their cages, so we've been trying to wrangle them.

Brian closes the store early to take inventory. Aimee takes all the decorations down. Kendall had volleyball practice, so she left earlier. Brian tucks his clipboard under his arm. "Hey Kasey, can I talk to you for a minute?"

"Sure."

We walk to the back office. He closes the door.

"I got a complaint from a customer about you."

"Woah, stop the presses."

"And she complained about Aimee."

I inhale sharply through my nose, only aware I did so because the smell of hermit crab assaults my senses. "OK? So?"

"So, I want to know what happened."

"Aimee doesn't need to justify—"

"I'm not asking Aimee. I'm asking you."

It's then I notice I've absentmindedly been scratching at my palm. I force my hands to my side. Then I cross my arms and take a step back. "I don't know. The lady was pissed that Aimee was reading in the middle of the store. She said some stuff that I thought was out of line, so I told her Stacy McGowen wasn't coming to get her to leave. She had already bought the book, so you didn't lose a sale. Honestly, I don't know why it matters."

Brian nods slowly. "Maya said that Aimee was in the bathroom for a long time."

I look away from him. I'm tired from the day. I'm sore from unboxing. My back hurts from sweeping. I'm sweaty from wearing two shirts. My finger was pinched by a crab. I don't want to hear about this. My eyes start to sting. "Yeah, I think I might have freaked her out." I don't feel my throat say anything and my ears don't pick up the pitiful squeak that is my voice, but Brian just sighs.

For some reason, I keep going.

"It was my fault. I tried to impress her by telling the lady off and I think I got too loud. You know I stomp my feet when I walk, and she was on the floor, so maybe the visual was freaky or something. I think I made her feel weak?" I look up at Brian for permission to cry.

"You know, when I texted Aimee to see if she could come into work today, she said she was feeling a little fuzzy."

"Then why did you make her?"

"I didn't make her do anything."

"What did you say to her?"

"I told her you were coming in."

A tear falls and splashes on my right Sperry. Aimee walks in the door. I immediately turn away and wipe my eyes.

"Oh, sorry. Am I interrupting something?"

Brian steps forward and covers for me. "No, not at all. Are you heading home now?"

Aimee nods. She walks over to where our backpacks are stored and takes hers. Mine slouches over and she gently sets it upright again.

By now my face is back to normal and I turn to her.

She smiles shyly at me. "You know, we probably could get the Sea Dragon to do a full 360."

I nod in agreement.

She nods in agreement with my nod. "You just gotta believe."

"You just gotta believe."

Aimee waves goodbye to Brian and me and leaves. I pretend I don't see Brian looking at me.

"Welp, if that's everything Mr. Grossman, I'll be heading out as well."

"Oh, that reminds me. Can you come in early tomorrow? I need someone to help me secretly release all these extra crabs into Browseabout. I'm thinking we get a bunch of big coats and stuff our pockets full of them and strategically put them in different corners of the store throughout the day."

"Well, I don't know—"

"Aimee is coming in too."

"See, I don't like how you can just say that and have two workers completely at your disposal."

"Are you coming or not?"

"Does Stacy McGowen want to make tender love to the Oxford Comma?"

"See you tomorrow."

Madison Hallman is a recent graduate from Ithaca College, where she studied Writing for Television and Film. This is her first published work. Madison works at Bethany Beach Books as a bookseller and resides in Bethany Beach, Delaware. She often rides her bike to work and usually wears a blue button-down shirt. Madison first came up with the idea of a bookstore employee working an author event when she was working an author event as a bookstore employee. She would like to stress that although this story is set in a bookstore, the events and characters are entirely fictional, and this narrative in no way reflects her attitude toward her job, coworkers, boss, customers, author events, hermit crabs, or beach reads. Madison doesn't really use social media, but she can be reached (theoretically) on Twitter at @MaddiHallman.

Judge's Comment

*From her khaki shorts and leather belt to the snarky words that fall from her mouth, the author paints an image of Kasey so vivid that you swear you know her. The gruff but dutiful Kasey powers through Stacy McGowen Day, an author event at a fictional rival bookstore of Browseabout Books. "Take a Chance on Me This Summer" is humorous, heartwarming, and a great beach read.*

# Mummers in the Time of Y2K

### By Nina Phillips

"Why mummers?" I asked, as my mom and I strolled arm in arm along the Rehoboth Beach boardwalk, gazing in the shop windows. "Don't they have something to do with New Year's Day?"

It was June 1999 in Rehoboth Beach, just one week before the big July Fourth celebration. The festive red, white, and blue banners were already in place. This was a momentous holiday, after all, the last Fourth of July before the new millennium.

We had just left Candyland, a colorful candy store where Anna, my mother's lifelong friend, was the manager. Anna was a plump, self-assured senior who ran her store with the precision of a drill sergeant. Today, she had been the messenger of exciting news of an upcoming concert.

"Irene, this Saturday, a mummers string band from Philadelphia is playing at the bandshell," Anna had announced, as she leaned over to put the rainbow-colored candy into a plastic bag. Gummy bears were my favorite. "Tony and I will be there for sure," she had added, handing us the bag.

We stopped to get an order of the famous Thrasher's french fries, then ambled over to a white bench next to the beach, where we could see the ocean waves twinkling invitingly, like shimmering silver against the beige sand. The smell of the ocean mingled with the delights of the boardwalk—french fries, pizza, and cotton candy. We each put a golden french fry in our mouth and sat back to watch the tourists promenading on the boardwalk in their brightly colorful beach regalia.

I pictured a mummers parade I had watched on television New Year's Day. Hundreds of brightly colored, costumed merrymakers marched and danced down the streets of Philadelphia, reminiscent of the pageantry of a New Orleans Mardi Gras parade. Somehow, as we neared this strange point in time they're calling Y2K, when 1999 will become 2000, watching a mummers string band on the Fourth of July didn't seem so odd.

We were halfway into the year, and one could not escape the hype surrounding Y2K. "Are you Y2K-ready?" was the war cry. What would happen on Y2K? It seemed as if the whole world was afraid that computers wouldn't recognize the year 2000 and would cease all operations. Malfunctions of that magnitude could wreak havoc by shutting down everything from banks to transportation to grocery stores. Although I knew there were conferences, meetings, lectures, and essays about the possibility of an impending disaster, I did not buy into the mass hysteria. There was time to rectify the situation and many governments were investing time and money in hopes of solving the problem.

Still, Y2K was proving to be an emotional topic, and even my closest friends were doomsday predictors. My ladies' group was alarmed; they all believed Armageddon was near.

A few months ago, the three of us gathered for our usually delightful lunch rendezvous, with its wonderful conversation and delicious food. The happy conversation quickly took a more serious turn with the introduction of the Y2K controversy.

"Trains will stop, and grocery stores will be affected," Wendy predicted, as she passed around a plate of meatballs. She gently patted her orange cat, C.S., named after her favorite author, C.S. Lewis, while he rubbed against her legs in contentment. Her country home, complete with lots of children, pets, and plants, smelled fragrantly from the many lit candles and seemed like Narnia itself. I loved coming here and our infrequent luncheons were a rare treat.

"John and I stocked up on toilet paper and water," Mary Lou said as she ate her famous pina colada dip. Mary Lou, or Lou Lou, was a down-to-earth woman who regaled us with stories of her adventures and her colorful family. I loved both women for their loyalty, candor, humor, and great faith that they exercised in life's difficult waters. She stopped and looked at me seriously, handing me a piece of paper. "Here's a list of the items you should have on hand to be prepared."

I scanned the list quickly. Water: check. Toilet paper: check. Dried fruit: check. Dried beans. *Hmm.* A survival bunker filled with people eating beans. I couldn't help but smile, but I managed not to laugh out loud.

My merriment was not lost on my two unusually dour friends; they both turned to me with deep concern that bordered on rebuke.

"Nina, this is serious," Mary Lou stated emphatically.

"Yes, I know. Just don't forget the garlic."

"Garlic? Why garlic?"

"Garlic kills gas," I retorted. With that conclusive argument, all three of us laughed uproariously and fear of Y2K seemed to fade into the crisp fall air.

Saturday night's concert came quickly, and I walked with my mom to the opalescent white bandshell. Mom looked great. Rested from her vacation and completely turned out with her hair, makeup, and jewelry in perfect place, she looked much younger than her seventy-five years. I made a note to myself to preserve her wisdom, for both her physical and mental attitudes were inspiring.

I had the dubious honor of accompanying her alone to our night under the stars with the mummers. My two brothers, their wives, and my daughter had quickly scattered to pursue their own interests on the boardwalk.

On this sultry Rehoboth night, the dire Y2K predictions seemed distant. The area around the bright white bandshell quickly started filling up with happy tourists, and we quickly secured a front-row seat on a hard white bench. A family with two small children sat next to us.

"We're from Pittsburgh." The pretty mom wore a Pittsburgh Steeler T-shirt and had her dark hair pulled up in a white scrunchie. "Isn't it a beautiful night?"

My mom, always friendly, said, "Yes. Delightful. Your children are lovely. Pittsburgh. That's quite a distance—was it a long drive?"

"About five hours. But it was worth it. The beach was great, although Tasha got a little sunburned."

"Aloe works well," my mom suggested. "And you can buy it anywhere. Tasha? My granddaughter's name is Natasha."

"Thanks. I'll get some tomorrow." The woman patted her small daughter on the head. "Yes, this is our Tasha." The little girl in the bright-red Rehoboth Beach T-shirt eyed both of us with mild interest.

While we waited for the band, I reflected on what I had learned about mummers from the Lewes Library. I had been there to check out some beach reads, and while I was there, I did some research about string bands and the mummers.

The roots of the mummer's tradition ran deep in Philadelphia. Centuries ago in England, the mummers were traveling performers, going house to house to display their talents. Later, when the English came to the New World, the tradition of the mummers came with them. George Washington was entertained by mummers outside his Philadelphia home on New Year's Day 1790. The Mummers New Years' Parade was started in 1901 and now, the year 2000 parade was being welcomed with great anticipation. What better way to bring in the new century than with a huge celebration?

As we waited for the concert to start, I thought about string bands, which are an important part of mummers parades. I had learned that string bands in America trace their roots to the music of African American bands of the 1870s that later morphed into contemporary country and bluegrass music. Music is key to the mummer's performance, and each band uses musical instruments such as saxophones, banjos, accordions, violins, basses, fiddles, drums, and glockenspiels. Mummers groups have the look of marching bands: precision drills and Broadway-style choreography.

"Hey, Irene, you made it!" Anna appeared with her usual energetic stride and a huge smile.

"Yeah, a beautiful night," my mom said. "But where's Tony?"

"He's over there." Anna motioned toward the other side of the bandshell.

Tony was with a group of other seniors, prominently perched with his cane and clenching his trademark cigar in his mouth. The seniors were holding court by the bandshell, presiding over their nightly boardwalk tradition. They had held forth there on various nights for more than fifty years through local and national disasters, like the Vietnam War and Hurricane Hazel, and they had deservedly earned their special boardwalk position.

The all-male band, wearing colorful uniforms and carrying their instruments, took their seats in front of the waiting crowd. They reminded me of a high school marching band, and I half expected a team of cheerleaders to magically appear behind me yelling, "Y2K! What do you say? Yay! Yay!"

As the music began, the beach-weary audience became quiet with anticipation and even I got caught up in the lively tunes. They performed long-ago classics such as "Let Me Call You Sweetheart" and "You Are My Sunshine."

The crowd clapped their hands with great enthusiasm, and I glanced over at my mom. One look said it all—she was thrilled by the sweet sentimental melodies.

"God bless America! Land that I love!" The lyrics of the last song invigorated the patriotic crowd. Several energetic tourists attempted the mummer's strut, a Charleston-like dance characterized by vigorous arm flapping. I tried in vain to picture a solemn George Washington—as depicted in the famous Gilbert portrait—breaking out in an enthusiastic mummer's strut.

"Goodbye! Enjoy your vacation." The Pittsburgh mom stood and prepared to leave.

"You too. And don't forget that aloe," Mom said, ever the mom.

The woman motioned toward her husband, who carried a sleeping child in his arms. "Looks like this one had too much beach."

As we watched the crowd disperse, the bandleader, whom I had quietly dubbed Main Mummer, approached. A distinguished white-haired gentleman, splendid in his bright maroon uniform, he loomed over us with Old-World charm and elegance.

"Did you enjoy the concert?" he asked Mom. I could see she was flattered by his attention.

Uncharacteristically at a loss for words, Mom mumbled, "Wonderful," looking more like a smitten teenager than a senior citizen. Main Mummer nodded, and with a tap of his stick, he rejoined his band members, who were preparing to leave.

Suddenly, out of nowhere, Nick, my baby brother, came into view. With his athletic build in his trendy exercise attire, complete with a Phillies baseball cap, he stood out from the crowd that was pouring onto the boardwalk now that the concert was over. I realized he had probably been shadowing us and knew that the concert was over; it was like him to be concerned for Mom and me, for he was as kind as he was handsome.

"How about some ice cream?" he asked.

We gave him our order and off he went to the ice cream store of a million and one varieties, a local Rehoboth Beach legend. He returned with the ice cream and presented it to us as excitedly as if each ice cream cone were an unopened Christmas gift. His evident delight in servitude to his adored mother and sister was touching; he was simply the best brother ever. We happily dove into the cold gooey delight, and his act of kindness was not disappointing to either of us.

With a conspiratorial grin, he said to me quietly, "How did you stand that music anyway?"

"Surprisingly, I enjoyed the concert and so did the crowd. Mom certainly did," I replied, between determined licks of my quickly melting ice cream. We had moved away from the bandshell and now faced the beach on a white bench. Behind us was the hurly-burly noise of the tourists, but here in front of us was complete tranquility. The moonlight shimmered and danced on the ocean waves—a perfect end to a perfect beach day.

All Y2K predictions were now far away from this peaceful Rehoboth Beach evening. In a pleasant union of both New Year's Day and July Fourth, Old George, the father of our country, would not have been more pleased.

*In loving memory of Irene, Nick, Wendy, and Mary Lou.*

A TEACHER, NINA PHILLIPS LIVED ALMOST TWENTY YEARS IN NEW MEXICO BEFORE SHE RETURNED TO HER NATIVE DELAWARE IN 1995. SHE HAS BEEN PUBLISHED IN *BAY TO OCEAN 2020: THE YEAR'S BEST WRITING FROM THE EASTERN SHORE WRITERS ASSOCIATION* AND *BEACH SECRETS*. ALSO, SHE SELF-PUBLISHED A PLAY ABOUT BULGARIA'S RESCUE OF THEIR JEWS, *THE CRUSHING OF THE ROSES*. THE PLAY HAS BEEN ACKNOWLEDGED BY THE FORMER AMERICAN AMBASSADOR TO BULGARIA, ERIC RUBIN.

A DELECTABLE ICE CREAM TREAT FROM A DEVOTED BROTHER ON A HOT REHOBOTH NIGHT WAS THE INSPIRATION FOR HER STORY. REHOBOTH BEACH IS A FAMILY RESORT OF BOARDWALK SIGHTS, BEACH NAPS, AND ALL-AROUND BEACH ENCOUNTERS. BUT JUST FOR EXTRA FUN, THROW IN A MUMMERS CONCERT AND WORRIES OVER A POSSIBLE GLOBAL MELTDOWN. WHERE WERE YOU IN Y2K, THE WORLD CRISIS THAT WASN'T?

# The Cottage on Washington Street

## By Denise Stout

*"There's no place like home. Except the beach."*
-UNKNOWN

Jessi Carmichael had her hands full of overstuffed plastic grocery bags after shopping at a farm stand and The Fresh Market, intending to get all her supplies into the cottage in one trip. She was relieved to have made it to the beach in record time and excited at beating the Fourth of July traffic.

Her first trip to Rehoboth in years, it was a gift from Uncle Vic, to stay one last time at Aunt Dottie's bungalow before it was sold. It had been her happy place as a child and saying goodbye would be bittersweet.

As she closed the liftgate of her Honda, one bag snagged and ripped, and its contents fell through the gaping hole into and out of the car. One orange took off, rolling down the street.

Mood deflated, Jessi managed to unlock the door of the cottage with one hand while holding a half-dozen bags in the other, then wrangled the groceries into the kitchen. Before she could get the perishables into the fridge, there was a knock on the open front door. A man's voice called "hello."

Jessi pushed her tortoiseshell-framed sunglasses atop her head as she walked toward the door. She caught her breath at the sight of him. Six four, at least. Sandy hair, peppered with a little gray at the temples. Muscular but lean, suntanned skin standing out against his white polo shirt and khaki shorts. He was holding the errant orange. Quite the welcoming committee.

"Thanks. I see you found my wayward orange." *Humor covered embarrassment, didn't it?* When she took the proffered fruit from his calloused hand, there was a frisson of energy. *Could he feel it too?*

"The little rascal stopped right in front of me." His smile could light up the night sky. "I see you had a few other things escape. Would you like help getting everything in the house?" He nodded toward her car, still open, groceries on the ground around it.

"I'm good, thanks." People always seemed a little nicer here, even strangers. And his kindness had lightened her mood. Helpful, like Aunt Dottie's summer neighbors, the dad offering a hand when Uncle Vic wasn't around. The family had a son who surfed with Cousin Rooster. *What was his name? He had a silly nickname...*

"Vic mentioned he had someone staying here this week. I made sure everything was in working order." Pulling a business card from his wallet, he offered it to her. "If you need anything, call or text. Vic will vouch for me."

"Patrick Radcliffe, Radcliffe Remodeling & Renovations." *It couldn't be the same guy?* "I'm Jessica, but my friends call me Jessi."

"Everyone calls me Trick."

The memory clicked into place. "One-Trick Pony?"

"Messy Jessi? Rooster's little cousin?" They laughed in unison.

"I think we were teenagers the last time I saw you. No one calls me Messy Jessi anymore."

His finger pointed at the groceries spilling out of her car and they shared another laugh.

"You caught me. But I'm guessing you do more than surf now. More than that one trick?"

Trick picked up the loose groceries and grabbed her luggage. "I rehab homes, sometimes flip, general contracting." As he walked in, Trick motioned around the kitchen. "I'm fixing this place up after you leave so Vic can get top dollar."

"I jumped at his offer of a one-week stay. The last time he did that was right after I graduated from college." Jessi's eyes searched the room; it was nearly bare bones with most of Aunt Dottie's stuff gone. She continued to put the groceries away as they talked. "It's sad to see it go, but I'll always have the memories."

"Those were great times. How's Rooster?"

"He's a big-shot attorney to the stars in LA. I'm sure you know Uncle Vic and Aunt Mary retired to Florida after Aunt Dottie, Vic's mom and my grandaunt, passed away. It was a matter of time before they let the cottage go." She filled two glasses with water and offered one to Trick. "Where are my manners?

"Thanks."

As he took a long drink she wondered how fate could put this hot guy from her past right in front of her, just moments after arriving. He was the first man to catch her eye since she broke off an engagement a year ago. Probably because he was the gallant knight in shining armor who rescued her recalcitrant orange. Those ocean-blue eyes still shown bright like the Delaware Bay at noon. Shaking it off, she realized he had noticed her staring at him like the little girl who had had a crush on her older cousin's beach friend.

"Are you chilled? I turned on the AC before you arrived, but I can change the temperature for you."

He had noticed. *Calm down.* "No, I'm fine."

\* \* \* \* \*

Trick drove home, surprised to have seen little Messy Jessi all grown up. She had been a cute, slightly annoying kid with freckles and messy hair. While there was a resemblance, she was no longer the bothersome girl who had tried to tag along while he and Rooster surfed and hung out at the beach. Her frizzy brown hair was now tamed and wavy, her chocolate-brown eyes sparkly, and she was curvy in all the right places. Grownup Jessi wouldn't be a nuisance. The attraction was real. He thought she may have felt it, too, when she took the orange.

The July Fourth holiday might be a little more exciting with her around. He didn't have much work scheduled with all the tourists in town; no one wants to hear the buzz of a saw or pounding of a hammer on vacation. He had a few guys on standby for an emergency, but other than that, he was free the next few days. Too bad he hadn't thought to get her number.

* * * * *

Jessi awoke early, with plans to head to the beach a few blocks away before families arrived en masse. As she walked, she noticed new shops and old, as expected in an established beach town. She made a mental note to stop at the bookstore to grab some new reads for the week.

The sand was still cool from the earlier tide, and there were a few pretty shells to pocket. Slipping off her sandals, she let the water ebb and flow over her feet. The surf breaking on the shore, seagulls arguing over a scrap, and the salty-sweet breeze off the ocean were her only companions. Feeling refreshed, she went to higher ground and sat on a towel to soak in the morning's glory.

When she got back to the cottage, Jessi took a quick shower. As she got out, something seemed off. It shouldn't be this humid inside, even after a shower. Jessi finished getting ready, drying her hair, applying minimal makeup, and opting for a casual pink floral sundress. Checking the thermostat, she realized there was a problem with the AC.

Seeing Trick's business card on the counter reminded her he said to call if there was a problem. He *was* going to be fixing up the house, *and* he was a contractor. Debating for a moment, she called.

"Trick, this is Jessi, Vic's niece. I'm having a problem with the AC. What should I do?"

"I can check it for you."

"I hate to be a bother."

"It's not a problem. Is this a good time to come?"

"Sure."

"I'll be there soon."

\* \* \* \* \*

Trick knocked on the door, and Jessi answered his knock right away. She looked beautiful in a flowy dress and bare feet, like a mermaid on land, tempting him. He checked the thermostat and the outside unit. Although the motor was working, it wasn't cooling.

"What do you think is wrong?" Jessi fanned herself with a takeout menu.

"It might need a shot of coolant." He looked up at Jessi. She seemed at home at the cottage—the opposite of his ex, who would have found the place too small. "We're going to take the cottage down to the studs for the reno, so we wouldn't replace it now. I'll call someone to bring over portable units for you to use and have him see about the coolant."

"OK, sounds like a plan. Let me know the cost."

She seemed like a go-with-the-flow kind of woman, and he admired that. "There's no charge."

"You can't do the work for free." She had her hand on her hip, just like he remembered Messy Jessi doing when she was raring to argue.

"It's part of your uncle's maintenance contract. I've done this work for him for years."

"Whew. I thought I'd have to spend all my book and vacation money on a repair." Her smile combined with a slightly dramatic hand to her forehead revealed her sassy sense of humor which Trick found adorable.

"You have book *and* vacation money?"

"I'm a voracious reader and an English teacher. Books are integral to life." Another smile assured him she was teasing. He wanted to know more about grown-up Jessi.

"Why don't I take you to Egg for brunch, then we could walk around town so you can spend some of your book *and* vacation money." He winked. "By the time we're done, my guy will be here with the portable units, and I'll set them up for you."

They enjoyed a casual meal, catching up on each other's lives—his divorce and move back to the beach after years in banking, starting over by fixing up his parents' cottage rental, then going for a contractor license; her broken engagement and continuing ed classes taking up most summers, leaving little free time to relax.

They explored the shops on Rehoboth Avenue and surrounding streets, stopping at Browseabout Books for Jessi's beach reads, musing through a few galleries, and grabbing Italian ices to cool off before the walk back. Somewhere along the way, they began holding hands. It felt right.

He decided, on impulse, to give her the full Rehoboth welcome in one shot. They hit Dolle's for saltwater taffy, and since they couldn't agree on Grotto or Nicola, he bought a small pizza from Grotto and a Nic-o-Boli to split for dinner.

\* \* \* \* \*

Jessi set the table as Trick placed the portable AC units around the house. It cooled off quickly. She reflected over the afternoon on how easy it was to hang out with Trick. The moment he took her hand, she felt the surge of energy between them. Realistically, nothing could come of this. They lived nearly the length of the state apart. It's not like they would fall in love…

The next several days were a whirlwind. Jessi spent her mornings at the beach alone, reading, but the afternoons and evenings they spent together. Jessi was relearning the Rehoboth area, reminiscing about old times. A visit to the new botanical garden, shopping at the outlets, and visiting other towns along Coastal Highway were outings they enjoyed together. Trick had taken her to see his business office in a small industrial park, and he showed her his house, which was several miles inland.

Jessi and Trick were eating their way through town with funnel cake from Starkey's, beer and pub fare from Dogfish, and fries doused in malt vinegar from Thrasher's. A few nights Jessi cooked supper for them with the groceries she had brought, or Trick made seafood or steaks on the grill. It was downright domestic. It felt normal. Too good to be real.

The week was winding down. Their plans included the Fourth of July concert at the bandstand and fireworks. Leaving was going to be hard. They got along so well, saying goodbye was going to be harder. It was enough for Jessi to reflect on what she wanted for the future and who she would spend it with. They had talked so much about life, but never about the tomorrows. Just like any summer romance, it would end, and she'd go back to teaching in the fall. For the first time, it wasn't enough. She wanted more from life. Someone like Trick.

\* \* \* \* \*

Trick couldn't believe his time with Jessi was almost over. The past week had been eye-opening. He'd finally found a woman he could see being a part of his life, but she was leaving. It would be a lot to ask her to stay and relocate her life. Who makes that kind of decision after one week? It was crazy, but they were so in sync with how they spent time together, their interests, nearly everything. Was it a fluke? Could there be something they could build on?

He had a lot to think about, weighing the options. His business was going well, and it had become a year-round full-time gig. One he really enjoyed. Plus, he had employees depending on him. He had work lined up for more than a year out. He wasn't able to move back to northern Delaware. His life was here.

* * * * *

Jessi had spent the morning going through some boxes for Uncle Vic, looking for anything valuable. Most items weren't worth saving. She repacked what she thought was important, so she could ship them to Florida.

Then, at the bottom of one box, she found a treasure: Aunt Dottie's charm bracelet, which spelled out the letters R-E-H-O-B-O-T-H B-E-A-C-H in different colored charms. It had a Delaware-shaped charm on the end. Even though it was just costume jewelry, it was timeworn and well-loved, and it evoked so much emotion. Aunt Dottie, her grandaunt and pseudo grandmother, had let her wear it when she visited. Jessi ran her fingers slowly over each letter, thinking about the past, then snapped the clasp over her wrist. She planned to tell Uncle Vic about it later, but for now she was going to wear it. She hoped he would let her keep it.

Jessi dressed casually in a blue-and-white gingham sundress, to which she added a red belt, plus a pair of white slip-on sneakers, embracing the patriotic holiday. They were going to brave the crowd and walk to the concert. Trick mentioned he had found a quiet place where they could watch the fireworks afterward. A quick spritz of her favorite Philosophy scent and she was ready to go.

She heard his truck pull up and met him at the door. He wore a white polo shirt and navy-blue shorts. The sight of him had been giving her flutters all week, but tonight they were in overdrive.

She noticed him looking at her and he seemed to appreciate what he saw, which only increased the butterflies. He surprised her with a kiss on the cheek. They were friends and friends kissed on the cheek. *It didn't mean anything, did it?*

"You look beautiful." He handed her a small bouquet of mixed flowers she hadn't noticed him carrying.

"Thank you." She took the flowers and placed them in an old blue Mason jar she had found earlier in the week. "I made chicken salad."

"Sounds delicious."

"Since we didn't have time to make plans for a picnic, and the beach is so crowded, I thought it would be nice to have a quick meal here to use up the last of the groceries."

"Oh, right. You're leaving in the morning."

"I originally thought if I left on the Fourth, I'd beat the traffic home." *Ask me to change my plans; give me a reason to stay another day.*

"We'll have to make the most of our last night."

\* \* \* \* \*

It was a perfect evening for a concert. Clear night skies and air that had cooled to a comfortable temperature, with a light breeze coming off the water. They had walked hand in hand to the bandstand and stood near the back of the audience. Trick felt Jessi lean into him as the music played. He pulled her close and put his arm around her shoulder. It felt right with her by his side. If only there were a way to get her to return.

As the music played on, Trick whispered to her that it was time to beat the crowd for the fireworks. They walked back to the cottage, where he told her they were driving to one of his newly acquired rentals. It was empty and awaiting renovations.

They pulled up to a large multilevel raised home that backed up to the ocean near Silver Lake. It was one of his largest projects. He led her to the rear deck, where he had already set up a table and chairs;

a cooler sat nearby.

"This place is beautiful. And huge."

Trick watched her take in the ocean view. "It will sleep several families. Bring in steady revenue." He offered her a drink, but she opted for water.

"Great investment. Much larger than those cottages on Washington Street where we spent our summers."

"True…"

"Not quite the same charm, but most people don't want those quiet carefree days we had."

"That's spot on. I have every outlet wired for charging devices in this place."

"I hope whoever buys Aunt Dottie's place has a family and fills it with love. The cottage should always be a home, full of life."

\* \* \* \* \*

Jessi watched the fireworks erupt in the distance, bursts of red, white, and blue splaying across the sky. Standing behind her, Trick tugged her closer in his embrace. She relaxed into him, sighing at the comfort. It felt like home. After the finale, she turned to look into his ocean-blue eyes, sparkling in the moonlight.

"Thank you for the best beach vacation. I came to Rehoboth not knowing what to expect." She braced her hands on his shoulders and stood on her tiptoes to give him a light kiss on the lips. Leaving tomorrow, Jessi had nothing to lose. But she would have regretted not kissing Trick one time before she left.

"You're welcome." Trick had deepened the kiss, drawing her in and encircling her waist as she put her arms around his neck.

Jessi finally released her hold on Trick. She didn't want to, but this was ending when she left. There was no reason for false promises or to take things further. Just the memory of his kiss to treasure in her heart.

Trick couldn't believe it had been more than a month since Jessi had left, and he still missed her. *Could she feel the same way?* Knowing he couldn't ask her to leave her life, he was still unsure what to do with his feelings, so he poured the energy straight into his work renovating the cottage.

He had been cleaning out his truck when he found the bracelet. It was old and worn. *Why was it there?* His thoughts ran to Jessi. It had to be hers.

He texted Jessi about the bracelet. She called immediately, excited to know it wasn't lost. She gave Trick her address and asked him to mail it.

Trick knew it was a foolhardy plan, but with the Labor Day weekend coming up, he decided to deliver it in person. It was the only way to know if what had happened over the summer was real.

The look on Jessi's face when she opened her door and threw her arms around his neck told him everything he needed to know.

* * * * *

It was a year later and another July Fourth. Jessi and Trick exchanged vows on the beach in Rehoboth. It was a small wedding with only a few friends and family. She wore a simple but sleek white silk sheath gown. Perfect for a beach wedding. A lovely reception with a beach-themed tiered cake topped off the day.

Jessi knew the honeymoon location was a surprise. When Trick pulled up in front of the cottage on Washington Street, Jessi laughed, thinking it was a joke. It looked pretty, all freshened up, still emanating the charm of Aunt Dottie's bungalow.

Trick came around and helped her out of his truck. He picked her up and carried her to the door. "What are you doing? Uncle Vic sold this house."

Trick unlocked the door, carried her over the threshold, and then put her down. "Mrs. Radcliffe, how do you like your wedding gift?"

For the first time in her life, Jessi was utterly speechless. Looking around, she saw furnishings matching her ideas from a vision board Trick had asked her to make. Love filled every corner. The realization hit. This was now their beach bungalow. Their cottage on Washington Street. *Home.*

DENISE STOUT IS A HOPELESS ROMANTIC WHO DREAMED OF WRITING WHEN SHE DIDN'T HAVE HER NOSE BURIED IN A BOOK. SHE GREW UP IN NORTHERN DELAWARE, IS A GRADUATE OF THE UNIVERSITY OF DELAWARE, AND HOLDS A PARALEGAL CERTIFICATE. SHE WORKED IN THE BANKING INDUSTRY BEFORE FOCUSING ON HER WRITING AND HER FAMILY FROM HER HOME IN SUBURBAN MARYLAND.

DENISE WAS FIRST PUBLISHED WITH "CHRISTMAS MIRACLE ON OYSTER BAY" IN THE AWARD-WINNING ANTHOLOGY *THEN COMES WINTER*. SHE PRIMARILY WRITES IN THE CONTEMPORARY ROMANCE GENRE BUT HAS WRITTEN WOMEN'S FICTION, HISTORICAL FICTION, AS WELL AS TWO FULL-LENGTH NOVELS, AND SHE HAS A STACK OF REJECTION LETTERS TO PROVE IT.

DENISE WAS FEATURED WITH LIFESTYLE EXPERT KATIE BROWN IN *FAMILY CIRCLE* MAGAZINE, AND SHE WAS QUOTED IN VOX ABOUT BOOKS-TO-FILM HOLIDAY MOVIES. DENISE WAS RECENTLY CHOSEN BY BROOKE SHIELDS FOR THE 40 OVER 40 CAMPAIGN FOR HER BEGINNING IS NOW BRAND. DENISE IS A REGULAR CONTRIBUTOR TO THE WIC PROJECT LIFESTYLE BLOG AND WORKS AS AN AUTHOR ASSISTANT FOR SEVERAL WRITERS. SHE VOLUNTEERS AND READS WHEN NOT WRITING.

# The Best Worst Holiday Ever

### By Jeanie P. Blair

Paige Strickland was seething as she glared out the window of the black Range Rover driven by one of her father's hired musclemen. If she'd had her way, she'd be in her convertible Audi, cruising to her family's beachfront mansion in East Hampton, New York. She had planned to spend the next month enjoying her annual trip with her besties, celebrating summer and the July Fourth holiday, sipping margaritas and hopefully getting to know the hot young lawyer who had recently purchased the house just down the beach from theirs. Instead, thanks to her father, she was spending it alone with a stranger—some psycho for all she knew—at their other vacation home in Bethany Beach, Delaware. Dean Strickland was well-known for his fierce negotiating skills, of which his daughter was on the losing end once again. *Worst. Holiday. Ever.*

After several miles of deafening quiet, Paige broke the ice. "So, are you planning to talk to me, or are we going to ride in silence for the next four hours?"

Her driver stayed focused on the road. "I figured I'm the last person you'd want to talk to." Brodie Crawford was built like a linebacker, his thick, spiked hair matched his shiny black Ray-Bans.

Paige shrugged. "I guess it's not your fault my father's a jerk."

"Your father loves you and wants to keep you safe."

Paige rolled her eyes. "Yeah, right. He just wants to control me. As always."

The biggest land developer in the region, Dean Strickland was no stranger to threats from disgruntled real-estate moguls who had lost bundles in negotiations with him, but this was the first time a threat had been directed at his daughter.

"He *knew* I had plans to spend this holiday in the Hamptons like I do *every* year. I'm twenty-six years old and I can take care of myself. I'm so pissed!"

"Well, he'd rather you be pissed at him than see you get hurt. I'd say that's love." Brodie paused. "Not everyone gets that kind of love."

Paige wondered if Brodie was referring to himself. Though she barely knew him, it still saddened her to think that he might be.

"Well, when you put it that way, I guess I should be grateful." Paige sighed. "I think I liked it better when we weren't talking."

Brodie chuckled.

It was the first time she'd seen him smile, and she liked the way it softened his features.

\* \* \* \* \*

As the pair continued their trek they engaged in brief chats, mostly dominated by Paige. During a lull in conversation, Paige had succumbed to the hypnotic hum of the tires against the asphalt and drifted to sleep.

Brodie couldn't resist taking a few glances at her. Her wavy auburn hair slightly covered her face, and he found himself fighting the urge to reach over and brush it aside. What she didn't know—and he couldn't tell her—was that it wasn't an idle threat that had derailed her holiday. This time, it was an envelope sent to her father, containing photos of Paige with her friends and a note threatening her life if her father didn't back out of his current bidding war with other developers. Keeping her safe was paramount.

Paige jumped when Brodie tapped her arm.

"We're here."

"Wow. How long was I asleep?" She groaned.

"A good hour or more."

Paige stretched as Brodie removed their bags from the SUV. "Need help?"

"Nah. I'm good."

Brodie hauled their luggage up the steps of the enormous gray-and-white Sussex Shores house. Once inside, he peeled off his Ray-Bans and disarmed the beeping security system. He synced his cell phone with the keypad, then texted Dean to let him know they'd arrived.

"I'll disengage the security system every morning at five o'clock when I get up, so if you get up earlier than that, you'll have to wake me to turn it off before you go downstairs."

Paige laughed. "Me? Up before five? No chance of *that*, I assure you."

Paige couldn't help but notice how Brodie's muscles flexed when he lifted the heavy suitcases, though he handled them as if they were empty. After the bags were deposited in their respective bedrooms, the two proceeded to the main-floor kitchen.

"I'm sure there are cold drinks in the fridge, but we'll have to go shopping for some food," Paige said.

"Done," Brodie said. "Your father already took care of it."

"I should've known. When Big Dean speaks..."

Brodie shot her a look, and she noticed his striking, dark-brown eyes for the first time. They were so expressive she could read his thoughts.

"I know. Be grateful," she mocked.

"Exactly."

"So...what's *your* deal, Brodie Crawford? What do you do for fun?"

"Well, I'm always working, sooo..."

"Wow. You need to loosen up."

"I'm not being paid to loosen up. I'm being paid to protect you."

"Relax, Brodie. This isn't the first time my father overreacted to a threat from some pissed-off land developer. He couldn't care less about who he steps on to get what he wants."

"Maybe so, but he *does* care about you."

"He smothers me. That's why I was *so* looking forward to my trip."

"Well, unfortunately, you're stuck with me this holiday."

"Great. Well, if you think I'm staying cooped up in here the entire time, you're wrong."

Brodie glared at her with furrowed brows. "Fine. But no leaving the house without telling me. Wherever *you* go, I go."

Paige was surprised to find that statement more appealing than annoying. It was probably just his gravelly voice. *Snap out of it. This muscle-head is far from your type.* She rolled her eyes. "I'm gonna get a shower. I should hope you won't be accompanying me there."

\* \* \* \* \*

Brodie fixed a quick sheet-pan supper with food from the well-stocked fridge. Once it was in the oven, he grabbed a chaise on the screened porch to admire the breathtaking view. His boss's net worth was no secret, but this level of wealth was way beyond Brodie's comprehension.

The beeping timer snapped Brodie back to reality. He returned to the kitchen to check on dinner.

"Wow. Something smells good in here." Paige pranced into the kitchen in white shorts and a pink tank top, her shoulder-length hair still damp.

"Thanks. There's plenty if you're hungry."

"Actually, I *am* kind of hungry," she said, eyeballing Brodie's creation. "Impressive. A superhero *and* a chef." She arranged two place settings on the counter.

"Would you mind if we ate outside?" Brodie asked.

"Fine by me."

Brodie loaded their plates while Paige grabbed two wine glasses and a bottle of Chardonnay from the wine fridge.

"Just water for me, please," Brodie said.

"Really?"

"I rarely drink alcohol. It clouds the judgment and slows the reflexes."

Paige rolled her eyes. "Great. Of all the bodyguards on my father's payroll, I get stuck with Mr. Rogers."

Brodie shook his head and followed her out to the porch.

Dinner conversation was limited. They mostly just relished the scenery while they enjoyed their meal.

Paige took her last bite. "That was delicious, Brodie. Where'd you learn to cook?"

"Thanks. I had to fend for myself during most of my tours."

"Tours?" she asked.

"Marines."

"Oh. How long did you serve?"

"Twelve years."

"Wow. I guess you've seen a lot of this big ol' world, huh?"

"Yep."

"That's so cool!"

Brodie frowned. "*Cool*? It was no vacation, Paige."

"Jeez!" Paige snapped back at him. "I'm sorry. I was just making conversa—"

Brodie snatched up both plates and stomped off to the kitchen. He set the dishes in the sink and took a deep breath. *Easy, dude. She didn't choose your career.*

Paige stewed for a bit, then entered the kitchen just as Brodie had finished loading the dishwasher. "I'm heading up for the night. Thanks for dinner, Brodie."

She was gracious, but her stern expression told him she was still peeved at him. Brodie forced a half-smile and nodded at her. "Goodnight, Paige." He wanted to apologize for snapping at her, but the truth was, he had no idea what to say. Expressing his feelings was far from his strong suit—courtesy of twelve years in the Corps. Brodie suddenly realized he was gripping the edge of the countertop so tightly he might just snap it off. He released his clutch on the granite and put his hands on his head. He knew he had to right things with Paige.

\* \* \* \* \*

Brodie awoke the next morning before his alarm. He hadn't slept well after his tiff with Paige. He changed into his exercise gear, disarmed the security system, then headed to the fitness room. After clearing his head with an intense workout, he made his way toward the kitchen.

The smell of coffee permeated the first floor. *She's up. Time to make things right.* The kitchen was empty, so Brodie continued out to the porch. Except for an empty coffee mug on a side table, there was no trace of Paige. He proceeded out to the path that led to the beach. There was Paige, in a yellow sundress and a wide-brimmed straw hat, sitting cross-legged on a blanket atop the sand just beyond the pathway.

Brodie stopped and took a deep breath. Though he hadn't planned on starting the day with another battle, he wasn't happy she'd left the house without telling him.

"Good morning."

Paige jumped at the sound of his voice.

"I thought I asked you not to leave the house without telling me."

"And I told *you*…I refuse to be a prisoner."

"Fine. But I meant what I said. Where you go, I go."

"OK. Don't get your boxers in a bunch."

"Look, Paige. I apologize for snapping at you last night. And I don't mean to treat you like a child, but if I have to sleep outside your bedroom door, I will."

"OK...OK! I promise to behave myself, Yoda. I promise to play by the rules if you promise to lighten up a little."

Annoyed as he was, Brodie couldn't help but find humor in her sarcasm.

"C'mon. At least promise me you'll try," she said, and offered her hand. "Deal?"

"Deal." He shook her hand, but nevertheless, he didn't trust her completely. There was no way he was letting his guard down with this one.

\* \* \* \* \*

Following their pact, the next several weeks went smoothly. Brodie loosened the reins a bit, and Paige kept her promise to keep him apprised of her whereabouts. Seaside picnics became a ritual, and the pair spent many evenings watching movies or playing vintage board games from the study closet. Paige had even convinced Brodie to take her into town for the July Fourth festivities, including the fireworks and a concert by *Broken Lullaby*, her favorite local band.

\* \* \* \* \*

Paige called to Brodie from the porch dining table. "According to the town website, they're showing a movie on the beach tonight—*Jaws*. Wanna go?"

Another evening at a large gathering was against Brodie's better judgment. It would be too easy for someone to snatch Paige and disappear into the crowd. Brodie hesitated, trying to avoid getting sucked in by her enthusiasm, but it was becoming harder and harder to refuse her.

"C'mon, big guy. It'll be fun!"

"OK," Brodie conceded. "But we sit where I choose." With the right vantage point, he could keep her safe.

"Deal!"

Brodie laughed and shook his head. She'd clearly inherited her father's negotiating skills.

\* \* \* \* \*

When they arrived at the movie site, Brodie scanned the area and chose a spot at the foot of the grassy dunes.

Paige spread out a blanket. "I've seen this movie a million times, but it still scares the hell out of me."

Brodie chuckled. "Don't worry. I think we're far enough from the water here."

The ocean breeze made Paige's loose curls dance around her face. She wore just a minimal trace of makeup which, in Brodie's opinion, she didn't even need. She was perfect without it.

As the movie got underway, Paige moved closer to Brodie, who was watching the crowd more than the flick. He laughed when Paige jumped whenever it got intense. When Captain Quint met his bloody demise, Paige clutched Brodie's arm and buried her face in his bicep. Brodie laughed and laid his hand over hers. "It's over now. You can look."

"I'm sorry. That part gets me every time."

"No problem. It *is* pretty tough to watch."

On the drive back to the house, the two shared a few stories. Paige was easy to open up to, which was something Brodie rarely did with anyone. They both laughed hysterically as he told her about a drunken calamity with his fellow recruits at the end of basic training, which landed him ass over tin cups in a public fountain.

"You know, you should do that more often," Paige said.

Brodie laughed. "What, get drunk and face-plant into a fountain?"

"No." Paige chuckled. "*Laugh*. Your whole face lights up when you laugh."

Brodie smiled. His cheeks flushed, and he was damned glad it was too dark for her to notice.

\* \* \* \* \*

When they returned to the house, Paige persuaded Brodie to join her for a drink before calling it a night. "OK. *One* beer," Brodie conceded.

Paige grabbed two ice-cold Coronas from the fridge, and they headed up to the balcony off the third-floor game room.

"Brodie, thanks for making this nightmare bearable. I'm sorry I was so difficult in the beginning."

"You? Difficult? Naahhh."

Paige reached over to punch Brodie's arm but missed, striking the wooden frame of his chair. "Oww! Dammit!" She winced as she shook her hand.

Brodie jumped up. "Oh, crap. Let me see it." He sat down on the edge of Paige's chaise. She winced as he gingerly took her hand to assess her injury. "I think it's just bruised. Nothing appears to be broken." He grabbed her cold beer from the table. "Here, just hold this on it for a bit."

"Thanks. Let me guess. You're a doctor too?"

"Not exactly. But I *was* trained as a corpsman in the Marines."

A short while later, Brodie looked at his watch. "It's nearly one a.m. We should probably call it a night."

Paige agreed, and they both stood.

Brodie turned toward her. "How's the hand?"

Paige slowly flexed her fingers. "Fine. Especially compared to the time I punched Marty Mallek in the fourth grade."

Brodie laughed out loud. "You punched a boy?"

"That bully pulled my hair. Besides, I'm tougher than anyone gives me credit for."

Brodie took her hand and softly brushed his thumb across her knuckles. "I'm beginning to see that."

Their eyes locked. "Thanks, Brodie. For everything. This holiday hasn't been so bad after all." Paige leaned in and softly kissed his lips.

Brodie put his hands on her shoulders and gently pushed away from her. "Paige—"

"I…I'm sorry. I shouldn't have…Goodnight, Brodie." Paige made a swift exit to her room.

\* \* \* \* \*

Brodie awoke just before sunrise. After a long night of tossing and turning, he resolved that it was likely the Coronas that triggered Paige's kiss. Though he'd always dreamed of being with someone like her, he knew she'd never have any real interest in someone like him. Besides, he couldn't afford to get close. It was his job to keep her safe, not to get involved with her. He opted for a run on the beach to clear his mind. On his way down the hall, he noticed Paige's door was open, and she wasn't inside.

Brodie reached an empty kitchen and noticed the back door to the porch was open. He rushed over to the alarm panel and saw that it had been bypassed. *Damn her!* Somehow, she'd disengaged the alarm without it alerting his cell phone. He raced through the porch and down the wooden pathway. Still no sign of Paige. Brodie's blood boiled. He should've known last night had been nothing but a ploy to make him drop his guard.

\* \* \* \* \*

Paige strolled along the edge of the softly swishing surf. While she toed the cool, wet sand, she tried desperately to forget the kiss she'd planted on Brodie. What was she thinking? The man of her dreams wasn't supposed to be a hired gun employed by her overprotective father. Worst of all, based on Brodie's reaction, her feelings clearly weren't reciprocated.

The cackle of a passing seagull caught her attention. She admired the gracefulness of the soaring bird and envied its freedom. The amber glow of the sunrise was just beginning to breach the horizon. It was her favorite time of day, so peaceful and serene.

Suddenly, a large rough hand came from behind and covered her mouth at the same time a strong arm cinched her waist, lifting her off the ground. She struggled to get free—kicking her legs, trying to reach the sand. *This CANNOT be happening.* At that moment, everything Brodie had warned her about had become all too real. The thought of what might happen next terrified her.

Paige elbowed her attacker, and her feet were once again in the cool surf. Weak and out of breath, she fell to her knees. She looked up at the silhouette looming over her. The intensity of the sun blinded her, concealing his face. Paige gasped when her assailant stepped in front of the sun.

"Brodie! What the hell?!"

Brodie breathed hard. "I'm sorry. But I had to teach you a lesson."

"Are you *serious*?"

"Dead serious. If I had been a real attacker, I could've easily abducted you just now. And that's the *best-case* scenario. Now do you understand how quickly things can go bad?"

"OK. I get it. But why do you really care? Afraid you'll disappoint the boss man?"

"Really? You think *that's* what I care about?" He was clearly steamed. "Dammit, Paige. When I couldn't find you, I panicked. And not because I give a damn about your father." Brodie paused and combed his fingers through his thick hair. "Paige, someone's been following you."

Paige stood and brushed the sand from her legs. "Wait. What?"

"That's why I've been so intense. I wasn't supposed to tell you, but you've left me no choice." Brodie told her about everything, including the photos her father received.

Paige still struggled to catch her breath. "Oh. My. God."

"Exactly. Now you know why I've been on you so much."

"Oh, Brodie." Paige was still trying to wrap her mind around the horrific reality. "I had no idea. I'm sorry I've been so difficult."

Brodie stared down, hands on his hips. "But that's not all, Paige...I..."

"What is it, Brodie?"

"Dammit. I care about you, Paige. The thought that something had happened to you..."

"Brodie." She took a step toward him.

Brodie put up his hand. "Forget it, Paige. I don't expect you to feel the same way."

Paige palmed her forehead. "You idiot."

"Excuse me?"

"Who kissed *who* last night?" she asked.

"Oh. I figured that was the Corona." Seeing by her expression he'd been wrong, Brodie took her face in his hands and gave her a deep lingering kiss. "There. Now we're even."

Paige laughed. "Yeah? Well just don't forget who did it first."

Brodie's cell phone chimed. He tapped the screen. "Hello, sir." He listened intently for a bit. "That's great news. Thanks."

Brodie ended the call and turned to Paige. "That was your father. Your stalker's been apprehended."

"Oh, thank God!" Paige threw her arms around Brodie's neck.

"It's all behind you now."

Paige pulled back. "Speaking of behind me, how did you sneak up on me so quietly?"

"Not my first ambush," he said. "How did you bypass that door alarm?"

"Not my first jail break. So, I guess that means you'd better not let me out of your sight again. Deal?" She extended a hand to him.

"Deal." Brodie laughed as he took her hand and pulled her in for a long, passionate kiss. Now *that* was a negotiation he'd gladly concede to.

The pair took a seat on the sand as the sun continued its ascent. Paige rested her head on Brodie's shoulder. "Brodie, remember when I said this holiday wasn't so bad after all?"

"Yeah."

"Well, turns out it's been my best one ever."

Brodie put his arm around her and kissed the top of her head. "Mine too, Paige. Mine too."

A NATIVE DELAWAREAN, JEANIE PITRIZZI BLAIR RESIDES IN NEWARK WITH HER HUSBAND, SAM, AND THEIR MINIATURE SCHNAUZER, SOPHIA. "THE BEST WORST HOLIDAY EVER" IS HER SEVENTH SHORT STORY ROMANCE PUBLISHED IN THE VARIOUS ANTHOLOGIES BY CAT & MOUSE PRESS. ALONG WITH HER AFFINITY FOR WRITING, JEANIE ENJOYS SKETCHING AND CARTOONING, AND IS AN AVID MUSIC LOVER AND COLLECTOR OF MEMORABILIA FROM SOME OF HER FAVORITE BANDS. AS A SELF-PROCLAIMED SCIENCE NERD AND SHARK AFFICIONADO, SHE IS RELIABLY PERCHED IN FRONT OF THE TV FOR DISCOVERY'S SHARK WEEK EVERY JULY, HENCE THE REFERENCE IN HER STORY TO JAWS, ONE OF HER FAVORITE MOVIES.

THOUGH SHE WORKS FULL TIME AS AN OFFICE ADMINISTRATOR, JEANIE CONTINUES TO PURSUE HER DREAM OF BECOMING A SUCCESSFUL ROMANCE NOVELIST. AND—IF SHE CAN ONE DAY TALK HER HUSBAND INTO A COLLABORATION—SHE'D LOVE TO TAP INTO HIS CINEMATIC EXPERTISE AND TRY HER HAND AT A SCREENPLAY. AS ALWAYS, JEANIE WOULD LIKE TO THANK HER FAMILY AND FRIENDS FOR THEIR ENDLESS LOVE AND SUPPORT.

# Homebase

## By Anna Beck

Their story started out like most; it began with a meeting. He worked in middle management, doing a job that was of little interest to him and the people around him. She was a secretary but spent the rest of her time performing community service. It was during a beach beautification session that his world collided with hers.

She was picking up trash on the grainy sand dunes that had become very dear to her heart. She had grown up near the beach with her parents and enjoyed every splendor the boardwalk could offer. Long ago were the summers of childhood dreams and the possibility of becoming anything. Reality had hit her hard when she had to get a job and move out on her own, but the endless shoreline always gave her peace of mind, and it was important to her to help restore it. At that moment she was deeply upset with the amount of trash that had formed on her beloved dunes. Just then, a careless passerby walking on the boardwalk threw a coffee cup on the dune. Enraged, she started up toward the person to give them a talking to when she was startled by a voice behind her.

"Do you need any help?" a man asked.

Shocked, she couldn't manage a response for a few seconds. Never, in all the days she cleaned the beach, had anyone ever offered to help.

"I'm sorry to intrude, but I often visit here and always see you cleaning up. I don't know how you do it all by yourself, so today I figured I'd help." Truth be told, he had seen her a few weeks earlier when visiting the beach town and thought she was the most beautiful woman he had ever set his eyes on. Even with her hair slicked back into a tight bun and her stiff posture, she seemed as graceful and elegant as a swan. He knew he needed to meet her. It took him two more visits to the boardwalk to finally gather the courage to talk to her.

Both parties were equally shocked at speaking to one another. At last, she thanked him for his kind offer, declined his help, and continued walking down the beach.

*Now, what am I supposed to do with that?* he thought. Not one to give up a fight, he caught up to her and asked why not.

"Because I like working alone," she replied sharply, her green eyes sparkling with passion. "And another person would ruin the dynamic."

"Fine, then," he responded. "I'll just borrow one of your trash bags and walk ten paces behind you. You'll hardly even know I'm there." He took a trash bag and began walking behind her, picking up trash along the way.

She felt mocked and wondered at his persistence, but she held her tongue. They continued that way for some time, with him ten steps behind, until curiosity got the best of her, and she started asking questions. They ended up walking down the beach together, keeping up a light conversation and, when they had walked the length of the boardwalk, he asked her if she'd like to grab a coffee. She liked the idea of spending more time with this stranger, so she accepted his proposal.

Other dates followed, and after some time they were married.

* * * * *

Once the couple had settled, he got a promotion, and they were forced to move away. This was especially hard for her, as she was forced to leave everything she had known. But she knew it was for the best and looked forward to their new future together.

They moved into a nice suburban house in a neighborhood where all the houses looked the same. Their house had a playset and an old treehouse in the backyard.

They settled into their new home and eventually had their first child. Two other children followed. She was occupied mostly by the children, keeping the house clean, and preparing the meals. There was little time to do anything else. By the time they put the kids to bed she was exhausted. He was working long hours at his boring job, causing him to be exhausted as well. This cycle carried on long enough that he stopped caring and she lost her passion. They became strangers in their own household.

One day, he looked up from reading the newspaper and glanced at her. He realized his wife was fading before him. She was like a zombie, walking around helplessly, so in tune to her world and surroundings that nothing fazed her. She had stopped participating in community service years ago; her ardent love for volunteering had ceased to exist. A sudden sadness came over him and he realized that he had to do something before she was lost forever. But what?

\* \* \* \* \*

She awoke to find a suitcase at the end of her bed.

*How unusual,* she thought, *we are not scheduled to visit the children.* Thinking he must have gotten confused, she made her way downstairs.

"Why are the suitcases out?"

"We're going on a trip," he said.

Flustered, she ate her breakfast in silence and got into the car without complaint. He was in an enjoyable mood, which only annoyed her. He refused to tell her where they were going, simply humming in response. Slowly, she drifted into a restless sleep…

He felt giddy with the prospect of surprising his wife. He hoped this holiday would bring them together and restore the connection they had lost over the years.

She awoke as they crossed the bridge over the canal, signifying arrival at the beach. As she took in all the sights and smells around her, her demeanor changed. It was as if she were a young girl again, looking forward to frolicking in the water, getting ice cream every afternoon, face red from the sun, then chasing off seagulls and building sandcastles with her childhood friends. It was all coming back to her. She looked around and realized that even though this was the same location, the downtown had changed significantly. There were more tourists, more buzz, and more shops. This fact saddened her at first, but she was too overwhelmed by happiness to dwell on it.

"Are we really here?" she asked.

"Yes, we are," he replied. "I figured we could both use a break, and we haven't been back here in so long. I know you've missed this place, and so have I."

She reached over and squeezed his hand. Then, it dawned on her why he was doing this. She looked over at her husband and saw him, really *saw* him, for the first time in years. She was about to say something when the car stopped.

"We're here," he said, looking over at her, gauging her reaction.

He had brought her back to her childhood home at the beach. They had kept it in the family when her parents died but had neglected to visit it for years. The house was a little worse for wear, with its peeling white paint, fading awnings, and overgrown yard, but it would forever be her home. They unpacked the car and walked inside. Both were taking in all the sights and smells of the sun-beaten house. It was a little cluttered and covered in dust and cobwebs but was otherwise as they remembered it.

She took her suitcase upstairs and put it in her old room. She looked around and basked in the glory of her years spent at the house.

"We're going to need some fresh sheets and blankets. Want to check out the boardwalk with me?'" he asked.

"Yes, I'd love to," she answered.

Despite not finding any sheets or blankets to their liking, they had an enjoyable afternoon and bought fries and popcorn from stands along the boardwalk. The fries were crisped to perfection and they both doused them in salt and vinegar, creating the perfect sour combination. With the popcorn, they decided to stay on the safe side and get plain popcorn with butter but promised each other that they would be back tomorrow to try at least one of the many flavors available. It was as if something magical had happened. The ice had begun to thaw. They had been chatting and laughing for hours when she noticed there was trash scattered across the beach.

"C'mon," she said, pulling him across the boardwalk toward the sandy shoreline. She started to run, and he chased after her.

She had picked up all the trash she could hold when he produced a trash bag. She realized he was always there for her, even in the little moments, and smiled at this.

He realized that she was always putting others before herself and smiled back at her.

They continued their way down the beach, picking up trash and conversing easily with each other as the sun began its slow descent. He was able to drag her away from their beloved beach and they made their way back to the beach house hand in hand.

She was beginning to realize that he was not doing this for him or her, he was doing it for them, their marriage, and their life together.

At last, she spoke. "Thank you for bringing me here."

"You're welcome."

They looked into each other's eyes and smiled. A lot of feelings were exchanged in that one glance, a lot of vulnerability that was exposed after years of hiding.

\* \* \* \* \*

There was something about that beach that brought them together, relaxed tensions, and made them breathe easier. It was for those reasons and many more that after that day they decided to visit the beach as often as they possibly could. They began working their weeks away and counting down the hours until they would get a glimpse of the golden coastline. Once they both retired and nothing was holding them back anymore, they loaded up their belongs and headed to the place dearest to their hearts.

For the rest of their lives, they stayed at the beach and talked about the magical times spent there to their children, grandchildren, and even great-grandchildren, always making sure to bring up the importance of beach cleanliness. So, it was no surprise that all their family shared their love for the beach and decided to open an inn to share their love of the beach with as many people as possible. Their love for the beach was carried on for generations and some say, if you take a stroll on the beach during sunset, you can make out the soft outline of a young couple laughing while devoting themselves to make the beach and their home a better place.

Anna Beck is a rising sophomore at Cape Henlopen High School. She enjoys baking, reading, and spending time with friends and family, while challenging herself academically. Her interests in school vary from writing and English to math and science. She is an active member in her school's newspaper, *Viking Ventures*, as well as Leo Club and Mock Trial. Anna has very ambitious goals and plans to attend law school after college. She hopes to be a practicing lawyer working for the United States government. "Homebase" is her first published work.

Inspiration for her story stemmed from the thought that a writer could tell a complex story without naming the individuals and still create a compelling tale. It then evolved into a work about an older couple, reflecting the many retirees moving to Delaware and a possible reason for them wanting to move to the area. Anna wanted to showcase the ever-evolving Rehoboth Beach region, displaying how the basis of the town remains the same despite more traffic and a growing population. She included a community service aspect to her story as homage to her own involvement and to bring awareness to the issue.

## Judge's Comment

*This story is brisk and well-paced, while still leaving an emotional impact. With simple, straightforward style, the author follows relatable characters and touches on the way the beach has a special place in the hearts of those who love it.*

# Fourth of July Fundango

## By Doug Harrell

**From:** beachgeek@earthlink.net
**Sent:** July 5, 11:01 a.m.
**To:** angelica43@icloud.com
**Subject:** Fourth of July Fundango

Dear Sis,

I hope you and George are having a good time on your cruise. Thanks for trusting me with the little brats, I mean your lovely children, to whom I am deeply attached—mostly. While I am hardly a responsible adult, you will be happy to hear they are both still alive, and they haven't learned any bad words this time—at least none I didn't know when I was their age. I took a page from Odysseus and stuffed their ears with wax. ;- )

I know you're a worrier, so I'll fill you in on what we've been up to. The weather on Friday was sunny and hot, so we spent the day at the beach. The waves were great! Fortunately, so were the lifeguards. Did you know a rip tide can carry you thirty yards in less than a minute? On the bright side, now Amy and Billy are even *more* motivated to take swimming lessons.

Saturday would have been a great beach day, too, but we needed to stay indoors and drink lots of fluids. That's what you do for sunburn, right?

Remember when Mom and Dad used to take us for a "Fourth of

July Fundango?" On Sunday, the three of us set out to Fundango the night away.

We started at Grotto's. As soon as the little darlings had ingested enough pizza to make vomiting interesting, we made a beeline for Funland. They tried their darndest to give the pizza back, first on the teacup ride, then on the Freefall. I sat those out, but I did go with them on that big Viking ship that swings back and forth. Billy said it was boring, so I held him over my head until he screamed and wet his pants. Don't worry, I'm fine.

At the Haunted Mansion, Amy put both hands on her hips (remind you of anyone?) and announced she was big enough to go by herself. I was very proud of her. She stopped shaking as soon as the ride was over, and only cried for a few minutes after that.

Amy was also big enough to go on the bumper cars alone this year. I rode with Billy. He was laser focused on ramming his sister, just like I always was, and we got her good! I'll send you a picture of Amy in her pink neck brace. She's adorable!

At last it was dark enough for the fireworks. They were incredible this year, and we were super close to the launch site. Too close as it turned out, but how was I to know the Roman candle would set Billy's sleeve on fire? Good thing I still had some soda left!

It was a Fourth of July the kids will never forget—at least according to the caseworker from child protective services.

Before you place a ship-to-shore call to Mom to rescue your kids, let me put your mind at ease:

1) Beach, yes—*Baywatch* rescue, no—sunburn, no
2) Boardwalk, yes—peed pants, no—terror, no—whiplash, no—nephew flambé, no, no, no!
3) Fun, Yes! Yes! Yes!

Even without risking death and dismemberment at every turn, we've had a wonderful time. Amy and Billy really are the sweetest kids. (Are

you *sure* there wasn't a mix-up at the hospital?)
Love,
Your little bro
"The Man, The Myth, The Bad Influence"

NOTHING BEATS A DAY AT THE BEACH WITH KIDS: BOOGIE BOARDING, BUILDING SANDCASTLES, AND HUNTING FOR BURIED PIRATE TREASURE. THEN, IT'S TIME TO HIT THE REHOBOTH BOARDWALK AND FUNLAND. REMEMBERING PRECIOUS HOURS SPENT WITH HIS NIECES AND NEPHEWS OVER THE YEARS WAS DOUG'S INSPIRATION FOR THIS STORY.

FORTUNATELY, NONE OF THEM EVER HAD A NEAR-DEATH EXPERIENCE IN HIS COMPANY. HOWEVER, AMY AND BILLY GAVE HIM QUITE A SCARE EARLY ONE MORNING. THEIR BEDS WERE EMPTY, THE TOP SHEETS WERE MISSING, AND THEY WERE NOWHERE IN THE HOUSE. RUSHING OUTSIDE, DOUG FOUND THEM WRAPPED IN THE SHEETS WITH TOY SWORDS HELD HIGH, MARCHING THROUGH THE SAND PRETENDING TO BE LAWRENCE OF ARABIA.

DOUG HARRELL IS A RECOVERING ENGINEER WHO HAS TAKEN UP WRITING AS A SECOND CAREER, DIVIDING HIS TIME BETWEEN PIKE CREEK AND LEWES. "FOURTH OF JULY FUNDANGO" IS HIS SIXTH STORY PUBLISHED BY CAT & MOUSE PRESS. VISIT HIM AT WWW.DOUGLASHARRELL.COM.

P.S. NO NIECES OR NEPHEWS WERE HARMED IN THE WRITING OF THIS STORY.

# Summer Valentine's Day

## By David Cooper

Heat filled my cheeks and rose to the tips of my ears. I looked up and down the beach before taking the folded red-paper heart from my father's rough hand. Even though I was nine, I embarrassed easily. *This is stupid*, I thought.

My sister, Nina, contributed her usual huff and eye roll, but Luca, the oldest, smiled in my direction. For some reason, Luca always went along with Papa's Summer Valentine's Day.

"Don't open it yet." Papa held his matching valentine, took a long breath, and peered over the sparkling ocean. His brow wrinkled and lips pressed together from some passing thought but only for a moment.

Mom-mom stood with us, next to the waves and within the whirlwind of chattering seagulls, her hair pinned back, smile gleaming in the sun, and wearing her best dress. She enjoyed Summer Valentine's Day as much as Papa, but we all knew this was really his day.

Nina shuffled her feet. "Do I have to do this?" She always had somewhere else to be, and the somewhere usually involved boys.

Papa gave her a stern look. "You can give your brothers, grandmother, and me one day a year." He nodded his head. "OK, go ahead and open it, Antonio. Read the clues to us."

*Cursive.* I hated reading the swirling looping script. "First, love brews deep and brings a heart to the surface. Second, you need"—I struggled to make out the next word—"muscle to break the shell around a heart."

"Why don't you just tell us what to find, Papa?" Nina whined.

Papa put a finger to his lips. "Let your brother read."

"Third, this heart is almost as sweet as your Mom-mom. Fourth, with a light heart, you can have a whirly, twirly crazy time."

"Good, Antonio." Papa glanced at my brother and sister. "Your phones charged?"

They nodded.

Papa clapped his hands and smiled, flashing his teeth just like Mom-mom. "Text me your photos as soon as you get them."

"Can we split up?" Nina asked this question every year. "It'll make this whole thing go faster."

"No." Papa shook his head and pointed at each of us. "You never split up. Always stay together on Summer Valentine's Day."

Mom-mom hugged us, then placed her hand on my cheek. "Listen to your brother and sister. And remember, Frank and Louie's at noon for lunch. Don't eat too much junk. You'll spoil your appetites."

We trudged toward the dunes, climbed the boardwalk ramp, passed Funland, which wasn't open yet, and neared Zelky's arcade, blinking, beeping, and buzzing with activity. A game card loaded with four dollars lay tucked in my shorts pocket. "Can we play some Skee-Ball?"

Nina tugged my arm. "The faster we find these things for Papa, the faster we can all do what we want to do."

"Nina, this isn't a race." Luca put his hands on my shoulders and guided me away from the games. "And it'll be fun. It always is."

Luca would have had more luck ripping a chew toy from a possessive Doberman's mouth than convincing Nina of anything.

"Maybe *you* think this is fun," she said.

"I do, Nina."

"Why do we give up vacation time every year for this garbage?" she asked. "Valentine's Day is in February, and even that is a made-up holiday. I vote we make this the last Summer Valentine's Day."

I raised my hand. "Me too."

"We can't." Luca didn't show any signs of giving up. "You know how important this is to Papa."

Nina said, "This whole vacation is important to Papa. He crawls under cars all year for us to have this one week, then we do this stupid thing he thinks we like, and it only takes away one of those days."

"Look, just don't say anything like that to him." Luca turned away from her. "What is the first thing to find, Antonio?"

"Something about love brewing and a heart coming to the surface."

We passed families lugging beach bags, pulling carts filled with brightly colored buckets and shovels, and holding towels under their arms headed for their days on the sand.

Nina's voice softened a bit. "I think I know the first one. Papa's favorite coffee shop makes little hearts with the froth."

"The Coffee Mill, right?" I asked.

She didn't answer, but they headed for the narrow alley off Rehoboth Avenue. The shop's screen door opened with a squeal, and the smell of ground coffee washed over me. I looked up at the wall of canisters holding at least a hundred different kinds of beans. Papa used to make me read a few labels each time we went there.

Luca took a photo of the heart shape in his coffee's foam, texted it to Papa, and I got an iced hot chocolate. We went outside, sat at a metal table, and waited for Papa's reply. Nina pulled her phone from her pocket and tapped away at its tiny screen. The space between Luca's eyebrows wrinkled. He cleared his throat, but she didn't look at him.

I finished my drink and thought about the big sugar cookies I saw in the Coffee Mill's case.

Luca's phone buzzed. "Papa gave us a smiley face."

"What's next?" I asked.

Nina kept typing on her phone. "Read the list, munchkin."

I took the folded valentine from my pocket and followed Papa's flowing handwriting with my finger. "You need muscle to break the shell around a heart. What does that mean?"

Luca sipped from his paper cup. "We should go to the beach."

"Why?"

Luca stood. "The clue has something to do with shells."

"Just go to the Sea Shell Shop." Nina's fingers pecked at her phone. "They have those shells in the bins."

My metal chair made a grinding sound across the alley's bricks as I got to my feet. "Good idea."

Luca stared at Nina, who was still focused on her tiny screen. "You're right, Antonio. Nina does have a good idea. That's why she's going to lead the way."

Nina huffed, slid back her chair, turned from the table, and only looked up from her phone when she shouldered a man walking his dog. "Sorry."

She didn't sound sorry.

We walked the half block to the store with the sea-green metal awning and "Sea Shell Shop" in big letters across the front. An air-conditioned blast hit me when I opened the door, and we snaked our way through the pastel and tan beach-themed knick-knacks, ornaments, dishtowels—all of the things Mom-mom browsed along Rehoboth Avenue. We spent so much time looking through bins of polished shells, mesh gift bags of beach fossils, and decorations, I bet even she would have been ready to leave.

Luca rounded a shelf. "You see anything?"

I shook my head.

"Maybe we're looking at this wrong."

My stomach growled. "How long until we meet Papa and Mom-mom for lunch?"

"About forty minutes."

Something red with lots of legs dropped on my shoulder. I jumped, spun, and found Nina laughing at me. She knelt, picked up a stuffed lobster, and shook it in my face. "Why are you so afraid of me, Antonio? Because you ate my friend?"

"That's not funny, Nina."

Luca took the stuffed lobster from her. "What did Mom-mom get when we went to that seafood place?"

"She got those long black clams," I said.

"Those were mussels, Antonio." Luca put the lobster on a shelf. "And when you open them—"

Nina finished his sentence. "They look like a heart. Did you see any here?"

"Not those ugly things, but…" I headed for the door. "There are mussel shells on the beach near those wood posts going into the water—the jiffies."

Luca caught my shoulder and pulled me back to him. "Those are *jetties*, and stay together, remember?"

We explored the little pools along a jetty and sifted shells along the high-tide line. Nina found an opened mussel shell, and it looked just like a heart—even if it was a little long. Luca took a photo of me holding it in front of my chest, and Papa texted back another smiley face. We ran down the boardwalk and up Baltimore Avenue to Frank and Louie's.

Mom-mom waved to us from a table with an umbrella in the small lot next to the sandwich shop. "Your papa is getting the food. Antonio, go inside and help him."

She knew I liked seeing the meats, cheeses, oily olives, peppers, and the cream puffs—so many things we couldn't find at the corner store back home.

"We figured out two clues, Papa."

"You found those quickly." He passed me three sandwiches wrapped in thick white paper. "Take these to Mom-mom."

Papa followed a minute later with the rest of our order, and Mom-mom arranged five place settings of water bottles, plastic forks and knives, and napkins for us around the small plastic table.

We held hands. Papa said, "Dear Heavenly Father, thank you for our family and, especially, for this special day you have given to us. Bless each heart we find around this table and let us always remain together. Amen."

I unwrapped my sandwich, smelled the bread, opened it to see the soft mozzarella and thinly shaved ham, and wished Frank and Louie's could make the sandwiches I took to school. As soon as I did, I felt guilty, remembering how Mom-mom stood at our kitchen counter making our lunches every morning.

"So, you've found the first two." Papa took a bite, chewed, and sipped some water. "Any ideas for the third?"

Nina flipped her phone, which she had lying on the table, screen down. "Actually, Papa…"

I could tell from her tone what she would say.

"We've been talking. We—all of us— want to enjoy every day of our vacation. Do we really have to do Summer Valentine's Day?"

*If he says no*, I thought, *I can go to the arcade after lunch.*

Mom-mom looked at her lap and smoothed her napkin. "Maybe it's time to tell them, Sal."

Papa lifted his sandwich and just held it there. "They grow up fast enough."

"Yes, but…" Mom-mom smiled. I knew she faked it, because I couldn't see her teeth.

Papa pointed at me with his sandwich. "So, what do you think the third clue could mean?"

I looked at Luca and Nina. Everyone just sat there until I pulled the valentine from my pocket, unfolded it carefully, and read, "Third, a heart almost as sweet as your Mom-mom."

Mom-mom still looked down at her napkin.

Luca said, "You really like those heart-shaped chocolates at Kilwin's candy store, right Mom-mom?"

She nodded.

I didn't think before I spoke. "Does Summer Valentine's Day have something to do with my mother?"

Mom-mom reached over, put her hand on my arm and then slid it down to take my hand. "No, Antonio. This has nothing to do with her."

Papa took a bite, chewed, and said with a full mouth, "Be back at the cottage at 3:30. That gives you two and a half hours to figure out the last two clues.

We finished our sandwiches in silence, then backtracked to the Coffee Mill's brick alley. I felt bad for Papa, but Nina had told the truth.

I asked, "Why didn't Papa say anything about stopping Summer Valentine's Day?"

Luca answered while he walked ahead of us. "Because that question really hurt him."

Nina put her phone in her pocket. "Don't blame me. We all agreed. I was just the one with the guts to ask."

"We didn't all agree." Luca turned and looked right at her. "You shouldn't have said that."

"Why not? And what was that 'maybe it's time to tell them'?"

"Give it a rest, Nina." Luca said.

Nina grabbed Luca's wrist. "Why didn't you speak up, nature boy? You never like wandering around town. You could be fishing or riding your bike up to Cape Henlopen."

Luca yanked his arm free.

"You know something, don't you? That's why you always defend Papa."

Luca locked eyes with me, and I saw something in his face I didn't understand, like he remembered something bad and looking at me brought back the memory. He spoke to Nina, but he kept his eyes on me. "You said what you needed to say, so let's just keep going."

Kilwin's door stood open, but we had to wait until some people left to make room for us in the shop. A candymaker poured liquid fudge into a metal cooling tray. I watched her spread it into a long flat slab, fold it, and spread it again. Each movement made the air thick with the smell of chocolate, enough to leave a hint of it on my tongue. We walked along a windowed case holding a rainbow of sweets and chocolate-dipped wonders until finding what Mom-mom called her "chocolate sweet hearts." Nina bought a few, then we took a picture of one, texted it to Papa, and within seconds he sent back a smiley face.

"One more," I said. "A heart for a whirly, twirly crazy time."

"Sounds like a ride." Luca took a napkin from the counter and wiped sweat from his forehead. "Funland should be open by now."

"I bet Papa wants us to take a picture of my favorite one. The ride's name has the word crazy in it. Crazy Dazy, I think."

The sun baked us on the boardwalk. I soaked my T-shirt just walking to Funland, but the shade inside felt good. We stood under a large ceiling fan, watching riders spin and laugh in giant flowers decorated with patterns of leaves, petals, and all sorts of shapes. During one of the rider changes, I noticed a small pink heart on one of the flowers.

"There it is!" I pointed and almost jumped out of my sneakers.

We took the picture, sent it, and got a smiley face from Papa. All four puzzles solved, and we still had an hour for Skee-Ball and rides before going back to the cottage.

\* \* \* \* \*

Luca led us through the cottage's side door and into the kitchen where Mom-mom's heart-shaped Summer Valentine's Day cake lay waiting for us on the table.

Papa opened his arms for a hug from me. "You figured out the clues without any help this year!"

Nina plopped onto a chair and pulled out her phone. "Yay for us."

Luca frowned at her. "Papa, can I talk to you?" He left the kitchen for the living room and Papa followed.

I ran my finger along the cake's bottom edge and stuck some icing into my mouth. Mom-mom not only made the cake, but she always made her own icing.

Papa returned with Luca. "Nina, put your phone away please." He looked pretty serious. "Let's all talk for a little before we cut the cake."

Mom-mom took off her apron and joined us at the kitchen table.

"Your Mom-mom was right." Papa took a deep breath. "It's time you know why we have Summer Valentine's Day. Why we always do this together." He reached over and moved a sweaty piece of hair away from my eyes. "Antonio, you were so little you wouldn't remember, and your sister wouldn't, either."

Luca looked at me. "I just remember a little bit."

Papa was always so strong, so I never forgot the few times I saw his tears. "Your momma and I brought you home, and we were so happy." He looked around the table. "We all were. After a few weeks, we noticed something was wrong, and the doctors told us you had a small hole in your heart. Your mother and I were so scared."

Mom-mom twisted the apron balled in her lap. "We were all scared."

I put my hand on my chest. "A hole, like it was bleeding?" I started to cry.

Papa took my hand and squeezed. "There's nothing to be afraid of, Antonio. It's fixed. That's why this day is so important."

"You mean," Nina spoke barely above a whisper, "Summer Valentine's Day is for Antonio? Being here with us?"

Papa nodded. "The doctors fixed the hole on July 17th. Today. Summer Valentine's Day."

A thousand questions spun in my head. I couldn't hold onto one long enough to ask it, but I could feel my father's hand around mine and Mom-mom taking my other hand. I saw her holding Nina's hand and Nina holding Luca's. *We always stay together on Summer Valentine's Day.*

Nina asked, "Papa, can I write the clues next year?"

DAVE COOPER CLAIMS HE CANNOT TAKE FULL CREDIT FOR "SUMMER VALENTINE'S DAY." HIS EARLY DRAFTS STALLED WITH A CLICHÉD FAMILY SCAVENGER HUNT AND DIDN'T MOVE FORWARD UNTIL HE LISTENED MORE CLOSELY TO HIS CHARACTERS.

DAVE'S FIRST PUBLISHED ARTICLE APPEARED IN THE NATIONAL MIDDLE SCHOOL ASSOCIATION'S *MIDDLE GROUND* IN 2003. SINCE THEN, HE HAS CONTRIBUTED TO A VARIETY OF PERIODICALS INCLUDING *TEACHING HISTORY*, *MIDDLE LEVEL LEARNING*, *FAMILY CHRONICLE*, *BOY'S LIFE*, *COLLEGE BOUND*, AND *PENNSYLVANIA EDUCATIONAL LEADERSHIP*. HIS FICTION AND POETRY HAVE APPEARED IN *TIMBER CREEK REVIEW*, *YORICK MAGAZINE*, *NFG*, AND IN THE CAT & MOUSE PRESS ANTHOLOGIES *BEACH PULP*, *BEACH DREAMS*, AND *BEACH SECRETS*. DAVE TEACHES EIGHTH GRADE HISTORY, MARTIAL ARTS, AND WRITES IN LANCASTER, PENNSYLVANIA, WHERE HE LIVES WITH HIS WIFE, JUDY, AND PUGGLE, AUBREY. MORE OF DAVE'S WORK CAN BE FOUND AT DCWRITING. WORDPRESS.COM.

# Labor (Day) of Love

## By Katherine Melvin

The bus from Potomac Assisted Living Center, P-TALC, pulled to a stop at the end of Rehoboth Avenue. After the seemingly interminable four-hour drive, retired US Marine Corps drill sergeant Harry Partlow realized they were not paying him nearly enough to haul a busload of "people of age" anywhere, let alone from Maryland to Delaware at the height of beach traffic on the official last day of summer. He should have requested combat pay. And he should have made certain the beautiful Melissa Miller was riding in the bus with him and not with that weasel Tony Dilanio.

When Harry had agreed to drive, he'd imagined Mel sitting right behind him. They'd chat for hours. In fact, he'd counted on having the uninterrupted time to work up the courage to ask her out. Just the thought of the raven-haired, blue-eyed beauty made him want to swoon except, of course, drill sergeants don't swoon. They look tough and squint.

Instead, Mel had batted those long black eyelashes, waved her manicured fingers goodbye, then hopped into Dilanio's Volvo SUV.

Harry shook his head in disgust at his naivety regarding women and old people. *Elderly* meant *quiet* in his mind. He thought his biggest worry would be that one of them might go to the big beach in the sky on his watch. But no. Not this group. A bunch were playing strip poker in the rear of the bus. Strip poker! The rest were cheering them on. His recruits wouldn't have dared do that in the barracks right under his nose. After the crawl over the Chesapeake Bay Bridge, he was forced to stop the bus to remind them there was no stripping of any kind, anywhere, at any time, on *his* bus. He spoke with his sternest voice, the one he used for the first day of boot camp.

Fifty wrinkled faces topped with varying amounts and colors of hair stared back. Then burst out laughing.

"What are you going to do?" Louise Mulligan asked. "Give us detention?"

He'd been warned about her.

Before he reached for the handle to free the inmates, he leaned his large head—everything about Harry was large—on the seatback and sighed.

"Come on."

The troublemaker again.

"Open the door! It's hot in here."

Which it wasn't. The air was still running.

Harry stood, careful to stretch the kinks from his legs so his knees didn't buckle. "Now Mrs. Mulligan…"

"Call me Lou."

He ran a hand over his dark bald head, a habit from when he had hair. "Patience is a virtue."

That caused her to titter.

Was she choking? Should he start the Heimlich maneuver?

The taunting laughter grew louder as she walked to the front, rather quickly for an old lady. Harry corrected himself—*elder person.*

She stood five feet two inches in her sneakered feet to his overloaded six-foot-four frame. He looked down as she poked his belly.

"Who are you calling virtuous, bubba?" She thumped her hands on her hips and cocked her head at him just like the parrot his father used to have. She was as colorful as the bird too. Bright-red T-shirt. Canary-yellow shorts. The grass-green sneakers and royal-blue anklets put a period to the outfit. "You gonna open the door or not? Some of us need to pee."

"I'm one of them."

The troublemaker's sidekick.

She extended her plump hand. "Mildred O'Svenson."

He shook the bejeweled fingers.

"Call her Millie. She's with me," said Lou.

Harry squinted at Lou then looked at Millie, who wore the same colorful outfit. They were practically identical except this one was taller and a tad bit wider, with curly orange hair he'd be able to spot from anywhere on the beach. Good thing, since he was supposed to help Mel and Dilanio watch them.

"Listen up." Harry had to wait a minute for the passengers to stop shuffling and quiet down. "We leave at exactly six o'clock on the dot." Guessing what she was going to ask, he scowled at Lou when she raised a hand. "That's p.m. As in *tonight*. Be here ready to board." He counted on his fingers. "Make sure you have all your stuff. Eat beforehand. Pee." He heard Louise clear her throat. "Or whatever you got to do. Just be here on time. I'm counting heads, but I'm not waiting around." That was a lie, but he thought if he ruffled them a bit they'd listen. He made a dramatic gesture of putting his hand on the lever. "Have fun, kids."

Harry left Mel and Tony to help the passengers off the bus while he pulled out the walkers and two wheelchairs. How they were going to maneuver over the boardwalk and sand was beyond him.

It didn't take long to find out.

Millie, who a minute ago was so antsy to use the bathroom, put two fingers in her mouth and whistled. "Attention!"

Lou waved a neon pink hanky. "Everyone who's in the walker race line up here."

The racers formed two lines side by side along the sidewalk.

"Hey," Harry said. "You all can't do that here."

Lou grinned. "Wanna bet?" She held the hanky high. "On your mark. Get set."

Before she could wave *go*, Mel arrived and winked at him. "I've got this."

"Mm, mm, mm." Harry moved his body side to side on each "mm." "That is one fine woman. Smart. And funny, too."

Millie sidled up to him. "What are you gonna do about it?"

Her voice so close in his ear startled him and his face got a little heated. "Say what?"

"Don't be a Neanderthal. She likes you. You like her. Do something about it. We've been watching you two tap dance for months." Millie did a short soft shoe.

He rubbed his chin. It was already bristling. "I need to move this bus before I get ticketed."

Millie rolled her eyes. He cringed when she cackled like a chicken and called cock-a-doodle-do. She was probably flapping her arms too. He refused to give her the satisfaction of looking.

As he sat in the driver's seat, he heard Mel give in. "Oh, all right. Just one race."

To the sound of cheering, Harry shook his head. "Combat pay, my man, should've asked for combat pay."

* * * * *

On the way back from parking the bus, Harry bought two slices of pepperoni pizza from Grottos and two fruit smoothies from the coffee shop. He imagined handing them to a very impressed, very grateful Mel. He stopped at the gazebo. A few of his passengers sat in the shade of the building, fanning themselves. A couple of the tinier ladies sat on a park bench at the edge of the sand. They each held an umbrella over their heads.

Harry turned in a circle. Water from the perspiring slushies dripped down his arm. "Where'd everyone go?"

A gruff old man (his nametag read *Bob*), who looked like he'd been talked into the outing and regretted it, pointed to the ocean. "They went that-a-way."

"You all good?" Harry wondered if he should stick with them.

Five heads slowly nodded.

Bob said, "Better get on down there. That Mulligan woman was already pulling off her compression socks."

Harry turned to the beach. "What the…" He handed Bob the food and took off running.

About twenty people of age had Lou hoisted over their heads. She was tiny, but still, the ones carrying her were old. Graybeards. Advanced in years. Well preserved. Whatever.

"Hey!" Lou said. "Who pinched my bottom?"

Not too old, apparently.

"Me," one brave man said.

Another one added, "Wish I had."

"Well, go ahead. Do it."

Millie stood to the side, recording the spectacle.

Mel hopped around them, arms flailing, trying to prevent a disaster.

"Lou. Lou. Lou." The old codgers, ah, seniors chanted as if they were about to sacrifice her to an active volcano. Out of nowhere, Dilanio appeared. He was tall enough to wrest Lou away from them and set her on her feet.

"Hey," Lou said. "Put me back up there."

"Absolutely not. There are liability issues," Tony said. "You looked like you were surfing a mosh pit."

"Exactly."

Tony rubbed his knuckles under his chin. "How do you even know what a mosh pit is?"

"Who do you think invented them, Dilanio? Now lift me up."

"Oh, Tony." Mel sighed. "Thank goodness! I don't know what's got into them." Mel gave Lou and Millie The Look.

"OK," Tony said. "We're here to have fun and relax. Go back to where we set up the umbrellas and chairs. Water and snacks are on the way." He shooed them like children. Lou and a few others stuck their tongues out as they passed him.

Harry deflated. Another missed opportunity to impress Mel. What was Tony playing at? She wasn't his type. Mel wasn't a Volvo woman. Anyone could see that. She had spunk. She had fire. Her type drove bright-red Broncos. Maybe even a Ford Ranger.

"Ouch." Harry grabbed his arm.

"Too slow, mo." Lou tried to pinch him again, but he side-stepped away from her. "We didn't request this trip for you two to go your separate ways. Now get busy. It cost us money and time's a wasting. It's already mid-afternoon." She grabbed a pail and stormed off. "I've got shells to gather."

Harry squinted as he unraveled what she'd said. He couldn't believe they had talked the center into this trip so he could be with Mel. Nah. Couldn't be.

Harry watched as Mel arranged a low beach chair to face her charges. He was considering his next move when she gasped. He followed her gaze. Mr. Benton. He was snoring, spread eagle, skinny legs jutting from a large bathing suit. *Oh, geez*. He walked over and gently moved Benton's legs together. "Don't want any sandfleas in the nether regions."

Mel snickered.

Yes! She'd noticed. He suppressed a fist pump.

Mel lifted her sunglasses, tilted her head back, and peered at Harry. "You're blocking my sun."

"Ah," Harry said. "You do know you're not supposed to turn your back on the ocean."

"Would you prefer I turned my back on them?" She gestured to the P-TALC residents.

Just then, they heard an ear-splitting whistle.

"Millie has got to stop that," Mel said.

"How 'bout some bocce ball?" Lou said to Harry and nodded toward Mel.

Harry got the message and turned to Mel. "Care to join us?"

"Nah," she said. "I prefer to watch. You go on." Mel waved him away. "Before Millie whistles again."

Head down, he trudged through the hot sand with Lou to join Millie.

"No go, huh?" Lou said.

Harry shook his head and frowned.

"Drats. Millie, do your thing."

Millie whistled, loud and shrill. Right next to Harry's ear.

Harry winced. "Where'd you learn to do that?"

"Gave birth to four boys. Had to do something to be heard over their ruckus."

"Hey, Mella Bella," Lou shouted. "We need a fourth and you're it."

Mel looked around. "Where's Tony? Ask him."

"He's getting the cooler," Harry said.

"I still don't want to."

Millie said, "We don't care."

Mel stood and glared at Harry as if it were his fault she was being forced to play.

"Don't look at me." He figured his chances with Mel were dwindling the more the meddlesome duo butted in.

"You and Mel against me and Millie," Lou said.

Mel turned to Lou. "You're a bit bossy."

"Thank you."

Mel shook her head. Harry smiled and shrugged like none of this was his fault.

"Here." Millie handed him the jack. "And don't throw it too far. We are octogenarians after all."

"You're octa something all right." Harry squinted as he wound up into his star pitcher stance from high school.

"You're not supposed to—" Mel yelped as the little ball bounced off Tony's leg. "Throw it overhand."

"Now you tell me."

Mel and Millie took Tony by the arms and helped him into the cool water.

Back on the beach, Lou cranked her head to look up at Harry. "You like her and she's sweet on you." Lou raised her hand to stop any argument. "We know people who know things. Stay here. Leave it to us."

"What about Dilanio?" Harry heard the whine in his voice. He sounded like a recruit who wanted to go home to his mommy. Disgusting.

"What about him?" Lou squeezed his bicep. "Oooh, that's a big one. Don't you worry your pretty little head about it. We got this."

That's what he was afraid of.

Eventually, Mel trudged back up the beach, and Harry helped her spread a blanket.

"Thanks," she said, motioning him to sit. She handed him a drink. "Sweet tea, right?"

How did she know it was his favorite? "Yes, ma'am."

They watched Tony chat with each person who had made the trip. He poured seawater on their feet from a red pail.

"Working the crowd," Harry said.

"Checking on them." Mel corrected him. "Can't have them getting heat stroke or anything."

"He's a wanker."

"Harry! What is it with you and Tony?"

Harry didn't get a chance to respond. Apparently, they were on Dilanio's rounds too.

Tony arched a brow. "Dinner?"

"No thanks. Gotta bus to drive," Harry said.

"Wasn't talking to you." He nodded to Mel.

"I'd love to," she replied.

"Great," said Tony, and then he went to refill the pail.

"Why would you have dinner with him?" Harry asked Mel.

"Because, Harry, no one else asked me and I've got to eat."

"Well, I can't. I've got to get them back before they turn into pumpkins."

"Uh-huh."

Harry "harumphed" and turned on his side. "I'm taking a nap before the drive back. If I'm not awake, shake me at five."

* * * * *

At six o'clock on the dot, the bus was loaded and all was quiet. Everyone was tired from a great day at the beach.

Harry squinted. Something was off, but what was it? The calm. The silence. The peace and quiet. He walked the aisle counting riders. Two passengers short. That's when it hit him. The troublemakers. Lou and Millie weren't aboard. That's why it was so darn quiet.

Harry tore off the bus and ran after Dilanio's Volvo, which had just backed out of a parking spot and was headed west on Rehoboth Avenue. He waved his arms. He yelled. Finally, the car came to a stop in front of Browseabout Books. Tony lowered the window as Harry ran up.

"They're. Missing," Harry panted. "Lou. Millie."

Mel squealed. She jumped out of the car as soon as Tony had pulled into a parking spot. "Oh my gosh. Oh my gosh. Oh my gosh." Mel's arms flapped like a grounded bird.

Harry placed his hands, gently, on her arms, lowering them to her side. "It's OK. We'll find them. They couldn't have gone far."

"Are you kidding?" Tony said as he joined them. "If they hopped on the—"

"Jolly Trolley!" Mel wailed. "They could be anywhere."

Tony spoke with the authority of a man used to being in charge. "We will find them."

"Those sweet old ladies." Mel batted back tears.

Harry and Tony looked at each. Tony mouthed, "Sweet?" and made a face.

"I'll take the other side. You guys look here." Tony headed across the street.

"We were supposed to take care of them," said Mel, her voice cracking. "They may have been kidnapped."

Harry thought of O'Henry's short story "The Ransom of Red Chief," where kidnappers hold an unruly kid for ransom and then end up paying his father to take him back. He took Mel's hands. "I think that's unlikely."

Mel sniffed.

"Think for a minute. What did they say before they left the beach? Exact words."

"I don't know. Something about you needing help. What do you need help with?"

He rolled his eyes. "With you. I've been struggling with, you know, words. The last thing they said to me was *we've got this*."

Mel thumped him on the chest the way Elaine did to Jerry on the Seinfeld show. "*We've got this*?"

"Don't get mad at me. I didn't know what they were planning."

"Are you saying this…this…disappearing act could be one of their little schemes?" Mel's eyes narrowed. "Just to help you get a date? With me?"

Harry shrugged, self-conscious. "Maybe…"

"Wait till I get my hands on those two." Mel hopped to her feet and paced back and forth in front of the bookstore. "I'd say I don't believe it, but the daring duo are always up to their eyeballs in something. Why last Fourth of July they snuck fireworks to Lou's granddaughter's and almost set the house on fire. And then, there was the time they escaped…"

Harry raised his hands. "I get it. Darn. I have to admit I'd like to be that spry and on-the-ball when I'm their age."

Mel stopped moving. She stood in front of the window, squinting into the store. "Oh, for crying out loud."

"What?" Harry peered in the window, saw the orange head, and started laughing. "I don't believe it."

He opened the door and they entered.

The dangerous duo sat at a round table, books spread out before them—sound asleep. Lou's head was tilted back. A slight whiffling noise escaped her open mouth. Millie's head rested on the book she was reading.

Mel scanned the books: *Dating Secrets. Dating for Dummies. Shy Guys Dating Guide.*

Before they woke the sleeping beauties, Mel said, "I don't think you need any of these, do you?"

Harry shook his head. "No ma'am."

"Well?"

"So you'll go out with me?"

"Absolutely."

"Bout time." Lou snapped awake. "Sat here all afternoon." She patted her mouth for drool, then nudged Mille. "Wake up, woman. They found us."

"Did he?"

"He did."

"Then our work here is done."

"Say goodnight, Millie."

"Goodnight, Millie."

"Okay, you two sleepyheads," Harry said, as he and Mel led their charges out of the store. "Time for all good people of age to go home."

Lou threw her hands in the air in exasperation. "Tell it like it is, youngster. We're old. Not ancient. Old."

"It's better than the alternative," Millie said. "We're proud of our age." Arm in arm, the delightful duo ambled to the bus.

Behind them, Harry wrapped his arm in Mel's. "You know what?" Mel arched a brow.

"I want to be just like them when I grow up."

KATHERINE MELVIN STUDIED CREATIVE WRITING AT JOHNS HOPKINS UNIVERSITY, MONTGOMERY COLLEGE, AND THE WRITER'S CENTER IN BETHESDA, MARYLAND. HER HUMOROUS SHORT STORIES FOR REHOBOTH BEACH READS ANTHOLOGIES HAVE CENTERED ON TWO FRIENDS FACING OLD AGE. THEY ARE INSPIRED BY THE NEED TO LOOK OLD AGE IN THE FACE AND LAUGH. HER SHORT STORIES AND ARTICLES HAVE ALSO APPEARED IN MARYLAND WRITERS' ASSOCIATION ANTHOLOGIES, *TODAY'S CHRISTIAN WOMEN*, *CHRISTIANITY TODAY*, AND *CATHOLIC DIGEST*. A STRONG SUPPORTER AND A PROUD MEMBER OF THE MARYLAND WRITERS' ASSOCIATION, KATHERINE HAD THE PLEASURE OF EDITING THEIR ANTHOLOGIES *30 WAYS TO LOVE MARYLAND* AND *MARYLAND IN POETRY*. KATHERINE LIVES IN MARYLAND WITH HER HUSBAND, AND WHEN SHE'S NOT WRITING, SHE PLAYS GOLF WITH HIM AS MUCH AS POSSIBLE. SHE IS ON THE LOOKOUT FOR HER NEXT FOUR-LEGGED, WET-NOSED WRITING COMPANION.

JUDGES' COMMENTS

*Feisty seniors drive their driver crazy. It's zany fun. Revenge of the geriatrics, with humor. Sometimes all people need is a friendly nudge to find happiness.*

# DALD Day

## By David Strauss

"It begins with an assault on the beach at dawn. We'll march in loose formation down the roadway of Rehoboth Avenue. The group will stop and line up shoulder to shoulder along the boardwalk, facing east. Six locals will storm the sands, armed with beach chairs and a cooler; one will be chosen as umbrella bearer. As the sun rises over the empty Atlantic, the group of six will reenact the famous photo of Iwo Jima, staking the umbrella's wooden shaft firmly in the sand, reclaiming this beach—our beach—once again. Chairs will be placed in a wide circle around the umbrella, its canopy lifted and opened as the first rays of sun illuminate the colorful canvas panels. A cooler will be opened, and a single beer specially created as a collaboration between our local breweries, *Revelation Dog*, will be presented and poured onto the sand—a sacrifice to the hard-working men and women of Rehoboth Beach."

The six town commissioners sit in silence, all twelve eyes staring at this man and his stack of crumpled papers atop the podium. One begins to open his mouth to speak, but the man behind the podium continues.

"The group on the boardwalk will file onto the beach, followed by reinforcements moving down from Deauville Beach. Dogs and their owners will arrive from Poodle Beach, where the residents of Rehoboth will reclaim their spots of sand for the first time in months. Locals as pale as vampires will shield their eyes from the sun's rays, not used to seeing natural light or being awake at such an ungodly hour."

"And…uh…ah…Mr. Getz, is it?"

The man looks up, nods affirmative, and resumes. "After the locals have placed their beach chairs and coolers by their umbrellas in the sand and exchanged warm greetings to friends they haven't seen in some time, the gathering will file from the beach to the bandstand, where one of our local acts will be playing Jimmy Buffett songs for all to enjoy. The local coffee shops will be on hand to provide some much-needed caffeine, and then the mayor..." Mr. Getz looks up at the commissioners and smiles. "The mayor will arrive for the dedication ceremony."

"Ahh, Mr. Getz," one of the commissioners manages to break in, "Mr. Getz, I'm a bit confused by what you're getting at here."

Getz looks at the group assembled in front of him and then back down at his hand-scribbled dissertation. "Well, that's what I'm saying."

He continues, undeterred. "The mayor will arrive for the dedication ceremony, declaring this day, DALD Day, as a town holiday—for now and forever. The band will play something appropriate for an occasion like this, something like "Cheeseburger in Paradise," or "It's Five O'Clock Somewhere," and then there'll be a plaque or a sign, or something."

"Again, Mr. Getz, DALD Day? I think," the commissioner says, glancing at his co-commissioners and then fixing his gaze on the presenter, "I think we're all a bit confused by what you're getting at. For example, *DALD Day*. Could you explain that?"

Getz looks down at the wrinkled mess of notes and then smiles at his audience. "Sure. *D-A-L-D* Day—Day After Labor Day Day, or as I like to call it, DALD Day."

"DALD Day?"

"Yeah," Getz explains, "DALD Day, like bald day—but with a *D*. I think DALD Day rolls off the tongue better than *D.A.L.D. Day*, dontcha think?"

The town commissioners mumble and look at each other, perplexed.

A smartly dressed woman, mid-sixties, clears her throat, "Perhaps, Mr. Getz, if you could just tell us the reason for your appearance before us today." She takes a not-so-subtle glance at her watch, checks it against the time on the wall clock, and folds her hands neatly. "In one sentence—or less."

Mr. Getz flips through his papers, looking for the answer to this question. After a brief period, he folds the crumpled pages and stuffs them in the pocket of his cargo shorts. "Well, uh, I thought it was quite obvious. I am proposing that the town of Rehoboth Beach make the Tuesday after Labor Day an official holiday."

He looks up at the faces looking down from the dais and smiles. "You know, as a way of showing appreciation for all the citizens who work so hard and put up with so much over the summer. This is a kind of a taking-back-the-town holiday, you know, for when the tourists have gone home, the kids have gone back to school, and the town kind of belongs to us again—at least on the weekdays."

A town commissioner on the left end of the group looks up and nods, a wry smile crossing his face. "So, a holiday for the locals. What about a picnic and a parade? Perhaps a Ms. Local DALD Day riding on a float? We could get a nice sash and tiara for her to wear."

Getz nods excitedly, pulling the wad of wrinkled papers from his baggy pocket. "Yeah, yeah! I've got all that in here."

He begins to describe his vision for a town parade, complete with floats from the various establishments, all making their way down Rehoboth Avenue. "A giant green Dogfish being ridden by a local, a massive pile of Browseabout books with a small group of locals on top, a spinning pizza, skaters from Sierra Moon, a huge bucket of Thrasher's fries—all these cool floats being ridden by locals. And…" Getz pauses, a huge grin spreading across his face, "instead of a Ms. Local, I've got a DALD-Day Diva, who would ride on the final float—alongside the mayor, of course."

"Of course, of course," the well-dressed woman responds. "And let's not forget fire engines. You can't have a parade without fire engines."

Another commissioner interjects. "Mr. Getz?"

Getz stands behind the lectern, big hands clasping each side. His wrinkled dream of handwritten brilliance lies beneath him, uncrumpled and almost illegible, a million intersecting creases like an aerial view of the Nazca lines—mysterious and bewildering all at once. "That's my name! Johnny Getz." He smiles and chuckles. "And whatever Johnny wants, Johnny Getz!"

A slight movement in one corner of the commissioner's lips betrays a smile. "I suppose we'll have fireworks too? A closing ceremony of sorts?"

Johnny Getz raises his hand, ready to give a thumbs-up. At the same instant, a loud siren wails inside the walls of the room, making it impossible to hear anything else. Getz watches as the scribbled dream of DALD Day vanishes before his very eyes and then the lectern itself vanishes. He turns his attention to the six commissioners, but they too have vanished.

The wailing grows louder and louder, the room turns black, and Johnny Getz can no longer see anything. Then, in the distance, a small circle of light grows wider and wider, until Getz finds himself on his bed, the alarm clock wailing its annoying wake-up sound. Johnny sits up and rubs his eyes, looking at the time on the clock, banging the button to silence the noise with the palm of his hand.

He sits up, groggy from a late-night bar backing at Zogg's, stretching and yawning himself awake. Getz opens a bedside drawer and finds a stack of old work checks, some still in their wrinkled white envelopes. He grabs a pen and begins scribbling, *D.A.L.D. Day aka DALD Day…*

DAVID STRAUSS GREW UP VISITING THE BEACH, SPENDING HIS SUMMERS IN CLEARWATER BEACH, FLORIDA, AND OCEAN CITY, MARYLAND. HE SPENT HIS COLLEGE YEARS LIVING AND WORKING IN OCEAN CITY, WHERE HE DELIVERED PIZZAS BY BICYCLE AND ROAMED THE BEACHES WITH HIS FRIENDS, SEARCHING OUT THE BEST WAVES. DAVID HAS HAD POETRY AND/OR SHORT STORIES PUBLISHED IN *DAMOZEL* AND *DIRT RAG* MAGAZINES, AND IN *THE BOARDWALK*, *BEACH NIGHTS*, *BEACH LIFE*, *BEACH PULP*, AND *BEACH DREAMS*. HE HAS ALSO PUBLISHED TWO NOVELLAS, *DANGEROUS SHOREBREAK* AND *STRUCTURALLY DEFICIENT*, THROUGH CREATESPACE. HE IS TEACHING US HISTORY UNTIL HE CAN RETIRE TO THE BEACH WITH HIS WIFE, SPENDING HIS SUMMER MONTHS TRAVELING OUR SHORELINES SEARCHING OUT THE PERFECT COASTAL TOWN.

THE IDEAS FOR MANY OF HIS STORIES COME FROM TIME SPENT LIVING AND WORKING AT THE BEACH. "DALD DAY" WAS INSPIRED BY THE MANY LOCALS HE HAS WORKED WITH—THOSE YEAR-ROUND EMPLOYEES WHO CALLED THE BEACH TOWN HOME. THIS HOLIDAY, EVEN IF IT ISN'T REAL (YET), IS DEDICATED TO THEM.

# The Power of Three

## By Mary Ann Glaser

Under the pier where it meets the boardwalk, three shadowy figures sat in the nearly dark shade. Sitting in a tight circle, they appeared to wear identical shirts under ankle-length tunics tied at the waist, their hair covered and pulled back by headcloths like those worn by peasant women in the Middle Ages. One woman old, one middle-aged, and the third, young. As they leaned toward each other, the middle-aged woman spoke.

"Tell me again, sister, why came we to Boboboth?"

"*Reho*both, Macha! *Rehoboth*, ye dafty cow," snapped the eldest.

"Dafty cow!" The youngest giggled. "Hectate, you are funny."

Hectate shot her a look that killed the giggle.

"Macha." Hectate sighed. "Have ye forgotten all your whining at the thought of another season of damp cloudy days? Gasing on and on about your poor achy bones?"

"'Tis true, the *dreich* is more wearying than ever for me." Macha sighed. "I was craving sun."

"And so, here we be, sisters dear, in this American town, Rehoboth, having a sea holiday, with the sun shining and it being warmer here than at home."

"Oh, I did like the carousel last night, sister," said the young one.

"Aye, Bave." Macha giggled. "Changing those wooden horses to winged dragons and flying them about was fun. One can ride up and down in a circle for only so long."

"This night," said Hectate, "I'm thinking we'll try that thing called bumping cars. I hear they race about and crash into one another, yet they stay whole."

Macha and Bave looked at each other in confusion.

"But what be the point in that?" asked Bave.

"We'll see. America is a young country. I expect there be many senseless things here. Right now, I fancy a morning meal. I saw a picture of what looked like a banger roll on a sign yesterday. Shall we stroll out, sisters?"

They rose as one, and as they walked out of the shade, a shimmer appeared about them; instead of three women in medieval dress, there were three women wearing running shoes, jeans, hoodies, and sporting fanny packs, walking arm in arm up the boardwalk.

* * * * *

Maired watched as Belenus, The Fair Shining One, painted the long low gray clouds with glorious hues of peach, pink, and rose, veiling his passage. Closing her eyes, Maired listened to the sound of the waves beginning to bring the tide in. Suddenly, she was on Islay's shore, standing on the cliffs as she had every morn before the Norsemen came and the sisters fled to the North Kingdom.

A splash of water on her Doc Marten boots brought Maired back to present day. She sighed, silently thanking The Fair One for the day's beautiful beginning. Samhain, (she gave herself a pinch to remind herself that here it was called Halloween to most, All Hallow's Eve to some) was only a day away. The boardwalk would be awash with people for the Sea Witch Festival and the quiet of off-season Rehoboth would be, for a time, broken.

As Maired heard it told, *Sea Witch* was a famous clipper ship that held the record for the fastest time from Hong Kong to San Francisco from 1849 until 2003. While she never found a connection between *Sea Witch* and Rehoboth Beach, there was no denying the Sea Witch Festival made for a lively holiday celebration at the beach, with magic shows, bands, costume contests, and other Halloween fun, ending with the big parade led by the Sea Witch balloon, but she was a witch, not a ship. Which was weird but also proof that a good party needn't be based on anything but fun.

Maired had been busy with preparations to ensure those from the other side of the veil, so close to this side on Samhain, didn't slip through until after the parade was over and the non-magicals were safely on their way. People here often think it would be fun to meet a ghost or one of the *guid* folk until they do, and there you are, calling the EMTs and doing CPR. Maired turned to leave the beach when three streaks of green light flared across the clouds.

*Three streaks, three days in a row. There's no denying now.* That does not bode well. She called out, "Corvax!"

A large seagull swooped down, settling on her right shoulder. It shook violently. Feathers flew and colors darkened until a large raven emerged.

"Mistress?" Coughing, it dipped its head as it choked out the word.

"Seriously? Such a drama queen, you." Maired sighed. "It's a glamour, not a transfiguration, spell. I happen to know that appearing to be a seagull does not cause you pain, you beastly bird."

Corvax drew himself up, clacking his beak a bit in chastisement. "Pain is felt in many ways, mistress. A raven is a noble bird, but it is distressing to dress as something, well, lesser than."

"Noted. I praise your sacrifice, oh noble one. Now, did you see the green lights just now? I fear it's an omen."

"Aye, mistress. I saw and agree. It is perhaps a portent. But I have not sensed any magical presence unknown to us."

"Nor I; it could just be something celebrating the approach of Samhain, and yet... Talk with our friends. Check the thin places in the veil where the fae and shades usually cross. They shouldn't be able to cross until the witching hour, but let's be thorough, just in case. I'll go see Tassia. Maybe she's picked up something."

Corvax nodded and, shaking his feathers to activate the spell that made him look like a seagull, took off over the boardwalk.

Maired paused, watching the green steaks fade in the sunrise. *Yes, let's be thorough.*

With the toe of her boot, she quickly drew a circle in the sand around her. Seeing it was properly closed, she whispered a spell, while giving her braids a shake, activating the rune-etched glass beads woven throughout, powering up her magic. Reaching into a pocket in her black hoodie, she slipped a bracelet of black tourmaline, obsidian, and selenite crystals onto her left wrist. With this bracelet, she could summon a protective boundary if need be. Rehoboth Beach wasn't known for demonic happenings. Well, OK, occasional raves and biker brawls excepted, but things had seemed off for several days now and, well, a lass couldn't be too careful.

Maired brushed sand from her black jeans. The goth look was convenient for disguising the protective amulets on the zipper pulls and ties on her black hoodie, jeans, and boots. People looked at her and saw goth, not Wiccan, which was the point. Illusion was safe passage. Sadly, she could not disguise her pale Scots skin and red hair. She'd tried dying her hair black to complete her look, but every morning there it was, back again in all its flaming glory, so she made peace with her hair. One has to work with what one has, after all.

Walking toward the boardwalk, Maired decided to grab a couple of breakfast burritos at the Breakfast Guru to share with Tassia, as thanks for her opinion on the portents. Most people here knew Tassia only as a shop owner offering crystals and other things woo-woo, but in fact, she was a gifted Wiccan touched with The Sight and a solid friend. Crossing the street, Maired turned at the bandstand and walked a few doors down to the Breakfast Guru.

"Hey, Maired!" Stan called out as she walked in. "Usual breakfast burrito?"

"Make it two, Stan, I'm on my way to Tassia's, thanks. How's business?"

"Oh, weekends have been good, weather's been holding so the off-season's been a good one so far. There'll be more folks in for the Sea Witch parade, of course." He slid the two burritos into a sack. "There was something weird last night. I was here later than usual and, well, I could have sworn I heard the carousel's music playing in Funland. I mean, they've been closed since the end of the season—everything's locked tight—but…" He shrugged his shoulders as he handed her the bag. "I dunno; maybe I'm missing the beach crowd or something."

"Yeah, maybe that's it." Maired said as she swiped her card. "Thanks, Stan."

"Sure. Tell Tassia I said hey."

As she headed into Penny Lane toward The Salty Witch Candles and Crystals Shop, Maired mulled over Stan's maybe, hopefully, auditory hallucination.

"I come bearing tasty things, Anastasia!" Maired called out as she pushed open the shop door making the tiny Tibetan brass bells chime.

"Blessed be, Maired. I accept your offering of breakfast burrito. Well chosen."

Chuckling at Tassia's breakfast prediction, Maired made her way to Tassia's combined reading room/office in the back. Tassia stood with her back to Maired as she walked in.

"So, you've come to ask about the signs in the morning sky."

"Oh, Tassia, you are too good. Did you see it in the cards this morning?"

"No, love." Tassia turned, holding two mugs of tea. "I saw the streaks of green in the sky these past three mornings from my deck." She put the mugs on the table and turned back for plates and napkins.

"I'm thinking it's the Triple Three."

Tassia paused, then turned back to the table.

"A sign of the Triple Three manifesting just before Halloween?" She shrugged. "It may be something, but then…dare we assume, love? Sit. While we eat, tell me why you are uneasy."

"Well, there's been three streaks across the sunrise, three days in a row. I've felt something has been off for three days, but neither Corvax nor I have sensed a new presence. Stan just told me he heard the carousel music playing late last night." She hesitated. "And, just for a moment, during my morning ritual, I was back on Islay."

"Well." Tassia clapped her hands and stood. "That bit of a time slip tips the balance. Clear the table while I get the cloth. Time to see what the cards can tell us."

Maired quickly cleared as Tassia returned with a silk pouch and a dark blue velvet circular cloth, runes embroidered in silver along the edge. Laying the cloth, Tassia took her tarot cards from the pouch, and spread them out in a loose pile, quickly moving them around to wash off the last reading's energy. She gathered them, shuffled the deck, and placed it in front of Maired, who cut the deck into three piles and reassembled it. Tassia then drew the deck across the table, making a smooth line of cards.

"Choose six."

Maired carefully slid six cards, one by one, from the line, leaving them face down. Tassia arranged the selected cards in two rows of three in the order selected.

"As you know, the first card is the face of the challenge," she said, turning the card over. "The Empress. Hmm. Let's see the second, the crux of the challenge, before I begin the reading." She turned over the next, The Three of Swords. "Oh." Tassia sat back in her chair.

"What?"

"The Empress, the third card in the major arcana, followed by The Three of Swords?" Tassia leaned forward, holding her hands above the six cards. "I'm getting a weird vibe. Let's just see what we have here." She turned over the next cards: Death, followed by The Three of Wands, The Three of Pentacles, and The Three of Cups. "By the Goddess, all the three cards in the deck." She leaned forward, looking intently at the cards. "What I'm getting is a message that we are facing something very powerful already in our midst. I see the Triple Goddess: Maiden, Mother, Crone. I do not sense an evil intent, but in your vision of Islay I see the presence of the three Weird Sisters of the Hillock near Brodie Castle."

"The Scottish play witches? Macbeth was not who Shakespeare made him out to be, Tassia. There was a lot of murder for the kingship afoot, true, but it was never Macbeth."

"Well, you would know, Maired, but even though Will played with the drama, that doesn't mean the Three Sisters didn't foretell Macbeth's ascension, does it?"

"No, but it also doesn't mean the Triple Three portends the Weird Sisters are here in Rehoboth."

There was a loud crack, and the six cards flew up and burst into flames. Maired and Tassia watched the embers shimmer and slowly float down to the table.

"Well," said Tassia. "It seems we have visitors."

\* \* \* \* \*

The three sisters strolled the boardwalk, enjoying the sea air and the sun on their faces. They wandered through racks of clothing outside shops, casting spells that made the colors of the clothes change whenever a shopper moved the hangers. Small giggles, but fun nonetheless. Suddenly, Hectate, her nose twitching, lifted her face into the wind.

"Chips! I could murder a tub of chips."

"Oh, aye," crooned Bave. "With lots of salt and sauce."

"Sauce?" hooted Macha. "It's salt and vinegar, sister. That trip to Edinburgh ruined you." Arguing the merits of salt and sauce versus salt and vinegar, they hurried after Hectate, who had followed her nose toward Thrasher's. They lined up behind her, as she was already ordering sodas and fries. Bave and Macha fell silent as Hectate slid a plastic card looking for all the world like a credit card, into a box on the counter. Muttering, she tapped a finger on the side of the machine. Bave and Macha twittered appreciatively as the box dinged approval, and the clerk handed out their food.

"Oh, sauce for mine," said Bave.

"We only have salt and vinegar here, ma'am."

Bave leaned in to demand sauce.

"Come, sisters," snapped Hectate.

Bave made a face at the clerk, and as she turned, she cast a spell, covering her chips with brown sauce and for good measure changing the vinegar in the squeeze bottles to brown sauce. She rushed to catch up with Hectate and Macha.

"Hey! What's this brown stuff in the vinegar bottle?" cried out a voice.

Hectate turned and glared at Bave, who burst into giggles, quickly joined by Macha.

"Let us rest on one of those benches while we eat our chips," said Hectate.

As they walked toward the benches facing the boardwalk, two young girls just ahead of them touched one of the benches and it flipped to face the ocean. The three sisters stood in amazement. Macha carefully walked up to the girls.

"Please, good sisters, what manner of magic was that?"

"What?" The girl closest to Macha giggled.

Macha pointed at the bench.

"Oh, well, it does look a bit eerie that first time you see it. Look, it's just a push here." The girl made the bench move again, flipping it to face the other way. "Cool, right?"

"Indeed!" smiled Macha. "Blessed be!"

The three sisters walked to the next open bench and flipped it several times, cackling gleefully at each turn. Then they sat facing the ocean, watching the waves and the seagulls as they ate their chips. Bave, famously long-sighted, noticed a ship in the distance and gestured toward it with her tub of chips. Without warning a seagull swooped down, snatched a chip, and shot back into the sky.

"You!" commanded Bave, gesturing at the bird with her tub. It froze in mid-air. Bave gave the tub a shake. "Bring it back. *Now*." With a shudder, the bird wheeled back down to the tub Bave held out and carefully placed the chip back. It then fluttered to the ground before her and bowed deeply.

"Forgive me, mistress, I did not know. It is not often that one of your power and beauty are seen here."

"Hmm. You beg with style. Very well, be gone." Bave grandly waved the bird away with her chip wand.

As the gull bowed again and flew off, a large seagull who had been watching from the roof of the storefronts behind the sisters flew off toward Penny Lane.

* * * * *

Maired was on her way to find Corvax when she saw him flying toward her.

"What news, Corvax?"

He alighted on her shoulder. "I have news of spells." He told her of the spells cast, especially the seagull stopped in mid-flight.

"Corvax, remember the tales of the three Weird Sisters near Brodie Castle? I believe they are whom you saw."

"I do recall, mistress, but why would they leave Scotland for

Rehoboth? Are the English burning the witches again?"

"No, thank the Goddess, but your question is wise. Why are they here, to what purpose come all this way? We need to find them. Come, mayhaps they are still enjoying their chips."

They traveled the entire boardwalk, but though they heard tales of small spells being cast that created larky bits of mischief from the *guid* folk who chose to live amid Rehoboth, they were always two steps behind the sisters.

It was now near the witching hour. Maired lay on a bench while Corvax perched above her on the bench back. She stared up into the night sky as she tried a locator spell to find the sisters. After a long minute, the globed streetlights along the boardwalk flickered, then began to change colors sequentially from yellow to orange to green, like landing strip lights, leading up the boardwalk. Maired bolted upright, startling Corvax into the air.

"Funland! They're in Funland. Fly! I'll be close behind."

Maired arrived on the stroke of midnight; Corvax glided down to her.

"They are within, mistress, in the bumper car ride, if the sounds are true."

Maired found the door was open. Corvax alighted on her shoulder, and they quietly slid inside.

Each of the sisters sat behind the wheel of a car, driving slowly, as if figuring out how to operate their ride. The elder clapped her hands and suddenly all the cars were tearing around the rink, wildly crashing into one another, brightly colored sparks exploding like fireworks with every collision. When one sister would crash into another, they would laugh, as thunder rolled and multi-colored lightning flashed across the ceiling. After a time, the cars came to a stop and the three climbed out, a wee bit wobbly. Laughing, they hugged each other and, walking to the center of the rink, sent the cars into their original places.

Maired stepped from the shadows. "Blessed be thy feet, that hath brought thee in these ways, sisters. I, Maired, and Corvax welcome you to the fair city of Rehoboth." She and Corvax gave a polite nod.

"Merry meet," said Macha.

Hectate scowled and Macha took a step back and hung her head.

"Fair words, Maired and Corvax of Rehoboth," said Hectate. "So, you found the spell to reveal us. Impressive. I am Hectate, and these are my sisters Macha and Bave. We hail from Scotia."

"Scotland." whispered Bave.

"Aye, Scotland," said Hectate. "For what purpose have you sought us?"

"Forgive my boldness, sister, but why came you to Rehoboth for Samhain, so far from your home?"

"We came not for Samhain, Maired, but for a holiday away from the constant cold and damp of Scotland. It has been a merry and warm time here." Macha and Bave nodded their agreement.

"We thought you should know that there will be a celebration during the day tomorrow, with many non-magic folk in attendance. They call it Halloween and do not celebrate in the old ways."

"We know this Halloween of which you speak, the common have their fun whilst we light our bonfires to honor and speak with those who have gone before us. But you know this. Oh, you are concerned about our little bits of fun, yes?"

"I confess it, sister Hectate."

"Fear not, it is our plan to leave on the morrow to be home for the bonfires."

"Might you stay long enough to see the parade? It starts late in the morning and many people dress in costumes. There is music and fancy displays on wheeled platforms called floats."

"May we, sisters?" asked Macha. Bave and Hectate nodded, somewhat reluctantly.

"May Corvax and I join you to watch the parade?" asked Maired.

We can meet around ten o'clock at the bandstand."

"Agreed," said Hectate. And with a clap, the building went dark, and Maired and Corvax found themselves alone.

"Some exit that, eh mistress?" croaked Corvax.

\* \* \* \* \*

They met as agreed and walked to the parade route. The sun shone brightly, and the sisters were delighted with the parade, especially the floats. Suddenly, the sound of bagpipes filled the air, and a float with men in kilts with Scottish great pipes and drums playing "Scotland the Brave" rolled into view.

Maired turned to the sisters, but they were gone. Three rockets glittering green shot up into the sky, to the delight of the cheering crowd.

"Now *that*, Corvax, is indeed some exit," said Maired.

MARY ANN HILLIER, WRITING AS MARY ANN GLASER, WAS BORN IN CHICAGO, ILLINOIS. SHE GRADUATED FROM NORTHWESTERN UNIVERSITY WITH A BA IN ENGLISH LITERATURE, WITH HONORS, AND LATER FROM UNIVERSITY OF MARYLAND WITH AN MSM. SHE HAS THREE CHILDREN AND FOUR GRANDCHILDREN. SINCE RETIRING FROM THE US GENERAL SERVICES ADMINISTRATION AND HER NONPROFIT CORPORATION, PAPER & PENCILS, INC., SHE RELOCATED FROM THE EASTERN SHORE TO RALEIGH, NORTH CAROLINA, WHERE SHE HOPES TO RESTART HER GRADUATE PROGRAM, SHOULD COVID EVER DECIDE TO LEAVE TOWN. SHE HAS BEEN WRITING FICTION AND POETRY FOR YEARS; MOST NOTABLY, HER POEM "IN MEMORIAM" APPEARED IN NORTHWESTERN'S LITERARY JOURNAL, *HALCYON*, AND HER SHORT STORY, "THE KEY TO WINNING," WAS PUBLISHED IN *THE BOARDWALK*. SHE SERVED ON THE BOARD OF THE EASTERN SHORE WRITERS ASSOCIATION, AND, IN 2013, SERVED AS A READER FOR THE WRITER'S CENTER'S MCLAUGHLIN-ESSTMAN-STEARNS FIRST NOVEL PRIZE.

# Home for the Hallow Days

**By Terri Clifton**

The October morning started with fog from the sea that painted the whole day in softness, the gray lingering into the afternoon. A fine mist surrounded Sirena as she stepped outside onto the front porch. The others arrived at the cottage all at once, like a flock of migrating birds landing. Even Rosie, who was always late, pulled up out front right at three o'clock.

Instantly, the atmosphere of the house transformed. Calm, quiet, and empty only moments ago, it came alive with excitement and laughter. The sheer magic of having these women in her life again overwhelmed Sirena. She shook her head a bit at how quickly they fell into ease with one another.

The women abandoned their suitcases in the foyer and swept through to the kitchen, collecting wine and glasses and a corkscrew as they went, all talking at once but moving as one until they reached the back deck. Sirena wanted to hug them all again, to tell them how very much she'd missed them, but she instead settled onto a deck chair and accepted a glass of wine.

Rosie had always been her favorite, but Sirena would never say so.

Rosie winked at her as if she'd heard the thought and sat on the steps, next to the little white cat she'd found curled there in the shade of a planter of burgundy mums. Yvonne wiggled her pedicured toes and stretched long legs before her on a lounger. Veronica claimed the hanging chair, Constance the glider.

"Does she come with the place, Sirena?" The cat stretched under Rosie's hand.

Sirena nodded. "I'm beginning to suspect so. She's shown up every day this week. No one seems to miss her."

"You've been here a week already?" Rosie's fingers continued along the cat's spine. It arched and stretched. "You are going to need a name," she said, whispering to the cat, and eyeing Sirena.

"You know I like to get a sense for a place." Sirena shrugged. "It will be a busy weekend, so I came early to look around sedately. But you! I must say I'm amazed you braved driving in the traffic. You hate that."

Rosie smiled at the cat, which had crawled onto her lap. "It was crazy. People are so mean when they drive. But I thought we'd want a way to get around."

"So, a vintage convertible?"

"She's a gem, isn't she? Room for all of us." She paused. "I could have rented a beige sedan."

Faces scrunched and heads shook at the prospect. Rosie laughed in that way she had that invited mischief even from sensible souls.

"Red always was your color." Veronica absently braided the fringe on her chair. One toe pushed against the wooden deck to swing herself slightly. "We'll feel like old movie stars! It's going to be beautiful all weekend. Unseasonably warm."

"Oh," said Constance. "I was sure I heard a chance of rain and cool. I packed all sweaters."

"Nope. We'll go shopping."

"I salute your choice, Rosie," said Yvonne. "And yours as well, Sirena. An interesting and unusual choice of destinations." She was smiling over the rim of her glass.

"Rehoboth is a beautiful little town," said Sirena. Her eyes glittered but she kept her amusement and secrets to herself for now. "There's so much to do at the Sea Witch Festival. Life has been too serious, don't you think? We can just spend casual time and be ourselves. Play a little. A sisters' holiday.

"Hear, hear!" They lifted their glasses and toasted the weekend.

"In that spirit of play, I suppose this would be the time for your first presents, which you'll find in your rooms." Sirena had been preparing for this for weeks.

"Presents? Well now it is a proper holiday!" Veronica clapped her hands and headed inside. She lifted her long skirt as she hurried up the stairs.

The others exchanged glances and raised eyebrows but followed.

Each woman found her own room and the large orange-and-black wrapped box in the center of her bed. Inside was a head-to-toe witch's outfit—hat to boots. Each was different. Each was perfect for the woman who opened it, matching her personality.

Sirena stood on the landing to listen to the unwrapping and the exclamations that followed. She had enjoyed the selecting but the act of surprising was deeply satisfying. Their happiness was something she'd been hoping for.

Rosie came running, wearing her hat and brandishing a corset of dark cherry velvet. "You are just too much, Sirena. I couldn't love it more. You always did know us better than we knew ourselves. I can't wait to wear all of it."

Veronica swirled through her doorway, cape fanning out. Shades of green pulled out the color of her hazel eyes—eyes that had happy tears in them now as she put her arms around Sirena.

Soon it was a circle hug, all of them with their heads together, connecting. When it ended and they pulled away, Sirena watched their faces. Each had the same puzzled look. How had they forgotten the friendship? What about life had gotten in the way? So many years. The world didn't even look the same. But their smiles did.

They wore their hats while they made dinner.

"Tomorrow we will go out and adventure," said Sirena, grabbing plates from the cabinet.

"We'll have to." Yvonne picked up the last full bottle. "We're almost out of wine."

* * * * *

Awake early, one after the other they took their coffee on the deck, robes and sweatshirts to insulate against the persistent fog. Veronica was the last to arrive, her long kimono dragging behind her, pouring her first cup when everyone else was on their second.

"Thought you said it was going to be beautiful today," said Yvonne, as Veronica shuffled by, still looking half asleep.

"Wait for it." With her feet curled under her, Veronica sipped in silence while the others chatted.

Before Sirena had even finished her coffee, soft golden sunshine pooled in the backyard, setting the changing leaves ablaze in the trees. It was the kind of light that falls like golden dust on certain autumn days, precious in its rarity. There wasn't a moment to be wasted. Within the hour all five of them piled into Rosie's convertible and set out to find their Sea Witch spirit.

* * * * *

Strolling along the boardwalk, Sirena gazed at the calm ocean and listened to the talk and laughter around her she'd missed so dreadfully. You can't get it from strangers, she realized. It only comes with those you let your guard down around. She'd travelled the world and seen all the wonders and sacred places, only to realize nothing was more sacred than this. It wasn't the view as much as who you shared it with.

It was easy to say they'd drifted apart because they were so different, because they definitely were different. Veronica was quiet and happy, at ease in her patchwork sundress. Gentle and patient. A timeless flower child. Next to her walked Yvonne, her raven hair controlled in a high ponytail. Her chartreuse silk top and cat's-eye sunglasses gave her a bored celebrity air, but she was driven, brilliant, and vain, all of which she'd used to make herself rich. They shared cotton candy and giggled at things Sirena couldn't hear.

Rosie was the baby of the bunch and looked even younger than she was, wearing cutoffs and a *Wicked* T-shirt. She was also the daring one, occasionally the reckless one, but always the fun and loving one.

And then there was Constance, who seemed to be the only one who had really aged, and it went beyond the physical. Sirena couldn't help noticing that some of her friend's light had gone out, despite how hard she was trying to hide it. Secrets can't be kept long among soul sisters. The conversation would happen. At least she hoped so. There had been a time when they had known all the details of each other's lives.

In and out of shops and up and down the Avenue, the women talked about nothing and laughed about everything. Sirena began to relax about her decision to bring them here, despite the false pretenses. She'd already come to love the little town with its boardwalk and bandstand. The coast of Delaware was beautiful. The beaches and bays stretched for miles. The people seemed very accepting. The kind of place that could make a home for a while.

The sidewalk was crowded near the ice cream shop, busy on this warm day. The women wove their way through one shop after the other. Rosie was bringing up the rear when a man coming toward her read her shirt.

"How wicked are you, baby?" He laughed as if he'd said something clever.

"Uh-oh," said Veronica under her breath.

The first four women turned in time to see Rosie smile. All of them tensed. Rosie could have a temper.

"Fairly wicked." Her eyes glittered, amused and more.

The man looked dumbstruck, staring at her while he walked straight into a trash can. His milkshake lost its lid in the collision and spilled down his shorts. His face went red, and he looked confused.

She slid her sunglasses back in place and chuckled too softly for anyone to hear.

Yvonne laughed so hard she snorted.

"*Terribly* wicked," said Constance, but she was grinning too, and missing the judgmental tone she'd adopted on becoming a married woman.

* * * * *

They drove down the coast for dinner with the top down on the convertible, waving at all the people who stared at the ruby-red Cadillac.

Rehoboth Bay shimmered to the right and the unspoiled beaches of Delaware Seashore State Park shone to the left. They crossed the bridge over the Indian River where it flows into the Atlantic, the current strong, far below. The rushing air felt clean and smelled of salt. Veronica held her arms up as if she were riding a roller coaster and looked up at the bridge towers high above.

They walked into Big Chill Surf Club, pausing to admire the astounding view of both the ocean and the bridge's beautiful blue lights.

Sirena held up her margarita when everyone had a drink. "To soul sisters, and a most beautiful day together." Glasses clinked to the backdrop of the waves and sunset.

"This was such a good idea," Rosie said, when their meal was through. "Let's take a walk on the beach."

The golden day slid into a flawless October evening. Their bare feet sank into the cool sand as they walked. The first stars came out as the sky deepened to velvet blue. They sat, listening to the waves break, feeling the rumble. Out of that fresh darkness came Constance's voice. No preamble, not hiding the pain, just a flat declaration.

"I think he's having an affair."

There was a pause as each of them tried to comprehend what she'd said, then all at once they reacted.

"What?"

"Oh honey."

"The rat bastard."

"You *think*? Your intuition was always strong." Sirena took Constance's hand.

"I *know*." Constance's sigh rattled with tears she had held back. "I didn't want to know. I was afraid to know, but you all…make me braver. You always did."

Sirena's heart broke at how tired she sounded, how far from her center she'd drifted. "It was easier not to believe it. And you were in love."

"I was."

The rest of them had worried when she'd met Walt, and they had been right to. Constance had been the first to let go of their circle. She'd been younger and less wise but beautiful and endearing. Walt was clearly in love with her, but they seemed a mismatch. Constance's feelings had been hurt by her friends' tepid embrace of her choice. Time had passed, and for a while it seemed they'd all been wrong. A domestic life had suited her. Until now.

*****

Sirena bestowed the second and third gifts in the morning, completing her planned trifecta for the themed weekend. Opening the pantry door, she distributed the brooms.

"You'll need these for the parade," she said, handing them around.

Veronica reached for hers. "Parade? You mean we'll be in it? How fun is that?"

Sirena nodded, relieved; she hadn't been sure the others would be game.

"Are we riding these?" Rosie looked completely devilish, cutting her eyes at Sirena.

"Oh, that would be scandalous." Constance's words were at odds with the delighted prospect on her face. Some heaviness had left her overnight.

Yvonne held out a spike-heeled boot, protest written on her face.

"I would never make you walk, my dear," said Sirena.

"Rosie's convertible?" Yvonne looked hopeful, but Rosie was shaking her head. Yvonne's face fell. "I can tell by the look on her face that isn't her plan."

\* \* \* \* \*

They took to the streets on rented scooters in full costume, brooms strapped to the sides, waving to the cheers of parade watchers. As they neared the judges' stand, Sirena swung her scooter around, becoming the center of the circle of riders, shouting to be heard.

"You'll need to untie those brooms now." She looked at Yvonne. "I hope you can still dance in boots." With a mixture of emotions across their faces, they did as she'd asked.

Constance looked terrified. As the familiar music began, she turned to Sirena. "I don't think I remember." Her voice shook. She looked at the crowd.

It was Rosie who stepped forward and laid her hand on Constance's chest, over her heart. "You do."

It had been years since young girls danced under a summer moon, making their own steps, around a fire at the edge of the sea—where they had become sisters. A breeze, heavy with salt, wove through past and present. Time travelers for those few moments, their feet and spirits aligned. They danced their steps, and they danced with their memories. Returning to themselves. When the dance ended, they broke their own spell, to hear people cheering.

It was all such fun they broke their own rules, too, by making small magic right there in the daylight with everyone watching. It was hard to tell who was more delighted with the bubbles and sparks and illusions, the ones making them or the crowd watching. The Sea Witch balloon bobbed along in a cloudless sky, and the women followed it down Rehoboth Avenue with the floats and marching bands.

After the parade, they were asked for pictures and more magic tricks. They posed for the *Gazette* in front of the bandstand with their second-place trophy. People even bought them drinks at bars along the Avenue. Late in the evening, a badly besotted young man looked at Veronica with dangerously earnest brown eyes.

"I'd let you put a spell on me." He looked at her with a certain dreaminess around the eyes, as if she already had.

"Oh…" Veronica slid from her barstool slowly, eyes wide and interested. "You would? Really? Could you say that again?"

He opened his mouth but the other four never gave him a chance to finish. They bellowed "No!" in unison. Yvonne's arm moved the guy backwards and out of range. Rosie pulled hard on Veronica's arm to steer her away and everyone decided it was time to call it a night.

At the cottage, Sirena placed the trophy on the mantle. They stood side by side, looking at the Sea Witch medallion swinging slightly, the gold stars shimmering.

"We'll get first place next year." Yvonne crossed her arms, already determined.

"We will! We must come back," Veronica said. "And this house is perfect. Can we get it again?"

"Your rooms will all be ready. Anytime you want them, whenever you visit."

Understanding began to dawn on the faces she loved.

Yvonne was the first to speak. "You bought this place?"

"I did."

Their reaction was everything she could have hoped for.

They brewed a pot of tea and sat up until almost dawn reliving old memories and planning future get-togethers.

By morning, Rosie had decided to stay another day. Yvonne would return Rosie's rental car. She'd taken a liking to the convertible and thought she might make an offer on it and drop Veronica at the airport on her way.

Constance had grown quieter and quieter as the sun rose. After Yvonne and Veronica had said their goodbyes, Sirena took her aside.

"You haven't said what is next for you."

Constance rubbed her eyes. "I don't even know. I feel so lost and alone."

"Then go deal with Walt, and if you need to, come right back here. Alone is something you don't have to be anymore. None of us do."

Constance had a good cry then, the cleansing kind that happens when you are ready to let go of a struggle. By the time an Uber picked her up she was already wearing a look of resolve.

Sirena walked through the upstairs rooms. Silent now, but the essence of a wonderful weekend lingered, of her sisters, of joy and tears. The difference that was between a house and a home.

Rosie had straightened rooms and hung the costumes in the closets to wait for next Halloween. When Sirena found her on the back deck, she was sweeping away leaves with her broom and talking to the cat, which seemed to hang on every word. When she saw Sirena coming, she picked up her backpack.

"I thought you were staying."

"I lied. I was just waiting for it to get dark. But you and Spirit will see me soon."

Spirit recognized her new name and wove her way around the women's feet as they held each other in a long hug. A gust blew leaves from the trees and swirled into the night. The temperature was dropping quickly.

"The wind is shifting. Be careful out there." All her other words stuck in her throat.

"I love you too, Sirena." Rosie blew a kiss as she lifted slowly skyward, sidesaddle, delight and adventure shining from her eyes, reflecting a crescent moon.

Her laughter carried across the now-sleeping seaside town, but no one else looked up. Sirena watched until Rosie was lost among the stars.

"Shall we go conjure up a fire, Spirit? You can pick yourself a cozy spot for winter now that we're home."

All was still again, except for leaves skittering along the street. Sirena picked up the purring cat and held it to her chest, satisfied. Settled. Warm light fell from the windows of the cottage, and welcomed them in.

Terri Clifton is a writer of short stories, poetry, nonfiction, and novels. She was awarded an Emerging Artist fellowship for fiction in 2013 by the Delaware Division of the Arts. This story will be her fifth in the Rehoboth Beach Reads series, and her sixth for Cat & Mouse Press. A Delaware native, Terri lives on a historic farm along the Delaware Bay. She is a photographer, dancer, and advocate for the importance of the arts.

"This story has been in my head," she says, "waiting for the right themed book, and *Beach Holidays* was the one. Fall is my favorite time at the beach, especially those unexpected extra days of golden sunshine. I wanted to combine that with a story of extraordinary friends reuniting, and to put those human feelings and foibles into a fantasy story along with some fun and the magic of the season."

# The Legend of The Waxing Crescent Moon

## By Linda Chambers

The Sea Witch Festival was cancelled because of COVID in 2020, and Charlotte remained on the periphery in 2021 because of health concerns. Then 2022 came roaring back. Charlotte spent much of the weekend attending the events, oohing and aahing at the adorable kids and the equally adorable dogs and marveling at the elaborate conglomerations of costumes adults put together. She took part in the broom tossing on the beach. No bragging rights on that one, but her age category was mostly in it for the laughs. Besides, she had expended her energy in the 5K race earlier that day and hadn't done badly at all: thirty-five minutes and closer to the front than the back. A pretty good showing for a fifty-year-old. And she had still had enough energy to put on a costume and march in the parade.

Now, the weekend festivities had ended. The *Sea Witch* was back in dry dock and Hilda, the enormous green witch balloon that symbolized the festival, was flat and tucked away in her year-long resting place. Charlotte was exhausted, but she was also bursting with excitement. Yes, the festival was over but the holiday itself was just beginning. This year, October 31 was on a Monday.

At 7:45 a.m., Charlotte drove from her cozy mobile in Camelot

Meadows, found a parking spot in front of the bookstore on Rehoboth Avenue, and went inside. This was her ritual on October 31st. Not *every* October 31st; she had specific dates. She'd bought the first tarot deck in 2003 and subsequent decks in 2008, 2011, 2016, and 2019. These were the dates when Halloween occurred during the waxing crescent moon.

Browseabout had just opened. Normally she enjoyed the opportunity to walk unimpeded through the store and could spend hours perusing the books, cards, toys, jewelry, bags, socks, and journals, but she was in a hurry. Charlotte knew exactly where she needed to go.

The tarot decks were displayed on shelves in the center of the big wooden bookcase behind the counter. She examined them with a practiced eye. The Jane Austin tarot deck looked interesting; so did The Dark Goddess. She asked to look at them, and the young attendant reached up and brought them both down, laying them in front of her.

"They're new," Charlotte said, finally.

"I think so," he replied. He checked. "Says 2020. Pretty new."

"I'm looking for something a little older."

He nodded and turned back to the shelves. "Literary Witches?"

"Bought it in 2019."

"The 5-Cent Tarot?"

"That was 2016."

"Ah." He continued to look and then pulled out a small orange deck with black lettering and glanced at the box. "How about this? It's older."

"How old?"

He handed it to her. "Says 1989."

The Gypsy Witch Fortune Telling Playing Cards featured the silhouette of a witch, seated on a stool, stirring a cauldron over a fire. Smoke curled upwards and a black cat sat watching.

"Classic," she said. "I don't have these. Thanks, I'll take them."

He rang her up, bagged the cards, and handed them to her. "Happy Halloween."

She smiled. "The same to you."

\* \* \* \* \*

Back home, Charlotte put the unopened box of cards to one side on the table. She chose another, the 5-Cent Tarot, from the cupboard where she kept the rest of the decks and spilled the cards out on the kitchen table. Her ritual was to use an old deck for the reading on October 31$^{st}$ before noon and not unwrap the new one until the turn of the clock from midnight to 12:01 a.m. on November 1$^{st}$. The evolution of All Hallows' Eve into All Soul's Day, when the spirits were drawn back into the nether.

Charlotte poured herself a fresh cup of coffee and drank it black. She began to shuffle the cards. She would read them the way her mother read them every Halloween on the night of the waxing crescent moon.

Ruth, Charlotte's mother, was the epitome of Halloween. Everyone in the neighborhood said so. Halloween was Ruth's favorite holiday. She loved making costumes for Charlotte. An angel one year. A robot the next. A tiny vampire. A pumpkin. Martha Washington, complete with white wig.

When the leaves began to change and the air turned brisk, Ruth started assembling what she needed to decorate their mobile. Lights would be strung from the porch railing and encircle the bushes and the trees. Spooky music triggered by a footstep would emanate from a speaker hidden under the stairs. Ruth prepared the most sought-after treats: small bags of assorted hard candies and miniature chocolate bars, and individually wrapped caramel apples, decorated cupcakes, and cookies. The kids would line up at their door, bags open, demanding treats. Ruth always took the leftovers into the office with her, and her coworkers marveled at them.

Charlotte was pretty sure no one on the outside knew Ruth read the tarot at noon and at midnight or that she always bought a new deck on the morning of the 31st but kept it in the wrapper until midnight. At noon she read an old deck. When the clock struck twelve that night, she unwrapped the new deck and read those.

When Charlotte was old enough to go trick-or-treating by herself, Ruth called her into the kitchen to have a serious talk with her. Charlotte was expecting the usual "don't eat candy that isn't wrapped" and "don't bite into apples" or possibly "don't eat anything until you get it home and I can check it."

What Charlotte got was: "Halloween is the night when spirits roam the world, so you must be careful when you go out. *Especially* tonight. The best time for spirits is a night with a waxing crescent moon. Like tonight."

Charlotte had never heard this before.

"What's that?"

"It's the first phase after the new moon," Ruth had said. "Tonight, the moon is more fully illuminated. The crescent rises before noon and sets just before midnight, so they have more time to mingle."

Charlotte thought about that. "Are they friendly?" She asked finally.

"Usually," Ruth replied, "but you must be very careful because they may decide to snatch you up and carry you off to their land with them."

Charlotte wondered if any of her friends got the same Halloween instructions.

"What's their land like?"

"You don't want to know."

In fact, Charlotte did want to know but never asked her mother. She wasn't sure she wanted to hear the answer. By the time she decided she did, Ruth had passed away. Charlotte, then living in Baltimore, came back to Rehoboth and decided to stay.

That was in 2003, the first year she bought her own tarot deck and the first year she did the readings.

Now, the cards were arrayed in front of her. She'd been studying them for several hours. Night had fallen. The Ancient Celtic Method was her mother's favorite, but that involved more cards and a more complex layout. Charlotte used the simpler European Method. Three cards, representing the past, were laid out on the left. Three representing the present, in the center. The final three, divining the future, on the right.

Charlotte poured her third cup of coffee and studied them for the umpteenth time. One thing that was surprising: all the cards save one had been turned right way up. That was unusual unless the deck was brand new. This one wasn't. Charlotte had used it many times in the past because the artwork was so beautiful. Cards got turned around when you gathered them up and reshuffled and frequently appeared the right way down when turned over. This was important, as the cards meant different things depending on which way they were laid down. Right way up, the result was favorable; right way down, the result was unfavorable.

She read them again in order, from left to right, from past to future. First turned, first laid down: The Moon, indicating imagination balanced with illusion. Second: The Ace of Needles, signifying a breakthrough or clarity. Third: The Ace of Buttons, and this was the one that was right way down. The message that stuck out to her was "lost opportunity."

Charlotte took a breath and read through the second set of cards, representing the present.

First: The Three of Buttons, meaning collaboration. Second: The Knight of Matches, signifying adventure, passion, energy. Third: Death. Most people automatically misinterpreted the Death card. Yes, endings were part of its message but also change and transition.

Now she studied the final three cards, representing the Future. Another startling card—The Hanged Man—another card with frequent misinterpretations. She'd thrown that card various times in the past, sometimes right way down, where it meant resistance and indecision. Right way up it meant perspective, sacrifice, letting go. The second card was The Eight of Cups, signifying a journey. The final card was The Fool, indicating new beginnings, spontaneity, free spirit. *New beginnings.*

Charlotte closed her eyes.

How would her mother have read these cards? She was gone before Charlotte had the chance to ask her about any of this. About tarot card readings from dozens of decks bought over a period of years and stuffed into a hope chest in the bedroom. Or about spirits that wandered free on Halloween night, but not on *all* Halloween nights, just *some* of them, depending on the phase of the moon.

At the very beginning was The Moon.

She had no idea how her mother would have read them. It didn't matter. She left the cards where they lay, the brand new, bright orange and black Gypsy Witch deck beside them.

\* \* \* \* \*

At ten p.m. Charlotte was seated on a bench at Boardwalk and Olive Avenue, across from the Boardwalk Plaza Hotel. The lights still blazed on the balconies of each room. The tables in Victoria's outside dining area were filled and most of the patrons were in costume. Eventually she turned away from the hotel and stared out at the ocean instead, hands gripping the railing, watching the moon.

She felt the spirit first as she always did, sensing it rather than seeing it.

"Do you want to go in?" Dolly asked after a moment.

Charlotte turned to look at her. She felt a resemblance with Dolly, but it wasn't especially physical. They were of an age and of a similar build; their hair was different, and Charlotte was, possibly, half an inch shorter. The likeness was more in demeanor and character.

Charlotte shook her head. "Not hungry," she said.

Dolly smiled at her with great affection. "I meant in the *ocean*," she said, "not the *restaurant*."

Charlotte smiled back, because they'd done that in 2000. The two women had peeled off their costumes as they raced toward the dark water, leaving a trail of brightly colored clothing behind them. (They'd been gypsies that year.) They reached the water in their underwear and plunged into the nearly freezing waves.

"Not this year," Charlotte said.

"Hmmm," Dolly said. "No costume?"

Again, Charlotte shook her head. "Not this year." She grinned. "You either, I see."

They began to walk.

Charlotte's first real recollection of Dolly was from 1992; she may have met her earlier than that but she couldn't be sure. Sometimes as the years passed Charlotte would get a flicker of a memory of an earlier time. The memory couldn't even form itself properly; she'd been too young. A scent? A feeling? Years later she went back and pinpointed their meetings, and each one was on an October 31st during the night of the waxing crescent moon.

In 1992 she was twenty years old. Part of a themed costume tableau based on Stephen King's *The Shining*, Charlotte had been one of the Grady Twins. They were dressed in pale-blue dresses with pink ribbons tied round their waists, white knee socks, and black patent-leather shoes. At some point, members of the tableau drifted off, and Charlotte found herself wandering alone down the boardwalk, a little drunk, figuring maybe she should just find her car.

She had reached Rehoboth Avenue and strolled over to the beach. The moon shone across the water. Charlotte had stared at it and for the first time wondered exactly what phase the moon was in. She had seen the shadings on one side of it. She'd drawn in a breath of salt air and closed her eyes.

Suddenly a hand clasped hers. Someone said, "Let's go" and pulled her back into the boardwalk crowd. They'd walked about a half a block before Charlotte turned to ask her companion something and discovered she'd been holding hands with a stranger.

It was Dolly, wearing an identical Grady Twin costume. Charlotte just assumed she'd been separated from her own *Shining* group.

For a few seconds they had stared at each other and then they burst out laughing. They kept walking, hands still clasped, swinging their arms in a completely un-Grady-Twins manner, stopping occasionally to gaze balefully at other revelers. After a while they collapsed on a bench and sat and talked. And talked. And talked. Later, Charlotte couldn't remember what they'd talked about. It was near midnight when Dolly stood and said she had to head home.

"Do you need a lift?"

"No, I'm good."

"Let's keep in touch," Charlotte said. "I'll give you my number—"

"Just tell me," Dolly said. "I'll remember."

Charlotte did, and then said, "Wait, what's your name?"

There was just the tiniest hesitation before she replied, "Dolly."

For several months Charlotte thought about Dolly and waited for the phone to ring but it never did. Eventually, as disappointed as she was, Charlotte put her out of her mind. It wasn't until five years later that they met again, on the boardwalk, with crowds of people around them. In the middle of a conversation with a young man that had begun to bore her, someone grabbed her hand.

"My twin," Dolly said.

Oddly, Charlotte remembered her immediately.

"My twin," Charlotte echoed and with a quick apology to the man, the two scurried off hand in hand.

There was no discussion of the years in between. Charlotte didn't find it necessary.

In 1997, Charlotte was dressed as the White Queen from *Alice in Wonderland*; Dolly was the Red Queen.

By 2000, after her third encounter with no communication since the previous one, Charlotte considered discussing the situation with her mother. Charlotte decided not to; she was only in town for a visit, and she would be heading back to Baltimore where she'd moved for a job. All that aside, she wasn't sure how to adequately explain suddenly turning around to discover Glinda the Good Witch when she, Charlotte, was dressed as the Wicked Witch of the West.

The following year it was too late. In mid-June of 2003, Ruth died peacefully in her sleep. Charlotte came back to Rehoboth and decided to stay.

Charlotte and Dolly crossed Baltimore Avenue.

"I've been meaning to ask you," Charlotte said. "How did you do that, with the costumes?"

Dolly shrugged. "I can *do* things," she said.

"But how?"

Dolly smiled.

"OK," Charlotte said, "then *why*? Why *me*?"

"I *liked* you." There was silence, and finally Dolly said, "Charlotte? What do you want to know?"

"If you're real. Or," Charlotte said, "if I'm crazy."

"But you've felt safe with me, haven't you? All these years? You've never been afraid, have you?"

"No."

"I've obeyed the rules," Dolly said.

"Here by noon…"

"Gone before midnight."

Charlotte took a breath. "My mother was *right*. The whole waxing crescent moon business, and the spirits appearing…all that…that crazy stuff. The tarot? It's all true, isn't it?"

"There's truth in the tarot," Dolly replied, hesitantly. "And...time does matter."

They reached Rehoboth Avenue, and Charlotte stopped.

"Here," she said and took out the sketch she'd made of her own tarot reading. "I read the cards at noon, just like my mom."

Dolly studied it, then looked up, surprised.

"But this is...a journey."

"The signs are favorable," Charlotte said quietly. "Everything aligned."

Dolly smiled; her eyes grew bright in the reflected moonlight. She held out her hand. Charlotte reached for it, then hesitated and grinned.

"*Dolly*," she said. "Interesting choice for a name."

Dolly laughed. "I saw *you*," she said, "and looked up and saw *it*."

"It came down on December 15th. I watched; I took pictures."

The enormous sign advertising Dolle's Candyland had loomed over the corner of Rehoboth and the boardwalk for more than a hundred years. Now the iconic sign was gone.

"My mother was afraid the spirits would take me away to their land," Charlotte said, "but the truth is, that's exactly where I want to be."

"She'll be happy to see you," the spirit said, and clasped Charlotte's hand.

\* \* \* \* \*

When several days passed without anyone seeing Charlotte or her car, a neighbor with a key to the mobile had gone in. There was no sign of her. The police were called. A missing person report was filed.

On the kitchen table lay nine tarot cards spread out in a row, and a box of Gypsy Witch Fortune Telling Playing Cards, the seal unbroken.

LINDA CHAMBERS IS A BALTIMOREAN WHO VISITS THE DELAWARE BEACHES EVERY CHANCE SHE GETS AND IS THRILLED TO ADD "THE LEGEND OF THE WAXING CRESCENT MOON" TO THE FOUR STORIES INCLUDED IN PREVIOUS CAT & MOUSE PRESS COLLECTIONS. HER WORK HAS ALSO APPEARED IN FAE CORPS PUBLISHING'S *REMEMBERED NIGHTMARES* AND *HOWLING DEEP*. THE FIRST THREE PARTS OF HER FANTASY NOVEL, *THE SWORDS OF IALMORGIA*, ARE AVAILABLE ON AMAZON KINDLE AND MORE ADVENTURES ARE ON THE WAY. LINDA IS A PLAYWRIGHT AND STAGE DIRECTOR WHOSE RECENT WORK INCLUDED *LET THE FIGHT GO ON*, A ONE-WOMAN SHOW BASED ON UNION ORGANIZER MARY HARRIS ("MOTHER JONES"). ALSO AN ARTIST, LINDA IS IN THE PROCESS OF ILLUSTRATING A CHILDREN'S BOOK ABOUT BUTTERFLIES.

# Fall Ball

## By Doretta Warnock

### October 2021

"What do you mean Thanksgiving is canceled this year? COVID isn't a problem anymore," Alysson said to her mother, Rita. "We're all vaccinated."

"How can you be surprised?"

Alysson shouldn't have been surprised, but then again, she was. Thanksgiving had always been her mother's favorite holiday. Alysson's too. But then the last two Thanksgivings had ruined everything. Squeezed the joy out of the holiday. She had to think of something to get her mother back in the mood, to agree to provide the venue for the holiday. Thinking on her feet, she said, "Mom, the holidays are family time. If you host Thanksgiving weekend, I promise you won't regret it. I'll have a surprise for you to cheer you up. Come on, what do you say?"

After an agonizing pause, Rita agreed. Alysson knew she had only a small amount of time to throw something together, but with a mix of her neighbors, friends, coworkers, and students in the small south-Jersey town where she taught physical education, Alysson was sure she could come up with something. But she had a lot to overcome: the worst Thanksgiving ever and the even worse worst Thanksgiving ever.

### Thanksgiving 2019

Alysson pulled her car into her parents' Rehoboth Beach driveway, greeted by the sight of her brother-in-law Tommy, sitting in the passenger seat of his car, puking into a yellow wastebasket. This was not a good way to begin the Thanksgiving holiday.

Alysson headed toward the house, grateful for the crunching sound her feet made on the broken shells in the driveway that muted Tommy's retching. She paused on the porch to admire Mr. Turkey. The familiar aluminum turkey, standing just over four feet tall, had a bobble head and a sign around its neck that read Give Thanks. As a child, it had frightened Alysson; as a teenager, it had embarrassed her; but now, as an adult, she adored it. It wouldn't be Thanksgiving without it. She spotted her sister Cathy in the living room, holding her thirteen-month-old nephew, Sean, and decided to give Cathy a piece of her mind.

"Cathy, you've got to be kidding me. Why did you come here when Tommy is sick? Didn't you think about Mom and Dad? At their age, they can't afford to get sick, especially with Dad's high blood pressure and cholesterol."

"Don't worry about it. Tommy will be fine tomorrow for Thanksgiving dinner. It's probably just something he ate."

"I hope you're right."

Thanksgiving Day began with all the usual Whalen family traditions: eating cinnamon rolls for breakfast while watching the Macy's Thanksgiving Day Parade, listening to Alysson's dad, Joe, brag about bagging the biggest turkey on his hunting trip to Maine, and seeing Mom happily reclaim the space in her freezer when she finally cooked the bird. Cathy and Alysson helped Rita with the cooking while Joe entertained his grandson.

Dad's sister, Eileen, and her husband, Paul, joined the Whalen clan for dinner, bearing their contributions: apple pie and a big pot of peeled white potatoes in water, which Aunt Eileen swore would make Mom's cooking easier. Aunt Eileen never offered to cook at home. She always had an excuse—her leg hurt, her back hurt, she was too tired, she was too depressed. Dad felt sorry for his sister. He always invited her to Thanksgiving, even though Eileen never added anything to the conversation, and this year she looked more tired.

By contrast, Tommy seemed to have improved. The color was back in his face, and the twinkle was back in his green eyes. Judging by the amount of food he was eating, Alysson assumed all was right with the world until she looked at her sister Cathy. It was like an invisible force had transferred the sunken face and dead eyes from Tommy to Cathy. Alysson glanced at her sister's plate to see Aunt Eileen's potatoes, which were now mashed, sitting alone on her plate. Was that all she was eating? Was her stomach bothering her? Cathy jumped out of her seat quickly, knocking over the dining room chair on her way to the bathroom.

Apparently, they were now dealing with a stomach virus. Everyone knew it, but nobody said a word, choosing to eat the rest of the Thanksgiving feast in silence. Cathy never left the bathroom. When Alysson checked on her, she was huddled over the toilet bowl, moaning in pain. Alysson's first-aid training as a physical education teacher kicked in, and she knew the risk of dehydration was high. She handed her sister a glass of water from the bathroom sink, forcing her to drink.

There was a knock on the door. "Is everything all right in there?" It was Aunt Eileen. "Can you hurry up? I really need to use the bathroom."

"Go use the bathroom upstairs in the loft," Alysson yelled through the closed door. She wasn't ready to deal with her aunt right now. She was trying to get Cathy to drink another half glass of water when the crash occurred.

Alysson ran to the vestibule and found that her aunt had tumbled down the stairs. Eileen had a gaping head wound on her forehead. Alysson froze when she saw the blood.

Uncle Paul sprang into action. He grabbed Mom's specially made handwoven Thanksgiving dish towel, applied pressure to the wound, and got his wife out the door, while explaining they were on their way to Beebe Medical Center. That wound was going to need stitches.

Joe and Tommy were diehard sports fans. The commotion didn't seem to bother them as they sat, unfettered on the leather couch, watching the Dallas Cowboys lose to the Buffalo Bills.

Alysson cleaned up the bloody mess and put her sister to bed, while Rita got stuck with all the dirty dishes. By the time all the work was done, Alysson collapsed on the couch with a glass of white wine from the Salted Vine Winery. Dad sat in his red La-Z-Boy recliner, bouncing Sean on his lap.

Alysson had only taken a sip when Sean threw up violently and started crying. Alysson felt sorry for her little nephew. No amount of coaxing would get the one-year-old to drink fluids, no matter how hard she tried. He needed Pedialyte, and he needed it fast.

Alysson drove all over Rehoboth, looking for an open drugstore and finally found an open CVS on Route 1.

The Pedialyte worked wonders. Alysson put her nephew to bed, then herself, planning her day of shopping at the Tanger outlets on Black Friday. She wanted this nightmare of a holiday over. But it wasn't to be because on Friday morning, Alysson woke up with a queasy stomach. She waited another hour, but when she threw up, she realized she wouldn't be doing any shopping today and her Thanksgiving was officially over.

**Thanksgiving 2020**

Everyone decided to put last year out of their minds. They wouldn't even talk about it. The only reminders of last year were Mom's missing dish towel and the scar on Aunt Eileen's forehead.

But this year created a whole new set of problems. Should the family gather while COVID was so prevalent? The Whalens decided they would all quarantine for two full weeks and then take their chances. They weren't going to miss Thanksgiving. This year Joe had won a prize for the biggest turkey—and Mom outdid herself with all the fixins'. Everyone ate more than they should have, so Cathy suggested the family get the circulation going with a brisk walk on the Rehoboth Beach boardwalk.

The Whalens bundled up accordingly and walked the two blocks to the boardwalk. With all the shops closed, there were few pedestrians on the boardwalk. Cathy felt free to let Sean, now well into the terrible twos, set the pace for the group. He ran ahead, but everyone kept up except for Dad, who lagged behind. Alysson turned around just in time to see her father fall to the ground like a rag doll right in front of the bandstand. "Cathy, call 911."

Alysson ran to her father and immediately began CPR. It seemed like an eternity until the rescue squad arrived, but in reality, it was only minutes. She was exhausted from her efforts and relieved for the professionals to take over. The paramedics used a defibrillator to get her father's heart going again.

"What's his name?" one of the paramedics asked.

"Joe."

"Joe, Joe, are you with us?" the paramedic asked.

Alysson couldn't bear to watch.

The rescue squad whisked him into the ambulance and drove off. This would be the second year in a row that a Whalen family member would occupy a bed in the emergency room at the hospital. Alysson hoped this wouldn't become a Thanksgiving tradition.

Rita rode in the ambulance with her husband, while Alysson, Cathy, Tommy, and little Sean followed behind in Cathy's Jeep Cherokee.

It was a long night of waiting for the family. Sean fell asleep on his father's shoulders, but the others stood around anxiously. In the end, there was nothing anyone could do. Despite all the heroic measures, the damage to the heart was too extensive. Alysson's father was pronounced dead at 10:37 p.m.

## Thanksgiving 2021

Alysson arrived at her mother's house the night before Thanksgiving. The first thing she noticed was that Mr. Turkey wasn't on the porch to welcome her. Not a good sign. She entered the house and greeted her mother. Was Alysson in the wrong house? Her mother wasn't wearing any makeup, and she had stopped coloring her hair. The gray hair and flowing white dress made Rita look as if she had dressed for Halloween instead of Thanksgiving.

Without the family patriarch, the group dynamics changed drastically. Rita had chosen not to invite Aunt Eileen and Uncle Paul. Alysson thought that was a good idea; one depressed person was enough to deal with. Cathy and Alysson took over all the cooking duties while their mother sat glued to the couch, staring at her husband's empty recliner. It took effort to get Rita to join the family at the table for dinner. She said nothing through the meal, barely listening to Alysson and Cathy make small talk about their jobs and travels.

It wasn't until dessert that Rita spoke. "Alysson, you lied to me. You told me you would make this Thanksgiving special. That hasn't happened."

"Thanksgiving is one of the few holidays that can be celebrated for more than one day," said Alysson. "Your surprise will be tomorrow. You'll just have to wait and see." Alysson thought she detected a small smile on her mother's face.

Alysson got up the next morning and met her collection of coworkers, students, and neighbors at the Cape May Ferry. She led the caravan down to Rehoboth Beach. As a team they unloaded the cars, quickly setting up beach chairs, folding tables, food, coolers, and a volleyball net. Alysson started a bonfire and anchored a sign into the sand that read Fall Ball. It took three attempts to secure it firmly in the relentless wind. Finally, she texted her sister to bring their mother to the beach.

"Alysson, what is all this? Who are all these people?"

"This is your surprise. I know how much you liked to watch sporting games with Dad, so I created a beach volleyball tournament for you to watch. Eight teams, six players each. The four winners move on, then the two winners move on to play the championship match. You sit here in the guest of honor chair next to the fire."

Rita plopped herself in the low beach chair with a confused look on her face.

"Let Fall Ball begin," Alysson yelled. She reached into a hat and pulled out the names of two teams. "The first two teams up are The Beach Boys and The UTC WAPs. The Beach Boys were a bunch of very competitive seniors. The UTC WAPs were a mixed group of Alysson's neighbors. "Do you mind if I ask you what *UTC WAP* stands for?" Alysson asked.

Her neighbor Janice answered, "Up the Creek Without a Paddle."

Alysson laughed to herself. That was the perfect name, because these guys were going to kill them. "Let the games begin. The team that wins two out of three games moves on in the tournament."

Alysson did not find the match entertaining. The Beach Boys set up the kill shot and spiked the ball on almost every play. She looked at her mother and saw that she seemed bored. Rita let out a big yawn.

"Are you all right, Mom?"

"No. I'm cold and hungry."

Alysson realized this wasn't going well. She roasted a hot dog on the fire and gave it to her mother, along with a blanket and some hot chocolate. Still, Rita seemed to find looking at the waves more interesting than watching the game.

The next match featured two sophomore girls teams facing off. The Diggers and The Volley Dollies were very evenly matched. She glanced at her mother. Rita's head was bouncing back and forth like a ping pong ball, following the match. That was a good sign, but there was still no smile on Rita's face when The Volley Dollies won.

Rita slept through the next few matches but woke up on cue for the final match. The championship game paired The Beach Boys against a mixed faculty team called The Teachers' Touch. Alysson was rooting for the faculty team to teach the aggressive seniors a lesson, but she had to appear impartial. She needn't have worried, because the faculty team won hands down.

"We have two winners today," said Alysson. "First of all, congratulations to The Teachers' Touch. Your prize is a case of beer from our local Dogfish Brewery."

Stan Novak, a math teacher, accepted the award for the team, bouncing the volleyball on his head.

"And I need Rita Whalen, my mother, to come up here, please."

Rita maneuvered her way slowly through the sand to her daughter's side.

"May I present to you this $1,000 check, made out to the American Heart Association in memory of our father, Joseph Whalen?"

Rita just stood there, stoic, unemotional.

"Mom, react. What do you think? Are you happy?"

Rita nodded, looking stunned. "Yes. But where did this money come from?"

"Each player paid $20 to enter the contest. Eight teams; six players on a team. That's $960. Cathy and I chipped in the other $40 to round the check off to an even $1,000."

Still no reaction.

"Say something, Mom. Do you like it?"

Rita came to life. "I love it! I know your father would approve if he were here." Rita hugged her daughter. "There's just one thing," she said wiping a tear from her eye.

"What?"

"I see you gave a case of beer to the winners. What would have happened if those underage high school boys or girls had won?"

"I don't know. That would have been a problem."

"Next year you better hand out a case of soda to the winners, just in case."

"Next year?"

"Why not? Can't we extend the weekend next year? Maybe include more days, more teams? If all the money we raise can help even one family to avoid going through what we went through, that would be a blessing."

"Sure, all right," Alysson said, giving the thumbs up to her sister.

And so, the first annual Fall Ball was about to become a new Thanksgiving tradition. Alysson's head was already reeling with ways to make it better. Maybe she could add an apple pie bake-off or a costume party with prizes to the best dressed Pilgrim, Indian, or turkey. The possibilities were endless.

DORETTA WARNOCK HAS A BA DEGREE IN COMMUNICATIONS AND AN MA IN SPECIAL EDUCATION. AFTER SHE RETIRED FROM TEACHING, HER WRITING HOBBY BEGAN TO BLOSSOM. DORETTA LOVES TO TRAVEL AND PEOPLE-WATCH, WHICH GIVES HER LOTS OF IDEAS FOR STORIES. "FALL BALL" IS A COLLECTION OF THANKSGIVING EXPERIENCES FROM FAMILY AND FRIENDS ALL MASHED INTO ONE STORY. SHE HAS BEEN PUBLISHED IN *FUN FOR KIDZ* MAGAZINE AND *CALLIOPE*, MENSA'S LITERARY MAGAZINE. THIS IS DORETTA'S THIRD PUBLICATION WITH CAT & MOUSE PRESS. SHE RECENTLY COMPLETED HER FIRST FULL-LENGTH NOVEL, MOTHER MATERIAL, WHICH IS STILL SEARCHING FOR A HOME IN PRINT.

# The Bench

## By Krystina Schuler

Sydney had no idea what a treasure she'd bought when she discovered the old bench in the antique shop near Rehoboth Beach. Like all the furniture she lovingly restored, she had spent hours removing grime, paint, and damage to find the beauty beneath. This piece turned out to be particularly special. She secured the big bow to the bench, tapped her fingertips together under her chin in anticipation, and went inside, moving toward the kitchen.

Today was not only Thanksgiving; it was her parents' wedding anniversary and the day they had gotten engaged. They always celebrated on Thanksgiving Day, completely disregarding the actual date on the calendar. And regardless of the weather, it meant an afternoon at the beach.

A glance around the cottage satisfied Sydney that everything was ready. Appetizers enticed from the living room coffee table. Wine and her dad's favorite local whiskey from Painted Stave chilled on the bar. The only thing that would make this celebration perfect was if her sister MacKenzie, who had just started a new job, had been able to travel home from England. They would Skype with her soon.

Sydney was sliding the duck—her father preferring anything to turkey—into the oven, when a rap sounded at the door. On her way, she fluffed the mums on the entry table. Sydney could hear her parents bickering outside, a recently revived bad habit that triggered her childhood anxiety from a time her parents had hit a rough patch. She plastered on a smile and opened the door.

"Happy Thanksgiving, Sydney!" her mother said. "Sorry we're

late. The car needed gas." Her mother gave her dad a serious dose of side-eye and forced a smile at Sydney, offering her a one-armed hug. Her other hand balanced a pie carrier.

"Happy Thanksgiving," Sydney said, "and you're not late."

Sydney's father, whose posture was stiff, echoed her mother and kissed Sydney's cheek.

"I couldn't decide which pie to make, so we have pumpkin, pecan, and apple."

"One for each of us," Sydney said, taking the carrier from her mom and leading her parents into the living room. "No one ever claimed Thanksgiving wasn't the holiday of gluttony." She set the carrier down, removed the pies, and put them on the end of the buffet.

"Where do you want the deviled eggs?" her dad, an expert at Grandma's recipe, asked.

She pointed to the coffee table. "Over there with the other appetizers." She couldn't wait to sink her teeth into those creamy bites of heaven.

"New roof looks good," her dad said.

"They just finished Friday," Sydney said. Her little cottage was old, in need of many repairs, and totally hers. She was proud of her little fixer-upper, or she would be once she transformed it from derelict to beautiful. On a quiet river inlet, a bit inland from the bay, it would be a constant work-in-progress for the foreseeable future. "Kenz should be ready to Skype. Grab some appetizers, and let's head out to the studio where everything's set up."

Her parents helped themselves and passed through the kitchen to the back door. Her mother threaded her arm with Sydney's as they strolled across the grass. "How's the channel doing?"

Sydney was an interior designer by day, but by night she was a YouTuber with a furniture restoration channel that had almost half a million subscribers. "Very well," she said. "It's what paid for the new roof. That, and I sold five of my pieces for top dollar."

"Nice," her mother said, as she stepped into the shed Sydney used for filming.

Sydney turned the lights and camera on, logged into Skype, and dialed her sister.

Kenz laughed when she came on screen. "I think I'm the only person I know who gets video calls from a professional studio! Happy Thanksgiving and anniversary, Mom and Dad. Syd. Wish I could be there."

"We do too, baby," her mother said.

They chatted with Kenz for almost an hour, when Sydney said, "I gotta go check the duck. Talk to you Tuesday?" Kenz nodded. "Just shut everything down when you're done and lock the door, Dad."

Inside, Sydney discovered the duck was perfect, so she set it on the counter to rest and slid some dinner rolls into the oven. Her parents were bickering on their way in but stifled it once inside. She shook her head. "Why don't you guys go refresh your drinks and appetizers? I want to hear about your weekend away while the duck rests."

Her father filled a tumbler with ice and poured a generous helping of whiskey. Her mother loaded her plate with fresh veggies and tucked herself into the corner of the sofa. Her dad assumed a position in the armchair, as far from his wife as he could get in the small room.

Sydney sipped her wine, selected what appeared to be a perfect deviled egg, and sat opposite her mother on the sofa. She braced herself. Given the tension in the room, she was afraid to ask. "How was the getaway to Roanoke?"

"Awful," her father said, at the same time her mother said, "great." They glared at each other without a hint of humor.

"Well, I liked being in the middle of nowhere with spotty cell and Wi-Fi service," her mom said. "It was nice not having to listen to every single one of your Zoom calls, Mark."

"Those Zoom calls pay the bills—"

"Oh, here we go again." Her mother rolled her eyes and crossed her arms.

"Besides, how stressful can it be drawing all day long, Lisa?" he asked.

Sydney cringed. Her father, the director of Cloud Computing, often undervalued his wife's job as a storybook illustrator.

"Plenty," she said, "especially when there is a constant drone in the background about buckets, containers, ports, developers, and salespeople who don't understand technology."

Now he rolled his eyes. Sydney guessed that after almost thirty years, people really do start to resemble each other. "It was boring, and you never wanted to go anywhere," he said.

"Sorry I asked," Sydney muttered. She rose and topped off her wine, figuring she'd need it. Her parents probably should have vacationed separately. They'd both been working from home for the past two years due to the pandemic, and Sydney feared it was taking a toll. Her mother was an introvert who was quite content to work for hours without needing any interaction. Her dad, on the other hand, quite enjoyed the camaraderie of an office. His was still closed, however, a situation unlikely to change any time soon. They were probably driving each other nuts.

"You could've gone into the city and wandered on your own if you wanted. I was enjoying walking in the woods and kayaking around the pond."

"And leave you to be eaten by a bear?" He crossed his arms over his chest and raised an eyebrow.

"What would you have done if there had been a bear? Thrown your tablet at it?"

He scowled. "Think of how much fun we could have had in the city."

"Wasn't there anywhere you wanted to go that you both could agree on?" Sydney threw a questioning look at her parents and waved her hand in the air. "Like one of those all-inclusive places? Mom could have lain on the beach all day and you could have gone on excursions or something?" Sydney hated that her parents were at odds. Even as an adult, it still made her feel insecure. Her parents had had such a romantic start. If they couldn't make it, she wondered what the point was of even trying.

"Well, the prices of flights are outrageous right now," her dad said.

Her mother shook her head, pinched the bridge of her nose, and opted to ignore her husband. "What's new with you, love?" her mother asked, clearly wanting to change the subject.

Sydney brightened. "I've been put in charge of the interior finish work for the new hotel going up in Rehoboth."

"It's about time the partners at your firm recognized your skill," her dad said.

Sydney laughed. "It's a big project, Dad. They aren't just going to give that sort of job to a noob."

"And how about that nice young man you were giddy about last time we talked? The new guy? Sam was it?" her mom asked.

She shook her head. "Seth. And he's out." She grinned at her own unintentional pun. "In more ways than one."

"Out?" her dad said, raising an eyebrow. "Oh," he said, with sudden realization. "*Out.*" He waved his hand dismissively. "Well, I'm sure you'll meet someone eventually."

Sydney shrugged. If her parents' current relationship was any indication, she might be better off just getting a dog.

"Want me to carve the duck?" her father asked. "It's probably rested long enough."

"Sure," she said, moving toward the kitchen. "I'll get the sides ready. Mom, want to pour the water and light the candles?"

Sydney's kitchen was just an exaggerated galley with a door to the dining room. It would be open once she tore down the wall, but for now she and her parents were trying hard not to bump into each other. Her mother, having removed the water pitcher from the refrigerator, turned and nearly collided with her father. Her mom huffed through her nose, a huff that said, "why are you always in the way?"

After a few minutes of the kitchen waltz, the duck was carved and arranged on a platter. Everyone grabbed a plate from the table, served themselves from the buffet, and sat down to list the things they were grateful for over the last year.

The food was good and the conversation lighthearted. Her parents appeared to have relaxed and didn't seem as if they were about to claw each other at any minute. Sydney was just about to suggest they break into the pies when her father's cell phone rang. He squinted, took a sip of wine, pushed some food remnants with his fork, but then pulled the phone from his pocket. Her mother pursed her lips. Sydney preemptively cringed.

"Let it go to voice mail," her mother said through gritted teeth.

Her dad rose. "It's Raj, from the India project."

"It's Thanksgiving."

"Not in India," he said, as he slipped into the bathroom and took the call.

Her mother seethed and slowly rose from her chair. She strode out to the screened porch. Sydney looked at the table to make sure all the knives were accounted for. She checked to make sure all the forks were still there for good measure.

When her father returned moments later, Sydney pierced him with a gaze that needed no interpretation and tilted her head toward the porch. He headed outside. Once her parents were together, Sydney got up and locked the porch door. The door to the outside was still painted shut. The inside door was the only way to exit the porch, and she wasn't going to open it until they worked it out.

Her mother attempted to leave the porch but couldn't get the door to budge. When she discovered the inside door was locked, she banged on the frame. "Let me in, Syd."

A small part of Sydney laughed at the implied *or else*. "No. Not until you stop fighting."

The only thing on the porch to sit on was the restored beach bench. It had a pretty orange and burgundy bow on it, her parents' wedding colors. Sydney was planning on giving it to them for their anniversary. Her father sat, arms crossed. Her mother paced for what seemed like several minutes, muttering. "I can't believe...today of all days...don't you even care anymore?"

"Of course I still care."

Sydney saw her mother stop and stare at her husband. Then she watched her mother's gaze shift toward the small, gold, and very off-center frame tacked to the backrest of the bench. Sydney started to clear the table and put away the leftovers, trying to give her parents privacy, however the windows to the porch, slightly opened to regulate the overzealous radiators, wouldn't keep her from overhearing their conversation.

"Mark, look at this." Her mother traced her finger over the carving in the wood. Shock settled on her face as she looked at Sydney through the glass. Sydney shrugged in response. *Let it work its magic.*

"Lisa." Her father started to laugh. "This can't possibly be the same bench."

"It sure looks like it," her mother said. "*M* plus *L* forever." She paused. "Do you think they made it?"

"I sure hope so," he said. "Syd. Come out here and tell us where you got this bench."

Sydney crossed the room, unlocked the door, and went out on the porch. She crouched down against the wall opposite the bench. "I was rummaging through the antique and resale shops around here looking for pieces to work on for the channel. This was hidden under a bunch of rubbish in a shop north of here on Rt. 1. It reminded me of your proposal story."

"I assume it didn't look like this when you found it, did it?" her mother asked.

"No." Sydney laughed. "It was a mess—about fifteen different colors, all chipping. Some deep gouges. The bolt had been painted over, so the backrest no longer reversed. I had no idea it was *the* bench until I'd stripped off all the paint and the inscription emerged. I thought it would make a perfect anniversary present. I hope I wasn't wrong."

Tears filled her mother's eyes. "It's perfect, Sydney."

Her dad shook his head and caressed the carving. "Man. This was the bench we were sitting on when we decided to go steady. We were sure it was a sign that someone else had already etched our initials into the wood. Then, a year later, I proposed to you on the very same bench." Her father's eyes shined with tears, and he reached out to her mother. She took his hand and stepped closer to him. "Every Thanksgiving, we took a drive to the beach, found our bench, and planned for the future. After a while, we couldn't find it anymore. We tried to make a game out of it, but most years it was too cold to spend that much time on the beach searching."

"Yeah," her mother agreed. Her face relaxed and her tone softened. "Maybe the magic wasn't in the bench. Even in the years after it was gone, we took the time to take stock and look to the future. Syd and Kenz would play on the sand, oblivious to the cold, and we'd stop to be grateful for the past year, plan for the next." She heaved a semi-strangled sigh. "When did we stop doing that? Checking in with each other? When did it just become a mindless routine?"

Sydney sat as still and silently as a cat, not wanting to break the spell that had fallen over her parents.

"I don't know," her father replied. "I know we've been out of sync lately, but I still care. I still love you. What do you say we all go to the beach, like old times, and figure it out? The pie can wait."

Her mother looked at her and Sydney nodded. "Let's go!" Sydney said.

They bundled up. It would be colder at the beach, a blustery wind pelting the mid-Atlantic. Her father drove them into Rehoboth and parked on the Avenue. The wind sandblasted their faces as they walked down to the boardwalk. A few other brave souls were out. They started to stroll south down the boards. Her parents made a turn down the path to the sand.

"You guys go on ahead," Sydney said, wanting to give her parents privacy. "Catch up on the checking in you used to do."

"Y'sure?" her dad asked.

"Yeah," she said. "I'll sit up here, watch the waves, and get ideas for my project at work."

"OK." Her parents stumbled down to the shoreline where the sand was firmer. She watched her dad take her mom's hand, and her mom lean in toward her dad. It made Sydney feel warm inside. She sat on the nearest bench, just like the one on her porch, and contemplated the different textures she saw and the way the grays, greens, blues, and browns worked together.

After a few minutes, a shout startled her. "Peaches! Get back here!"

Sydney looked around and saw the most adorable ball of fur running in her direction with a leash trailing behind. An English bulldog puppy skidded on the boards in front of her, lifted its paws on Sydney's knees and yelped. Sydney reached down, scratched the dog behind its ears, and cooed to it. "You must be Peaches."

Footsteps slapped against the boards, and a man appeared next to Sydney. He was out of breath and bent over. "I'm…sorry…" he panted. "Peaches…you bad dog. Heel. When are you going to learn what heel means?" He seemed to have recovered his breath and retrieved

Peaches' leash.

When they finally looked away from the dog and at each other, time stopped. A slow smile spread across the man's face. "Hi," he said, smoothing the front of his coat.

"Ha...hi," Sydney stuttered, and pushed a piece of hair back under her hat. Her cheeks now glowed from within and not just from the wind. Peaches grunted and nudged her stilled hand, seeking more affection.

"I'm Trey."

"Sydney. Happy Thanksgiving."

"You too," he said.

She couldn't seem to bring herself to look away from his unusual eyes, eyes that couldn't decide if they wanted to be pale brownish gray or rich grayish brown. Peaches asserted herself with an excited lick of Sydney's hand. She dragged her gaze down toward the dog. "Peaches, huh? How'd you come up with that name?" Sydney didn't want to stereotype based on looks, but nothing about Trey suggested that he'd have named a dog Peaches voluntarily.

"I didn't," he said. He knelt next to Peaches and started scratching her rump. "My sister dragged me to one of those adoption events, and this little demon decided I was her person." Peaches gave a satisfied rumble in her throat. "They said that was the name on her collar when she came in. She already answered to it."

"Ah," Sydney said. "She looks like a giant peach, doesn't she?"

He laughed; it was a melodious, pleasant laugh. "She does."

"Do you live in town, then?"

"No, I live in Georgetown. My grandmother lives a few blocks from here. She hosts Thanksgiving every year. And there was no way I was going to trust Peaches by herself with my new leather sofa. How about you?"

Sydney rubbed the dog under her chin, while thoughts of kissing

Trey on his sofa flitted through her mind. "Probably couldn't trust me either." She bit her lip, gave him what she hoped was a coy peek through her eyelashes.

"Huh?" he replied, but then a grin slowly slid across his face. He cleared his throat. "I, uh, meant where do you live?"

She chuckled. "I'm a short drive from here on one of the river inlets. My parents got engaged and married here in Rehoboth on Thanksgiving Day. It's family tradition to come to the beach for a little while, no matter the weather, to celebrate." She glanced toward the water. "They're down there." She pointed, and they waved.

Trey stood up. He scanned the shoreline, smiled, and waved back. He lifted his foot on the bench and tied his shoe. "Hey, look at this," he said, pointing to the lower rail of the backrest. "Someone carved something into the wood."

"Oh, yeah?" She shifted around to look. In the wood, someone had carved "S ♥ T."

Trey looked at her with wide, incredulous eyes. Sydney was pretty sure her own eyes looked just as shocked.

"Huh," she said. "It couldn't possibly happen twice." She had said it louder than she realized.

"What couldn't?"

Sydney laughed. "Do you want to hear a story about a bench?" Her gaze caught her parents kissing like love-struck teens. "It's got a happy ending."

"Yeah," he said with a smile. Trey slipped his hand into his pocket and retrieved a treat. "Here, Peaches. Good dog." The dog gobbled the treat from Trey's hand. He sat down next to Sydney. Peaches insinuated herself between them. "I love a story with a happy ending."

The Bench

Krystina Schuler self-published her first novel, *The Girl in the Gallery*, in 2015, and will soon be looking for a home for her second one. She has had short stories published in *Beach Fun, Beach Dreams*, and *What Sort of Fuckery Is This?*. Krystina is the facilitator of The Write Touch Writers Group, has served as a juror for the Delaware Scholastic Writing Contest, and is a volunteer tutor for Literacy Delaware. When she isn't busy writing, she can often be found practicing piano, ukulele, or guitar; listening to music; or dabbling in arts and crafts. She also enjoys long walks on the beach with her family and has fun dying her hair purple. She lives in Delaware with her husband and son. You can follow her on Facebook at: facebook.com/krystinaschuler.author.

"The Bench" was inspired by a trip she and her not-yet-husband took to Lewes on an unusually warm day over the Thanksgiving holiday many years ago. From there, she let her imagination run wild.

Writing is often a solitary endeavor; however, many people have a hand in bringing a story to life. Krystina would particularly like to thank Jamie G. and Amanda H., who graciously suffer through her early drafts and help her brainstorm through plot problems.

# The Hanukkah Bush of Rehoboth

By Mady Wechsler Segal

Growing up in a Jewish family, Sarah was always jealous of her Christian friends who got so many gifts for Christmas. Almost all of her friends celebrated Christmas. She begged her parents to get a Christmas tree because she loved all the decorations. They refused.

What kept her from being totally heartbroken during the winter holiday was going to her best friend's home to help her and her family trim their tree. Sarah vowed that when she grew up and had her own home, she would have a Christmas tree with brightly colored metal globes, twinkling ornaments, miniature teddy bears, knitted dolls, and all kinds of animals.

When she told her parents this, they scolded her for not appreciating her own religion and culture. She replied, "When I'm married and have children, I'm going to get a Christmas tree for my home."

Sarah grew up on a cul-de-sac in College Park, Maryland, near the University of Maryland. The neighbors were diverse in race, religion, ethnicity, and age, and their families had come from India, the Dominican Republic, Germany, the Ukraine, and countries in Africa. Some of the marriages were interracial. Nevertheless, Sarah's family was the only Jewish household on the street. All the neighbors got along and helped each other in times of need. Their street was a community unto itself.

When Sarah was graduating from high school, her parents

encouraged her to go to the University of Maryland, where her mother was an English professor, and her father was a math professor. But Sarah didn't want to go to a college that was within walking distance from her house. She craved living near an ocean. She had received many feelers from colleges and universities because of her high SAT scores, but the one that really intrigued her was from Salisbury University. She had never visited the Eastern Shore of Maryland. She Googled the area and discovered that it was not far from the ocean.

Her father said, "You can get into much better colleges. Why are you aiming so low?"

"I don't want a large campus. I want a sense of community."

Once at Salisbury, Sarah immediately bonded with her roommate, Christine. They had fun setting up their room and getting to know each other.

Rushing out the door one day, Sarah ran into a guy coming out of the next room—*literally* ran into him. "I'm so sorry! Are you hurt?"

"No, but I'm shattered that you didn't even notice me."

*Is he ever wrong*, Sarah thought to herself. *He has the most beautiful blue eyes I've ever seen.* She said, "How can I make it up to you?"

"Hmmm. Let's start with an introduction. I'm Adam."

"I'm Sarah."

"How about you treat me to dinner tonight after class? Meet here in the hall at six o'clock?"

Sarah liked the sound of that.

At that point, another guy walked up and introduced himself as Adam's roommate, Eddie. He asked the women where they were from.

Christine said, "I'm from Berlin, here in Maryland. Sarah's from College Park. Where's home for you?"

Eddie said, "I'm from right here in Salisbury, but Adam's family lives in Rehoboth, Delaware. It's a great place. My friends and I go all the time.

Adam said, "I've got to run, but I'm looking forward to that apology dinner with you tonight, Sarah."

After the guys left, Sarah said to Christine, "Wow, Adam is adorable! Did you see his eyes?"

"Oh, you think anyone with blue eyes is gorgeous. Doesn't anyone in your family have blue eyes?"

"No, everyone has brown eyes, but since my mother's mother had blue eyes, I might be a hybrid."

Over the next few months, Sarah and Adam spent a lot of time together. They often went to the beach in Ocean City, Maryland, since it was nearby. By the time of the holiday break, their relationship had turned serious. Sarah didn't dare tell her parents. She spoke to them often, telling them how much she liked her classes and her new friends.

Sarah decided not to go home for the break. She blamed it on not wanting to deal with driving on snow and ice, but her real reason was that Adam had invited her to stay in his parents' house in Rehoboth for the winter break.

Sarah was excited and a little nervous during the drive to the beach. She admired the large home as they drove up and parked. But when Adam took Sarah into his parents' house, she was shocked. There were Hanukkah decorations everywhere.

"Adam, I didn't know you were Jewish."

"Is that a problem?"

"Why would it be?"

"It is for some people."

"Adam, I know. *I'm* Jewish. If my grandparents hadn't emigrated from Europe to the US, I probably wouldn't exist. I can't believe it. Here I was worrying about telling my parents.

"Well, I'm glad you don't have to worry anymore."

Sarah adored Adam's parents and his younger sister, Emily.

"I'm inspired," she told them. "I've been wanting a Christmas tree, but now I think I'll decorate my room with Hanukkah ornaments. I might even get a small evergreen and call it my Hanukkah bush." Adam liked the idea.

Sarah and Adam walked on the boardwalk in Rehoboth every day they were there. She told him, "The sea makes me relax. I love this place, even with the chilly wind." Adam huddled closer and said, "I do too. It's something else we share."

Sarah said, "I want to live here in Rehoboth forever—after I graduate, of course."

"Any room for me in that plan?"

"We'll see about that."

"Sarah, I see a twinkle in your beautiful brown eyes."

MADY (RHYMES WITH LADY) WECHSLER SEGAL DIVIDES HER TIME BETWEEN COLLEGE PARK, MARYLAND, AND BETHANY BEACH, DELAWARE. SHE SPENT DECADES CONDUCTING SOCIOLOGICAL RESEARCH (ON THE MILITARY AND DIVERSITY), TEACHING AT THE UNIVERSITY OF MARYLAND, AND PUBLISHING EMPIRICAL RESULTS IN BOOKS AND SCHOLARLY JOURNALS. WHEN SHE RETIRED, SHE STARTED WRITING FICTION AND FOUND IT EXHILARATING TO GET TO MAKE IT UP. LIKE MANY FICTION WRITERS, SHE HAS DRAWN ON HER OWN EXPERIENCES. THE PARAGRAPH IN THIS STORY DESCRIBING WHERE HER PROTAGONIST GREW UP IS BASED ON HER STREET IN COLLEGE PARK. THIS IS HER SECOND STORY TO BE PUBLISHED IN A REHOBOTH BEACH READS BOOK. THE FIRST WAS "SALT AIR EVENINGS" IN BEACH NIGHTS, WHICH WON A JUDGE'S AWARD AND INSPIRED HER TO CONTINUE WRITING FICTION. MADY IS WRITING A NOVEL CALLED, THE PROFESSOR'S YARNS. THE DOUBLE MEANING IS INTENDED, AS SHE IS AN AVID KNITTER AND HAS STORIES TO TELL.

# Blue House

## By Justin Stoeckel

My dad died when he was forty-six. I was glad. I was eleven. The oldest girl. I'm twelve now. He was a drunk. Emotionally abusive. To himself more than to any of us. There are five of us. I know that was hard.

I'm digging my toes deeper into the sand as a sharp February wind slaps my face. It catches my hair and tosses it behind me. If only it was that easy to put things behind you.

I miss him. But I'm glad I don't have to see him destroy himself anymore. Or yell at my mom. When they were together. The fights stopped when they divorced. That was good and bad for us.

Rehoboth is still sleeping. No dogs walking their owners down the Avenue. No runners pounding down the boardwalk. Just a scuffed sky above waves not quite awake yet either. I turn my back to them, taking in the turn-around at the end of the Avenue, picturing summer's bustle.

We made it a day when we came. Thrasher's dusted with a bit more salt and a splash of vinegar. All the little fingers poking at them like their own kind of seagulls. All of us crammed on a boardwalk bench. My favorite is the one I'm walking to now, across from Dolle's. I stare at the naked skyline where the Dolle's sign used to fill it. I stop, hold up my imaginary french fry—my finger will have to do—and trace the curving red letters I pretend to see.

He liked their saltwater taffy. Twisting open piece after piece while we darted off for another ride on the pirate ship ride, swearing we were going to sit in the back this time but chickening out at the last minute. He would ride with us. Put the little ones on the fire trucks and tighten their leather belts just like he did for me. I liked our days.

Then we stopped going. It was about the time that sign came down.

It was so hard for him to be happy. He was a good dad when he was there. But he wasn't there most of the time. He had things in his head. Things that pulled at him.

We'd draw. Color. Play kickball. Ride bikes. But the whole time I could feel his struggle. He buzzed like a high-voltage wire.

We talked. We played. Puzzles or crafts. Coffee station with the little ones. That was their favorite for some reason. He did it, but inside he was fighting something. It kept pulling on him. Outside, he was there. But inside he had already broken out in a sweat. I knew he wouldn't win against whatever it was. It was in his eyes. It'd get to a point while playing, then he was gone. Lumbering downstairs or back inside the house. I'd watch from my bike.

"Look after the little ones."

Always my task when it should have been his.

I dust the bottoms of my feet and slip them into my winter socks, their warmth hugging my numb toes. I don't want to leave. I like the emptiness of the boardwalk. He's in too many places at the house. Unpacking the dryer. Scrubbing dishes used to make the dinner he didn't eat. Upstairs, shouting for the little ones to stop splashing. In my room on his belly, drawing his version of the dancing avocado, while I lie beside him, shading in the green on mine.

That picture still hangs on my wall. But I pretend I don't know it's there.

If we were drawing in my room, after he left I'd listen to his footsteps on the stairs, then hear him trundle into the kitchen. Upstairs, I'd scribble, pretending his absence wasn't there. Feeling the rawness of the same scab torn free again. Listening while I finished his side of the drawing.

Down there, pots and pans bang. Dinner for all of us. There's five. That's a lot. He always made dinner though. But most times the refrigerator opened early. And it wasn't for dinner.

I walk quickly past the arcade. The buzzing and bells silent. But I see us in there, tossing balls and hoping for new high scores. My sister and brother, fishing for ducks they already have too many of. It's not why I slipped out this morning. I lean into the wind.

It had to be terrible for him. Always fighting that fight. He was fidgety. When he got fidgety, he got edgy. When he got edgy, he yelled. When he yelled, he got drunk. When he got drunk, he quieted down. That was good. But I felt sad for him then.

Little things would eat at him. He wanted to hang outside. Play in our fort. Play cars with my brother. Play foursquare with me. Swing my little sister at the same time.

But the dishes weren't done yet. The laundry was piled up. Lunch boxes needed packing. Baths needed to be run. Grass needed cutting. Leaves swept. Carpets vacuumed. The same leak on the porch to patch. I'm sure there was more. Things I'll figure out when I'm older.

But I don't want to know them yet.

Those were things pulling at him. I see them still. Elbowing their way to get at him. Gripping him by the shoulders when they did. Tugging at his waist, his ankles, his arms, while he struggled to stay with us. When all he wanted to do was be with us. Not just pulling at him—*tearing* him. Those things had nails like talons. When they got him, and they always did, their nails sunk into his flesh. That's why he lost. That's when it showed in his eyes. Stupid things. Ugly creatures. That's what I like to think. No, I don't *like* to think, but I picture them that way. It was their fault. Because when he was with us, he was good to us. It was those creatures. Wired-haired, hunched-over creatures. Shark-mouthed. Claws like rats.

They bit and clawed at him until he was shredded.

I step off the end of the boardwalk and give the beach one last look. A whisper of morning speaks through the gray. I turn away, feeling my eyes stinging. I blame the wind, knowing it's not the reason why tears streak back to my ears. It's up Surf Avenue then down on Oak, where the sycamore-lined streets crawl with him.

He could have gotten help. More help. He tried. Twice, that I know of. But medicine made him sleepy. Upset his stomach. Fogged him over. I didn't like that version of him. It wasn't him. I was glad when he stopped.

He was good for a few weeks after. Just him winning over them. Almost a month actually. And I was glad because that month was December.

My dad hated holidays. He wanted to love holidays. But the pressure to make them was too much. The planning. The commotion. I think those creatures in him were hungrier then.

He found a corner and sat. I guess to quiet them?

But he really tried. For us.

That Christmas, the last Christmas, when he was off the medicine and was working to stay together, I was eleven.

It was my favorite Christmas but the worst Christmas Eve.

Yelling.

He didn't even want to read *The Night Before Christmas*. That was my favorite part so that hurt. He threw it down when my sister started complaining about something. One of us sitting too close to her or something. Overtired from a big day. It was late. She refused to sit on the couch with us while he read. She sat around the corner with her legs hugged to her. That was it. They got him after that. He had nothing for them. He was ashamed as soon as the book left his hands. I remember the sound of the book hitting the wall. It seemed so final when it struck. No echo. Just a final thud.

I looked at it on the floor. The pages flopped open. It looked like a dead bird lying on its back. Like it had just flown into a window. My grandmother said that was an omen. Death on the way. I guess she was right. Christmas was certainly dead.

He put us all to bed in the blue house. My sister was still crying. My brother was too. They both cried themselves to sleep.

I lay in bed and listened to them whine, wishing they'd fall asleep. But after they did, I wished they hadn't. What's that called? Hindsight?

Because after they quieted down, I heard him fussing with presents. That made me saddest of all.

The best part of Christmas Eve was staring eagerly into the dark. Picturing all kinds of things. Imagining Santa setting out presents until the bottom of the tree was stuffed with them. Struggling to fall asleep because I was too eager to let sleep in. I cried that night instead. The Christmas I knew was dead. Dead as that bird-book lying on the living room floor. Two birds, one holiday, but that's a dumb thing to say too.

That Christmas morning, he put on his Santa hat like he always did. I cried when I saw it and tried so hard to stop, because I didn't want to set him off. Mess it up for him. Open the gate and let the creatures pour in.

I scrubbed the tears away and willed myself to stop. I was so mad.

But he came over and gave me a hug and then the tears really broke. But I was OK with them then. Because I felt him there, hugging me, all of him. Hugging me like a dad. He kissed my forehead. Rested his cheek there. I felt his tears too, his chest working. It was the best Christmas after that because we were together in a new part of life.

Presents were opened. The wrapping paper didn't even bother him. He let it pile up instead of shoving it into garbage bags and muttering about the trash. Then apologizing. Then picking up again and not watching us open.

But that Christmas he watched. He handed out gifts. Put things together with us. We even ate Christmas breakfast—eggs, bacon, and scrapple real crispy—before the paper was cleaned up.

We cleaned it up together and that was perfect. It's dumb, but all that Christmas magic that had been ripped out me of the night before came back. It made the room buzz. Made the day buzz. He stayed with us all the way until he tucked us all in. I hugged that buzz until he got to me and smiled.

When he came in, he knelt on both knees and stroked my hair.

"You did great today. Still made it special for them."

I nodded. Feeling a rock in my throat.

"Now it's a new kind of special because you can be my elf. I'd love that."

"OK," I said, wanting to say more, but I didn't want to lose the rock. I knew what it was holding back.

"I think it'll be fun," he said. His voice broke. He cleared his throat then pushed himself up. He sat on the edge of my bed. He clicked on the light. I could smell beer in the room. Not a lot. But some. I blinked at the brightness. My eyes still adjusting. He was holding something. I pushed myself up against the pillows.

"'Twas the night before Christmas," he began. I put a hand on his arm.

"It's OK," I said. "You don't have to."

He looked at me kind of funny. I tightened. Waiting for the explosion. But he softly folded the book closed.

"OK." He clicked the light back off. The room was instantly black. I couldn't see anything, but I heard the bed springs whine. Felt him stand. He kissed my head and told me good night.

"Merry Christmas, girl." He always called me that. Then he said something I will never forget. "I love you for growing up."

Then I heard him pad out of the room. The bready beer smell lingered briefly. It made me wish he was still there. It felt like that old scab tearing off.

I still regret not letting him read the story. I knew he wanted to. I should have let him read. It would have been, should have been, his last time.

New Year's we stayed up because we asked to.

Dad got drunk.

We drank sparkling cider.

He let us taste his champagne. It reminded me of when I tasted the hummingbird bird food.

We walked up the beach and let the little ones sleep. We put our bare feet in the sand and shivered under the full moon, howling and whistling to a new year.

I slept most of the morning, then got up and made cereal for my brother and sisters so he could sleep more.

It's weird looking back. Knowing it was our last year with him. I always felt it that year. It hovered. Like it was sitting in another room when we were in the kitchen or the living room. I suppose he felt something similar. Like always feeling those creatures just outside the door. Or hearing them skittering in the walls. I don't know. That's dumb.

It didn't take long. And I don't know why he started drinking so much more that new year. Every night instead of most nights. I saw the change. His color got bad. Like the beer was erasing him. When we pulled into liquor store parking lots, I'd cringe.

"Watch them. I'll be quick. Nobody in. Not even the police."

He'd wait to hear me lock the doors.

I unlocked them while he put the big box of beers in the bed of his truck. Sometimes I hesitated. Not wanting that side of him to come home with us.

I step onto the porch of the blue house. His house. My mom is sleeping inside. She's here to clean him out. She's going to rent it in the summer. I wish she'd sell it. And I don't. I sit on the porch swing. The cold has snuck into me. My teeth chatter. But if I go in, he won't be cooking me scrapple.

He stopped doing anything with us. More yelling. We were just in the way. A nuisance. I tried to keep my brother and sisters from setting him off. But two- and four-year-olds can't be managed. He slammed the dishes when they didn't want to eat the dinner he made. Spaghetti on the wall. He cleaned it up while we watched the iPad.

My grandmother saw the change. Saw the higher speed he operated in. Rushing to drop us off. Rushing to pick us up. But she didn't say anything. I don't know why. Didn't want to set him off either, probably. Like the rest of us.

I wish we had, but I don't either.

How long would it have lasted?

Hindsight again.

But I guess the creatures would have found their way back in. Just like water finds the smallest crack. Like our leaky porch that still leaks. I guess it does.

On the porch swing, I listen to the quiet. I don't hear the yelling. Or see the stomping around. I close my eyes. Draw in a breath of cold air that stings my nose.

I see us drawing. Coloring. Building the 1000-piece puzzle of puppies and shaking our fists in the air when the final piece clicked in.

What I keep coming back to is that Christmas morning. The floor a mess and everyone together. In the day and all together. Then I go upstairs, and it's night, and there he is perched on the edge of my bed, trying to say *I'm sorry*. He didn't have to. The day did that for him. Still, I wish I had let him read *The Night Before Christmas*. Perhaps by not, I scratched open a tiny crack that the day had somehow sealed off, for good this time. One little crack. Then the creatures did the rest. Gnawed at it. Scratching their way in like rats.

But what good is it dwelling? Hindsight only hurts. I should be doing my homework. There's dishes to put away. Laundry to put away. All of him to pack away into boxes and the black garbage bags my mother brought. But all of it can wait. When I go inside, I'm going to draw. Then I'm going to play with my brother and sisters. Outside on the tree swing. I'll push them high, high, high like he used to do. Until they squeal.

As a father, Justin Stoeckel is constantly thinking of his children's perspectives and hoping like hell he's not making a train wreck of their lives. As a writer, and therefore maybe naturally neurotic, he goes to the worst-case scenario. In "Blue House," he tried to keep a child's perspective and a writer's perspective in sync. With all his stories, he never knows where they are going to take him. Stephen King said sitting down to write a story is like walking through a tall meadow and finding that string that will lead you out. This story lead Justin to a blue house and a child who comes out stronger after the train wreck.

Justin Stoeckel is a teacher and father of five children. When he's not stepping on Hot Wheels cars, painting nails, or arguing against the necessity of making slime every day, Justin fits in time to write. "Blue House" is his third published story with Cat & Mouse Press. He is currently at work on his fifth novel and holding out hope for an agent who will excavate him from the burial of teaching.

## Judge's Comment

*"Blue House" could be read as a sad story, perhaps not even one we would want to read on a vacation at the beach, but, underneath, between the lines, this is a love story, a story of Christmas in a town that is largely a summer town. A love of a daughter for her father. It is a coming-of-age story; who doesn't remember the new awareness of a twelve-year-old? The writing is choppy, like the seawater pounding the shore, like the emotions rocking the family, especially the narrator. Ebb and flow. This is a story that we know, and that we might not want to know, but we feel better after we have read it. The author provides a nice voice, nice inner monologue, nice use of time, and nice tribute to off-season, while choosing a tough holiday, no matter where, for a nice remembrance of a flawed father.*

# The Eternal Ocean

## By Eric Compton

Walter came out of the house in his dark-green L.L. Bean coat and beige khakis, both older than the grandchildren he had left inside. On his head, though, he sported a new bright-red Phillies cap, given to him by those same grandchildren that morning. It helped hide the thinning gray hair that had just been trimmed the week before.

As he left the warmth of the house, the cold December wind blew through him, and he felt the stark contrast immediately. But he was on a mission. Red, his faithful ten-year-old Irish setter, had been staring and nudging for the past thirty minutes, indicating his patience with present opening was to be rewarded with a walk. Despite any winds, and they were certainly colder and harder here at the beach than anywhere else, nature called. Walter knew his family let him keep the house a little warmer than they would like. Daughter Maggie wouldn't complain until she'd had a couple glasses of wine and was bustling over the hot stove with dinner. As happy as he was inside, it didn't make the transition any easier for the walk.

He looked at his navy-blue door, now adorned with an L.L. Bean wreath with bright bow, and considered an immediate retreat. He spent an extra minute on the wreath. It was real evergreen, unlike his Christmas tree inside, and he wanted to take in the pine smell. When the scent meshed with the sea air it was something unlike anywhere else. What was it about Christmas at the beach that was so unusual? In summer, things were spread out everywhere—all over the lawn, all over the beach, all over the town. Family was spread out as well, boating, kayaking, swimming, fishing, and it was rare everyone converged in one spot for long. Summer was the time of two-hour conversations on the back deck with one or two family members. But Christmas was the time everyone was together; the small cottage kept them all warm and close.

He looked back through the windows of his Rehoboth cottage. It was early afternoon, the sleepy time when the adrenaline rush of opening presents has passed, and the anticipation of Christmas dinner has not yet started. The lull in the action seemed the perfect time to address the needs of his companion. While the temperature wasn't pleasant, he welcomed the quiet. All through the fall, his beach house had been so calm. At night, with fewer cars, he could hear the waves crashing only a couple blocks away. People who lived in the city paid for artificial replicas of the sound to help them sleep, but here he got the real thing for free. But then his family had arrived—so noisy! He enjoyed it for a while, but these breaks helped restore him.

They started on the usual path, with Red checking all the key spots for the required smells that showed nothing had changed. A few blocks in, Walter suddenly altered course and headed toward the beach. His cottage, with its gray wood paneling on a double-sized lot, was only two streets from the ocean. Despite its size, it was worth ten times what he paid back in 1976, given its location.

He walked the boards and crossed the dunes to the sweeping view of the beach and the ocean. The wind picked up significantly without the dune grass and beachfront homes to block it. Red arched his nose and opened his mouth to capture the myriad smells carried on that wind, so very different than those on his normal route. Did Red hear something? He closed his eyes as if listening to a voice only he could perceive.

Walter looked out to the shoreline and watched the waves crash into the beach. In summer, the ocean, no doubt understanding tourism helped fund its maintenance, eased off its immense power and, for the most part, came down gently to allow tourists to wade into its waters. In winter, it did not hold back, bringing its full power to bear and hitting the shore with the sound of thunder. The sky was a bright blue, with no gray clouds to dim its brilliance. It was one of those days that looked perfect from inside your home, safe in your artificial warmth. The beach was empty, only the white sand stretching along the coastline.

*I am looking at the way it was one or two hundred years ago,* he thought.

Suddenly, he was a boy again, throwing himself into the rolling and cresting waves. Hands pointed to the beach, he is bodysurfing in the white-capped swells that break and propel him forward. The wave collapses, and his head thrusts out of the water, lungs filling with air, lifting his body up as he looks to see how far he rode this time. Laughing, he goes back for another try.

A thought struck him. Those waves were the same today. The ocean didn't change. It behaved this way when he spent his first summers crashing headlong into what seemed titanic-sized waves, and it would be this way after he was gone. The beach changed; it eroded, and only the efforts of man to rebuild it brought it back. The same was true for the houses along the beach. They, too, eroded and faded over time, sometimes to the point where they were replaced by new, bigger, versions. Nothing was eternal except the ocean.

He caught himself. Why was he thinking about these things? What was so important about whether something was eternal or temporary?

And then he realized.

It was the first Christmas.

Without her.

Red stopped taking in the smells, closed his mouth, and gave Walter a look. He seemed to know when Walter was thinking about her. He would come over and place his head on Walter's knee for comfort.

He missed her too.

"You are the silliest man," he heard, on the sea breeze. "How could you forget on today of all days?"

"What?" he answered.

"You are forgetting what else is eternal," it answered back, sounding like her voice. "Our souls are eternal."

He smiled. She was always the smarter of the two of them. Of course, she was right. He would see her again. But now was a time to focus on the people in that little warm cottage.

He turned around and headed home.

AFTER THIRTY-FIVE YEARS IN CONSUMER GOODS AND MEDICAL DEVICE BUSINESSES, ERIC COMPTON CHANGED CAREERS AND BECAME A PROFESSOR AT VILLANOVA UNIVERSITY. HE IS SERVING AS AN EXECUTIVE IN RESIDENCE IN THE VILLANOVA SCHOOL OF BUSINESS. IN ADDITION TO TEACHING, ERIC IS RETURNING TO HIS LOVE FOR WRITING, STARTING WITH THIS SHORT STORY AND, HOPEFULLY, FULL-LENGTH BOOKS (STARTING WITH A NONFICTION BUSINESS LEADERSHIP BOOK CURRENTLY IN PROCESS). ERIC'S INTEREST IN WRITING STARTED IN LATE ELEMENTARY SCHOOL, INSPIRED BY RAY BRADBURY, AND LED TO DOZENS OF PUBLISHED SHORT STORIES. THIS STORY WAS INSPIRED BY THE RECENT DEATH OF HIS MOTHER-IN-LAW, RIGHT BEFORE CHRISTMAS IN 2021.

WHILE ERIC AND HIS FAMILY HAVE LIVED IN OVER FIFTEEN HOMES IN EIGHT STATES, THEY HAVE BEEN VISITING BETHANY BEACH ANNUALLY FOR MORE THAN TWENTY-FIVE YEARS. THEY PURCHASED THEIR FIRST BEACH HOME ELEVEN YEARS AGO AND THEIR CURRENT HOME WAS ON THE BETHANY BEACH & COTTAGE TOUR IN 2022. MARRIED FOR THIRTY-FIVE YEARS AND FATHER TO TWO GROWN SONS, ERIC CAN BE FOUND ON HIS BOAT (CRABBING AND FISHING), DJING IN LOCAL RESTAURANTS, CYCLING AROUND SUSSEX COUNTY, TALKING ABOUT HIS BELOVED PHILADELPHIA EAGLES, AND SITTING ON THE BEACH.

# Tidings Of Comfort and...Lizards?!

## By Susan Walsh

"This is it, Mom? We're really here?"

"Ye—"

Lily laughed. She and her mother, Jenny, had been singing Christmas carols since Breezewood, and her mother's answer had turned into a croak.

"Oh, tidings of comfort and—"

"And the ocean? It's really as big as the sky?"

"It is. And it changes color depending on the sky too." Jenny couldn't wait to see daughter Lily experience the ocean for the first time.

"How still we see thee lie—"

"And I can play that Skee-Ball game you told me about?"

"Not sure about that. It might not be open this time of year, but we'll see."

"Deck the halls with—"

"And we'll walk down the street where you carried your fake baby? Tell me that story again?"

At ten, Lily seemed too old to hear stories over and over, but she was obsessed with this one.

"OK. On the main street in Rehoboth Beach there was—maybe still is—a joke store. My friend Lisee and I used to buy fake candy cigarettes there. Then, next door we got root beer—the old-fashioned kind that came in glass bottles that looked like real beer bottles. We'd take our beer and cigarettes and our dolls—they looked like real babies—and walk up and down Rehoboth Avenue. Your gran always walked ten paces behind like she didn't know us, but I heard her tell a friend of hers once she thought it was hilarious."

"All is calm, all is—"

"And you'll show me where you went to high school?"

"Yes, I promise." *Not really*, Jenny thought. Where you went to high school is where you graduated from, not the place you left after a year, leaving all your friends. Jenny felt tears start and tried to shake them off. She was just tired. It had been a very long drive from Iowa, and she was stressed and worried this trip back to the beach would be a mistake.

And now they were here. Back in the only place that had ever really been home for Jenny, a place she hadn't been in twenty-five years. She was equal parts excited and terrified it wouldn't be what she remembered. She wasn't coming home, she kept reminding herself. She was just a tourist visiting the beach for the holidays.

Her heart started pounding as she passed the Tanger outlets and realized how close they were to the beach.

She drove into Rehoboth, parked the car, and sat a moment, taking a deep breath. Lily was already out of the car and on the sidewalk, bouncing up and down in excitement. Jenny locked the car, and she and Lily started walking down Rehoboth Avenue toward the ocean. Jenny pointed out a few landmarks and found herself smiling. It looked much as she remembered.

"Just ahead, up First Street, was Nicola's—the pizza place—maybe if it's still there, we'll eat dinner there one night. And right up here on the right…" Jenny paused dramatically, "is the infamous toy and joke store. And no. We can't go in right now. We'll be here a couple weeks, Lil. Can't do everything at once."

At the end of Rehoboth Avenue, about to step onto the boardwalk,

Jenny asked, "You ready, Lily?"

Her daughter nodded solemnly, and Jenny took her hand. Halfway across the boardwalk, Lily stopped. Frozen. Jenny looked at her beloved ocean and once again felt tears welling. How had she ever survived leaving this place? She glanced down and gave herself over to watching her daughter, seeing her take it all in, eyes wide, a look of awe on her beautiful face.

"You were right, Mom. It's, it's just…" She shook her head as if she were seeing something not quite real, then suddenly hurled herself into Jenny's arms and hugged her tight. "We're really, really here! I'm so glad we came, Mom."

*Maybe I am too*, thought Jenny. *I hope so.* "All right, kiddo. I have a feeling we're too early to check in, but let's go ask, just in case. This way."

Jenny pointed north, and Lily looked toward the huge hotel.

"That's where we're staying?"

Her mom nodded as they walked up the boardwalk and entered the lobby of the Boardwalk Plaza Hotel. They took in the array of poinsettias and strands of fairy lights. The lobby seemed deserted, but after a moment a young man came through a door near the desk. *Young man.* Jenny grimaced to herself. *I sound like my own grandmother. He's probably almost my age*, she realized as she took another look. *And attractive. Sandy hair, nice smile and—*

"Hello, ladies. Can I be of assistance?"

"Probably not. We have a reservation, but I'm guessing we're too early to check in? The last name is Nelson."

"Your room isn't…quite…ready…" He paused, frowning at the computer screen. "Actually, there's a slight problem with the reservation." Before Jenny could burst into tears, he continued. "The room you'd reserved sustained some damage after a recent storm. We've had to upgrade your reservation—no cost to you, obviously—to a suite." Looking at Lily, he asked, "How'd you like your own bedroom, young lady? With a TV all your own?"

"Really? OMG, OMG!" Lily started jumping up and down. "Mom, did you hear that? Really? My own room!"

"That's very generous of you, but not necessary," Jenny said to the clerk.

"It is necessary, actually, unless you want to stay in a broom closet, because your original room is under construction. But no, the suite isn't quite ready yet. "Can you give us a couple of hours?"

"Of course. We knew we were early. It's been a long drive. Is there somewhere close that has good coffee?"

"Noela's. Go out to the boardwalk and head south to Baltimore Avenue. It'll be not quite two blocks down on the right. You can't miss it." He smiled.

"Baltimore? Is Grotto Pizza still on the corner?" Jenny asked.

"Ah ha. Not a newbie. You've been here before?"

"It was a long time ago."

"Well, welcome home. Once you've fallen in love with the beach, it's dangerous to stay away too long, you know."

*Yes, I do*, thought Jenny. "Thank you so much. You've been a great help."

Back on the boardwalk, Lily paused to take in the ocean once again—almost as if she couldn't believe what she'd seen just a few minutes earlier. She turned. "What's Noela's?"

"No idea," answered Jenny. "It must be a new place since I was here. I wonder if it's just open for Christmas time."

When they turned onto Baltimore Avenue, well before they reached the end of the first block, they could make out a storefront up ahead that seemed to have a lot of Christmas decorations. When they got close, they saw a beautiful little saltbox house, brown shingled with the front festooned with what looked like miles of garland and thousands of Christmas balls in shades of greens, blues, turquoise, and violet. Lily's favorites. Peacock colors she called them. Jenny loved them too, because they were the colors of the sea. A picture window took up most of the front of Noela's, decorated like the grand old department stores in Philadelphia and New York, with toys and a Christmas village and a stunning manger scene. Jenny and Lily were both mesmerized by all the details.

"Mom! There's a lizard in the nativity scene!"

Jenny was sure Lily was mistaken, but when she looked where Lily pointed, sure enough, nestled in with the sheep and donkeys was a lizard. Only then, did Jenny notice the sign over the little shop also featured a little lizard. *Odd.*

The entrance to Noela's was around the corner on the side of the building. Jenny and Lily pushed the door open, curious to see what the inside of this strange little place would be like. As they stepped in, Jenny registered that the older woman behind the counter looked startled and noticed the place was empty.

"Oh, sorry. Are you closed?"

The woman continued to look at Jenny. She slowly stopped wiping the counter and started to remove the apron she'd been wearing. "Not at all, come in. We're just between our morning and evening rush. Welcome."

Was she imagining it? Jenny had the uncomfortable sensation the woman behind the counter was staring at her. She seemed to keep her eyes on Jenny and Lily as she came out from behind the counter, walked over to the door, turned the latch, and flipped the Open sign over.

"You were closing. Really, we're sorry. We don't want to inter—"

"Jenny?" The older woman asked, still looking intently at her.

"Yes. Wait, what? How do you know who I am?"

"You look just like your mom the last time I saw her."

Once again, Jenny felt the slight pressure of tears gathering. "You knew my mom? I'm sorry…I don't recognize you."

"You wouldn't. You were a kid. And this lovely young creature looks just like Rene when she was twelve. Her granddaughter, I take it?"

Lily looked astonished. She'd never met her grandmother and here was someone who knew her. She probably had many questions, but what popped out of her mouth was "Why is there a lizard in your nativity scene?"

The older woman laughed a happy, warm laugh. "That's Noela, the Christmas lizard. But there are a lot of stories to get sorted out here, and I doubt that's what you came in for."

*Maybe this is exactly what we came in for*, Jenny thought. She expected the beach to still be the beach. She thought maybe some of the Rehoboth stores and landmarks would still exist. But what she dared hope, but never expected, was that coming back here after twenty-five years would feel like coming home. And yet…

"Yes, please. I would love a strong coffee, black. Feels like I've been driving forever. How about you, Lil?"

"Let me guess," said the woman heading back to the counter. "I'm Shirl, by the way. Shirl Moore. Lily, you look like a peppermint hot chocolate girl to me. Am I right?"

"How did you know that?" Jenny always steered Lily away from the super-sweet drinks, but she saw Lily looking at her hopefully.

"Sure, go ahead." Jenny smiled. "We're on Christmas vacation."

Shirl got busy behind the counter, first putting together a tray with a heavenly assortment of Christmas cookies and candies and bringing them out to the table for Jenny and Lily.

As Shirl worked on their drinks, the name finally clicked for Jenny. "I do remember you now. You're Charlie Moore's mom, right? I babysat for him a few times just before we moved. He hated me." She grimaced.

"He didn't hate you, Shirl said with a laugh. "He had a crush on you. He hated having a babysitter. Thought he was too old." Shirl paused. "Maybe he was right. He was almost nine. I guess I got a little over-protective after Charlie got sick."

"Charlie was sick?"

"Childhood leukemia. Your family moved in about 1996, right? He would have just been diagnosed. He survived," she added quickly, as she saw the stricken look on Jenny's face. "But it was bad for a while. That's where Noela came in, but I'm getting ahead of the story."

Shirl brought the drinks over for Jenny and Lily, then went back, grabbed a coffee for herself, came back to the table, and sat down.

"You're sure this is OK?" Jenny asked. "We don't want to get you in any trouble."

"My shop, my rules." Shirl laughed.

Wow. So, this laid back, grandmotherly lady owned Noela's. For a brief second, Jenny imagined herself behind the counter, then sitting down at a table after her shift, to write. Lily busing tables in another year or two. *OK, Jenny...getting ahead of yourself. Way ahead.*

"So, Jenny, how is your mom?" Shirl asked, easily drinking the coffee that was still too hot for Jenny. *Just like my mom did*, Jenny thought.

"My parents died."

Now it was Shirl's turn to look stricken. "Oh, sweetie, I am so sorry."

"They were killed in a car accident, right at the beginning of my senior year in college." *The senior year I didn't finish.* "Lily never got to meet her grands."

"I am so, so sorry. Why didn't you come home? You know, it broke your mother's heart when you had to move away from here."

"Really?" Jenny looked dumbfounded. "It never seemed like it bothered her."

"Well, she had no choice, when your dad's job transferred him. But it broke her heart knowing how unhappy you were, and she couldn't do anything about it."

"Wow. I really thought she didn't care. Anyway, by senior year, I was engaged to Lily's dad." *Another regret.* "Lily's father is from the Midwest and had zero interest in leaving. Even for a vacation. Not that we could have afforded one. Then Lily arrived." *The one good thing that came out of all my years away.*

"So, I take it…" Shirl paused, as if trying to choose the right words, "is Lily's dad…"

"We're divorced. He's no longer in the picture."

Shirl didn't press, with Lily sitting right there.

"What about Noela?" Lily piped up. She was a patient child, but a Christmas lizard story was too good to wait for.

"So. Noela." Shirl smiled. "I told you Charlie had gotten sick. After about eighteen months, we thought we were going to lose him. He just didn't seem to have any fight left. The illness had cost him everything he loved—baseball, boogie boarding, swim team. The headaches and dizziness made it excruciating for him to read or sit on the beach in the sun. I was working at the Boardwalk Plaza back then—"

"That's where we're staying! It's gorgeous." Lily interjected. "Except our room wasn't ready yet so we came here."

"The room wasn't ready?" Shirl sounded annoyed. "The tons of poinsettias in the lobby are a tradition going way back. One year, after they'd just been delivered, I was crossing the lobby, when there in the middle of the floor was a tiny lizard. It must have come in with the flowers, maybe all the way from Florida. One of the workmen decorating the lobby offered to catch it and take it outside to feed to the gulls. But…" Shirl paused. "For some reason, that little creature, looking so lost and scared…it just seemed urgent for me to try to save it."

"Like you were trying to save Charlie?" Lily spoke again, and Shirl and Jenny exchanged looks that said, yes, she's a smart kid.

"I ran and got a Tupperware container from the kitchen and scooped up the lizard. That night, on the way home from work, I stopped at the Shell Shop for supplies: a better container, a bottle for misting, some hermit crab food—I had no idea what lizards ate. I was late getting home, and Stan was furious. I was late. I'd wasted money. Anyway, I put the lizard on the end table in the hall and pretty much forgot about it the rest of the night." She paused her story. "Can I top off your coffee?"

"Yes, please. Lily, are you OK?" Lily nodded impatiently.

Shirl brought hot coffee to the table for Jenny, and more for herself too. "First thing every morning, I went into Charlie's room to check on him. That next morning, when I walked in, he wasn't in bed. I checked his bathroom. Nothing. I was terrified. I raced down the stairs, and there he was sitting on the floor in the hallway. With the lizard. He had an encyclopedia and a couple other books from the bookshelf out on the floor."

Shirl paused and smiled at the memory. "He was so excited. I hadn't seen him like that in months. He told me the lizard was an anole, *a-n-o-l-e*, and that was why he n—"

"Noela!" Lily exclaimed. "The letters rearrange to spell *Noela*!"

"Exactly." Shirl smiled at her. "Noela was the first thing Charlie had been interested in in months. He seemed to start getting better from that very day."

"So that's why Noela is in your nativity scene. A real Christmas miracle," Jenny spoke for the first time. She'd been transfixed by the story as much as Lily.

"So, I guess Noela isn't still...?" Lily asked.

"No, sweetie. I don't think anoles live all that long, and we had no idea how old she was when we found her. We had her about a year though. When she died, we buried her in our front garden and in the spring, we planted a little butterfly bush over her grave. The bush is huge now." She gestured toward the door. "When we bought the café, we took a cutting from the bush and planted it by the front door. So, there's a little piece of Noela here too."

The phone rang, startling everyone. Shirl answered, then glanced over at Jenny and Lily at the table. "Yes, as a matter of fact they are here." Shirl spoke for a moment, then hung up and returned to the table. "That was the hotel. Your room will be ready in about a half hour."

Jenny and Lily continued to ask questions about Charlie, Noela, the hotel, and the town in the last twenty-five years. A shadow crossed the table and Jenny realized there was someone at the door. She started to say something but before she could, the person at the door let himself in with a key. Jenny realized it was the same attractive young man who'd helped them at the hotel. In brighter light, his face was a bit more weathered. He looked not quite as young, but every bit as attractive as he had earlier.

"Hey, hon," Shirl spoke, getting up from the table. "We were just talking about you. Want your usual?" The man came right to the table and gave Shirl a hug.

Jenny and Lily looked at Shirl and then at the man from the hotel. Side by side, the resemblance was unmistakable. This was Charlie!

"Hi, ladies." Charlie smiled at the pair. "I see you found Noela's."

"It was hard to miss, with all the decorations out front." Jenny could hardly breathe at all the memories that were rushing at her. Could *coming home really be this easy?*

"We found it. And we're staying in Rehoboth Beach forever!" Lily shouted.

Jenny couldn't help it. Her eye was drawn to the nativity scene. She could see the Noela statue from where she was sitting. Did that little lizard just wink at her?

Susan Walsh graduated from Towson State University with a bachelor's in English and a concentration in writing. Her previously published efforts have been mostly essay/opinion pieces. "Tidings of Comfort and...Lizards?!" is her first published fiction.

A bit of Noela's story is true. Susan worked for many years for McCormick and Company. Once, when poinsettias were delivered to decorate the lobby for the holidays, a little lizard came along for the ride, and a coworker took it home as a pet. Susan thought that would make a great Christmas story. She tried several unsuccessful versions, but when she heard this year's contest theme was "Beach Holidays," she had a feeling Noela had found a home.

# Beach Holidays

## 2022 Rehoboth Beach Short Story Contest Judges

### Jackson Coppley

Jackson Coppley is the author of the bestselling *Nicholas Foxe Adventure series*, *Leaving Lisa – An AI Romance*, and numerous short stories. Coppley combines his insight from a career in telecommunications and computers with his knack for spinning a good tale. He resides with his wife Ellen in Chevy Chase, Maryland, and Rehoboth Beach, Delaware.

### Lois Hoffman

Lois Hoffman is the owner of The Happy Self-Publisher and award-winning author of *Write a Book, Grow Your Business*, along with *The Self-Publishing Roadmap*, and *Barriers*. She helps new and experienced writers confidently share their voice to make a difference in their lives and the lives of others through personalized writing, publishing, and book marketing services. She values a diversity of people, thoughts, and ideas to promote more knowledge and greater understanding in the world. And, because she believes in the power of words to change lives, a portion of course, workshop, and book sales are donated to organizations that support current and future writers. You can find her playing with her words at HAPPYSELFPUBLISHER.COM.

### Dennis Lawson

Dennis Lawson is an English Instructor at Delaware Technical Community College in Wilmington, Delaware. His fiction has appeared in *Philadelphia Stories*, *Crimespree Magazine*, the Rehoboth Beach Reads anthology series, and other publications. Dennis holds an MFA in Creative Writing from Rutgers-Camden, and he received an Individual Artist Fellowship from the Delaware Division of the Arts as the Emerging Artist in Fiction in 2014.

## Mary Pauer

Mary Pauer, a Pushcart nominee, received her MFA in creative writing in 2010 from Stonecoast, at the University of Southern Maine. Pauer publishes short fiction, essays, poetry, and prose locally, nationally, and internationally. She has published in The *Delmarva Review*, *Southern Women's Review*, and *Foxchase Review*, among others. Her work can also be read in anthologies featuring Delaware writers. She judges writing nationally, as well as locally. Her latest collection, *Traveling Moons*, is a compilation of nature writing. Donations from sales help the Kent County SPCA equine rescue center. Pauer was awarded the 2019 Delaware Division of the Arts Literary Fellow in Creative Nonfiction. This is her third literary fellowship from the DDoA. Pauer accepts private clients for developmental editing and may be reached at MARYMARGARETPAUER@GMAIL.COM.

## Dylan Roche

Dylan Roche is an award-winning journalist, novelist, playwright, and blogger from Annapolis, Maryland. When he's not writing about health and fitness for magazines, he can usually be found writing fantasy fiction. His first novel, T*he Purple Bird*, debuted in 2019. He serves on the board of Eastern Shore Writers Association, through which he hosts the monthly fiction writing group Get Lit. His plays have been produced onstage throughout the state of Maryland. He's also an ultramarathon runner and a corgi wrangler.

## Candace Vessella

Candace Vessella is the President of the Friends of the Lewes Public Library and an avid reader and passionate about libraries. She began her career as an intelligence analyst with the Defense Intelligence Agency and retired in 2009 from her position as the Vice President for Government Relations with BAE Systems Inc. In parallel with her civilian career, she served twenty-five years as an intelligence officer in the United States Navy Reserve, retiring as a Navy Captain. She received her undergraduate degree in communications from Southern Connecticut State University and her Master's in International Relations and African studies from The American University in Washington, DC. You will find her most days at the Lewes Public Library.

# Want to see *your* story in a Rehoboth Beach Reads book?

### *The Rehoboth Beach Reads Short Story Contest*

The goal of the Rehoboth Beach Reads Short Story Contest is to showcase high-quality writing while creating a great book for summer reading. The contest seeks the kinds of short, engaging stories that help readers relax, escape, and enjoy their time at the beach.

Each story must incorporate the year's theme and have a strong connection to Rehoboth Beach (writers do not have to live in Rehoboth). The contest opens March 1 of each year and closes July 1. The cost is $10/entry. Cash prizes are awarded for the top stories and 20–25 stories are selected by the judges to be published in that year's book. Contest guidelines and entry information is available at: *catandmousepress.com/contest*.

# Also from Cat & Mouse Press

## Eastern Shore Shorts

Characters visit familiar local restaurants, inns, shops, parks, and museums as they cross paths through the charming towns and waterways of the Eastern Shore.

## Beach Love

A diverse collection of beach romances, set in Lewes, Rehoboth, Bethany, Fenwick, Ocean City, and Cape May. Also available in large print.

## The Sea Sprite Inn

Jillian leaps at a chance to reinvent herself when she inherits the responsibility for a dilapidated family beach house.

## Sandy Shorts

Bad men + bad dogs + bad luck = great beach reads. Characters ride the ferry, barhop in Dewey, stroll through Bethany, and run wild in Rehoboth.

### Online Newspaper for Writers

Jam-packed with articles on the craft of writing, editing, self-publishing, marketing, and submitting. *Writingisashorething.com*

Other Rehoboth Beach Reads Books

## Fun with Dick and James

Follow the escapades of Dick and James (and their basset hound, Otis) as they navigate the shifting sands of Rehoboth Beach.

## Children's Books

## How To Write Winning Short Stories

A guide to writing short stories that includes preparation, theme and premise, title, characters, dialogue, setting, and more.

Made in the USA
Middletown, DE
12 October 2022